SPY'S MASK

Book five of the Aermian Feuds

By

Frost Kay

Spy's Mask

First Edition

Cover by Amy Queau

Formatting by Jay Cox

Copy Editing by Madeline Dyer

Proofreading by Holmes Edits & Kate Anderson

THE FIVE KINGDOMS

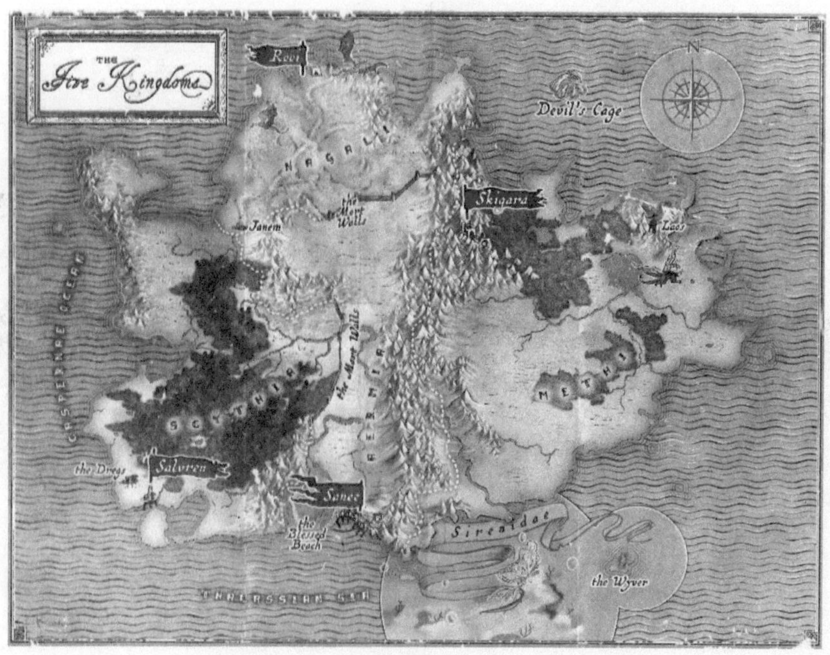

When I started writing this series over three years ago, Spy's Mask was supposed to be Sam's book. But my characters have a way of changing what I planned and doing whatever they want.

Spy's Mask demanded more of my heart and soul than any other book I've written. It's not for the faint of heart. Get ready for intrigues, war, and love in every shape and form.

This is NOT the last book in the series. There will be one more- Court's Fool, which I've already stated writing. *woot*

I hope you've enjoyed the journey as much as I have.

Hugs, Frost

PROLOGUE

Monsters.

Hell.

The myths and legends she'd once been told in the dead of night as a prank by friends weren't supposed to be real. It was all fun and games, a thrill. But what those innocents didn't understand was there were things in life, real things that rivaled any scary story. Hell and demons of their own making.

Sage wished what had befallen those around her was just a story, a fable to dismiss from her mind. But life was a cruel, fickle, and beautiful being that had no rhyme or reason. One never knew when whims would bless or curse you. Just the smallest detail could tip the scale.

From the beginning, life seemed to rage against Sage, a constant force that wore her down to her very bones. There were many paths for the rebel princess to travel, and they all led to one outcome:

Blood.

War.

Chapter One

The Warlord

Zane smiled as he watched the Aermian army scurry about like ants as they built their camps. They had thought they were so clever. But they were just children really, playing at being warriors. They had no idea what the future held.

Ignorant.

They were ignorant of his spies. Ignorant that their greatest enemy walked among them. A leren among babes.

He stilled and glanced over his shoulder as awareness tingled over his skin. His sixth sense. She was near. He narrowed his eyes at the approaching royal party. The crown prince led the group, but Zane didn't care. He only had eyes for one person: the goddess in armor and war paint.

"Sage," he whispered, his tone thick with covetousness. His consort stole his breath away, her beauty so bright it felt like it burned him where he stood. A spark of pride lit inside his chest at the Tia paint that adorned her face in savage strokes that he couldn't help but find lovely. He never imagined he'd see her in his people's war paint. Possession and something darker wriggled in his chest.

Ours, the voices in his head whispered.

Fierce. Bold. Deadly. A dark queen he couldn't wait to get his hands on.

Zane kept his head bowed as the group passed him. His fingers brushed her cloak for one second before he receded into the bustling camp, just another Aermian soldier following his orders. He could steal her away now, but that would be too easy.

His consort had challenged him, and Zane loved a good fight. No, he wouldn't take her this day. He'd wait for her to surrender, and it would be all the sweeter.

Zane adjusted his cloak and grinned.

Soon enough, she'd bow to him. All he needed was a little patience. His consort would grace him with her presence soon enough.

Then, he'd destroy her world.

Chapter Two

Sage

Her legs wavered as she approached Ezra. Her mind was screaming at her to stop, to turn back, but no matter how much she struggled, Sage found herself standing before the Sirenidae, the warlord's heat at her back as a thousand pairs of bloodthirsty eyes watched them. The large sword swayed slightly as she hefted it up, the tip hovering against the pale skin of the healer's neck.

Ezra smiled at her, his mouth twisting in a way that seemed like he was laughing at her, before he began to weep at her feet.

"I'm sorry," she choked out, hating that her fingers wouldn't release the blade. "This is not how it's supposed to be."

His cries cut off as he looked up, his eyes changing from magenta to black. "Murderer," he hissed.

Sage jerked as if he'd slapped her. "I don't want to do this. I can't do this," she pleaded.

"You have to," the warlord whispered in her ear, his warm breath tickling her neck.

The hair on her arms rose, and her stomach rolled as she cringed away from the body leaning over her from behind. "Leave me alone!"

"If I can't escape you, how is it fair that you escape me?"

She stumbled a step closer to Ezra, her blade slicing dangerously close to his neck. Tears burned the back of her eyes, but she wouldn't let them fall. How could she cry for herself when she was the one committing the crime?

"It's okay, Sage," Ezra whispered, his voice strangely hollow. He leaned closer to the blade, the sword biting into the delicate skin, just below his hammering pulse. "I knew what you were when I saw you."

She cried out as he impaled himself on her sword. "No, no, no, no," she screamed, releasing the sword and falling to her knees. Ezra's mouth pursed as his blood pooled and spilled over his lips.

"He's not the only monster," Ezra whispered as he fell to the ground, his white hair turning red as it splayed around him.

Sage held up her shaking hands and stared at the blood that coated her palms. She was a killer.

A hand cupped her chin and forced her to stare at the warlord.

He smiled, flashing sharp fangs as he brushed a bloodstained finger along her bottom lip. "You're perfect for me."

"I'm nothing to you."

He tsked and knelt so they were at the same eye level. "On the contrary. Like calls to like." He jerked his chin to the right. "Look at the ruin you've caused."

Sage turned and screamed as bodies upon bodies lay in heaps around her.

***

She jerked awake and sat up, her heart racing. Her nightgown clung to her body, soaked with sweat. Her own breaths were heavy in her ears as she tried to orientate herself. A lantern hung from the ceiling of her sprawling tent, giving off just enough light for her to see Tehl's still form next to her.

Sage placed a hand over her pounding heart and tried to calm it down. *You're not there. You're safe.* It had been two weeks since she'd arrived at the camp, and each night, her nightmares had escalated.

Throwing back the blankets, she rolled out of the makeshift bed, quickly donned her leather breeches and boots, and tucked her nightgown into her pants.

"Are you all right?" Tehl asked, his voice rough with sleep.

Sage peered over her shoulder at her husband who stared at her with concern. "I'm fine."

"You were talking in your sleep. I don't think you're fine at all. Plus, Sam says when women use the word 'fine,' it means the exact opposite."

She turned fully and crawled across their pallets to peck him on the lips. "Well, your brother doesn't usually give the best advice," she joked. She cursed internally at how, even to her own ears, her tone was off.

Tehl cupped her left cheek with his right hand and smoothed his thumb along her cheekbone. "I'm worried for you, love."

"I'll be all right." She had to be. There wasn't another choice.

"Is there anything I can do?"

"Hold me when I get back?"

He stretched and kissed her softly. "I'll be waiting."

Sage reached up and squeezed his hand before crawling out of the bed and moving through the tent in the direction of the door. She retrieved her discarded cloak from the simple wooden chair in the corner and threw it on to ward off the night's chill.

Tehl's voice caused her to pause as she lifted the tent flap.

"Be safe."

"Always."

Guilt assaulted her as she stepped into the crisp night air. Puffs of white steam escaped from her mouth. Damn. It was getting colder every night, and the weather in the plains was more frigid than anything she'd ever experienced in her life.

Sage stomped her feet a few times and lifted the cloak's hood to protect her neck from the chilly air, nodding at the two guards stationed outside their tent. Garreth whispered something softly to the other guard and stepped away from them, moving to Sage's side—her silent sentinel.

Without one word, they began their walk through the camp, and her protection detail melted from the shadows and fanned out to circle her. Fires burned low, softly crackling—the only sound except for the occasional snore and the rustle of her cloak in the breeze.

"Rough night?" Garreth asked, his voice no louder than a whisper.

Sage nodded, her chest tight. She couldn't get Ezra's hate-filled face out of her mind. Reaching the edge of the camp, she acknowledged the guards on the perimeter patrol with a tip of her chin and continued her walk. By now, the men were used to her unusual nightly routine.

They paced around the enormous camp until they reached their destination. A huge rock sat at the forefront of the camp, an old relic of the Mort Wall that was never used. She clambered up the side and plopped down. Garreth followed suit, only pausing to make some sort of signal to her protection detail.

At one time, she would have begrudged the extra men, but now she appreciated their protection and Garreth's discretion. She understood their necessity. Sometimes one had to give up a little freedom to stay safe. Plus, she rarely spotted the men that trailed her everywhere she went.

Seemingly satisfied, he sat beside her and loosely clasped his fingers between his legs.

A black shadow solidified below the rock and blinked reflective golden eyes. Sage smiled at Nali. The leren had made friends with the men easily. At first, they'd been wary of her, but after they'd been introduced to the fiilee, the maneater was considered the lesser of evils.

Nali chuffed and then slunk into the meadow, disappearing like a ghost.

"Still unnerves me," her guard muttered.

"Mistress of the night," Sage said.

"What I wouldn't give to have stalking skills like that."

A smile touched her lips. The man already did. "Your skills are nothing to snub your nose at. If I didn't know any better, I would say you're akin to Nali."

Garreth snorted. "What gave it away? Our temperament?"

She laughed, the sound surprising her, but, almost immediately, she sobered as she stared at the far-away lights of the Scythian camp. The fires burned brightly just beyond the Mort Wall, casting ghoulish shadows into the night.

He was there.

A shiver worked down her spine. He'd be watching her as surely as she was watching him.

"Do you want to talk about it?"

No, she didn't, but when she opened her mouth to say just that, something else came out instead. "I murdered someone."

The silence hung between them. She continued to stare blankly at the Scythian camp, waiting for Garreth's judgement.

"War is a nasty thing. We're all capable of things we never thought possible."

True, but not applicable to her situation. "He was my friend." Her whispered confession tore her heart.

"May I speak plainly?"

"Always," she answered.

"I have known you for some time now and spent numerous hours in your company. I'd like to say I know a bit about you. From my time spent with you, I know two facts: you love as hard as you fight, and you have more honor than a thousand men. I'm sure you blame yourself for your friend's death, but that doesn't make it true." A pause. "Nightmares aren't truth. They are all of our fears and insecurities twisted into something no one should suffer."

Sage blinked. "Astute." He wasn't wrong. "They're getting worse."

"Why do you think that is?"

"Because he's haunting me."

"There's no such thing. It's in the mind."

"Mine is broken," she blurted.

"Whose isn't?" Garreth shrugged. "We all have regrets and demons that won't leave us alone. It's what we do to get past them that shows what kind of person we are."

"Again, very wise. How did you get so smart?"

His face creased into an expression of despair and regret. "Trial and error." He inhaled deeply, then pulled his sword from his scabbard and held it out to her. Sage's brows knitted in confusion.

"What's this?" she asked, not taking the blade.

"I must atone for my sins."

She shook her head. "I'm not a confessor."

Garreth shifted onto his knees and lay the blade across both his palms, holding it out to her once again, his gaze glued to the rock beneath his knees. "I've done something horrible, and I can't continue on." He lifted his eyes and met her stare. "The guilt is crushing me. Every day I see you fight and struggle, I blame myself."

Sage whistled softly and stood, looking down upon Garreth. Nali launched herself onto the boulder and crouched near her side, looking for the threat.

"What have you done?" Sage asked.

"I betrayed you."

She pulled her gaze from her guard and scanned the area around them. They were on the edge of the camp, and warriors surrounded them. She wasn't alone, so it couldn't necessarily be an ambush. "Speak your piece before I set Nali on you, Garreth. You're scaring me, and she doesn't like it."

Nali snarled in agreement.

"Did you know I had a daughter?"

"I did not."

Garreth hung his head, the picture of dejection. "I was married young, and my wife became pregnant almost immediately. We hadn't been married a year when my wee one was born. But as my daughter took her first breath, my wife breathed her last."

"I'm so sorry." She couldn't imagine the pain he must have suffered.

He nodded but continued. "I raised her the best I could. She was a little wild, but I loved her." Pride colored his tone. "A year ago, she disappeared."

Chills erupted along Sage's arms. She knew how this story ended. "Scythia."

"That's what we thought. The spymaster sent spies into Scythia to find any information about my child, but nothing came back. She was just *gone*." He finally glanced up, tears in his eyes. "I never gave up hope, and one day, I received a message that she was alive."

Sage's heart stopped.

Garreth's expression morphed into one of pure hatred. "A man held her for ransom. I offered him money, my service, anything that he desired, if only he would release my little one. But he wanted none of those things."

"What did he want?"

"He wanted a way to access the tunnels."

Eight words. Eight words explained something she'd wondered about so often when in Scythia. How had Rhys known where to find her? She knew there had to be a traitor, but she had never guessed it was Garreth. Emotion after emotion slammed into her—betrayal, hurt, anger, hate, sorrow—but she kept silent, as did the disloyal guard.

"What happened to the child?" Sage bit out, finally able to speak without screaming.

A shudder worked through him. "I found her body in a shanty near the fishing quarter. From what I could discern, she'd been badly abused." Garreth's voice broke on a sob.

Her heart clenched. She couldn't imagine finding a child in such a state, let alone your *own* one.

"I don't deserve to live." He held the sword up higher. "My life is to be forfeit for my wrongdoing."

Sage carefully took the sword, and he hung his head, almost like he expected her to execute him on the spot. The moment he spoke his story, she knew what she was going to do, but there was one thing Sage needed to know. She placed the tip of the blade underneath his chin and pressed upward so he looked her in the eye.

"You betrayed me?"

"I did."

"And you make no excuses?"

"No. I knew the penalty when I made my choice."

"Do you regret your actions?"

"I regret hurting you when the Crown and you have been so good to me."

She nodded and cocked her head. Even though his revelation pierced her to her inner core, she knew Rhys would have used someone else if Garreth hadn't agreed. "Rhys would have found a way in no matter what. It wasn't your fault I was taken."

"I had a part in it. I'm not blameless."

"True, but you're not to be held accountable for everything that has befallen me since that moment. The warlord and his monsters are to blame." She sucked in an icy breath as the wind whipped her cloak around her body. "And I know what I've done for my friends would pale in comparison to what I would do for a child—my child. You erred badly, but I don't blame you for trying to protect your child, and, for that, you won't die." Sage lowered her sword.

Garreth shook his head. "I deserve death."

She shrugged. "All of us make mistakes." A wobbly smile

touched her lips. "I'm a murderer. Surely, I deserve death as well?"

"Don't forgive so lightly. Treason is not something to be swept under the rug."

Sage scowled at her guard and friend. He'd hurt her, but she could at least understand the motive behind his actions. "Stop trying to goad me into killing you. I can't imagine the pain you must suffer because of what happened to your daughter, but I'm not going to allow Rhys to take another good person from this earth."

"I'm not good."

"No one is wholly good. But one bad decision shouldn't ruin a lifetime of good decisions." She stared him down. "Will you ever betray me again?"

"Never," he breathed.

"Swear yourself to me, and we shall stay as we were."

"I give my life in service to you."

"Good enough."

Sage placed the sword on the stone and hugged Garreth.

He stiffened. "How can you even stand the sight of me?"

She squeezed him tighter. "Because I understand grief and guilt."

His arms tentatively wrapped around her as he hugged her back. "Thank you. You'll make a wonderful queen."

She pulled back and met his watery gaze. "Don't thank me just yet. You still have to tell the crown prince."

He nodded and re-sheathed his sword into his scabbard. "Now?"

Sage shook her head and gestured for him to sit with her. Nali wedged herself between the two and laid her head on her paws, big golden eyes closing. Sage stroked the feline along her spine and peered at the meadow.

"We'll let him rest a bit. First, tell me about your daughter."

CHAPTER THREE

Dor

Dorcus was going to be late, and that was the last thing she needed.

She rushed down the rough, stone hallway and joined the other stragglers rushing toward their respective jobs. Their faces were masks of strain that surely mirrored her own. Her pulse picked up as she turned right and entered the main cavern of the Pit. Even though she'd lived in the Pit her whole life, it still managed to take her breath away with its beauty and simultaneously terrify her. The giant, hive-shaped cavern soared above her and plunged below. Wide, sloping trails curved around its edges in endless circles, only illuminated by the soft lantern light.

Her eyes sought the top of the cavern where one lone shaft of sunlight pierced the domed ceiling, the light harsh and bright. She squinted as her eyes began to water. Every day, she stared at that one little bit of sunlight. What would it be like to feel it on her skin? To live in a world of night and day, not just one of eternal darkness and slavery?

Dor stumbled and cursed as she scraped her left toe on the black, porous stone beneath her feet. She placed a hand against the wall and lifted her foot to check the wound. Just a scratch. Good. She couldn't afford to catch an infection.

An older woman hustled by her and glanced over her stooped shoulder to frown at Dor.

"You best be hurrying up, or you're going to be late, little miss. I heard the warriors are in a mood today."

A shiver ran down Dor's spine as she scurried forward. She glanced to her right, eyeing the edge of the walkway. The last time the warriors were in a bad mood, they'd shoved a worker over the edge. Dor swallowed thickly and moved farther to the left. Even though her mother and father had taught her how to climb as a wee one, the immense drop still frightened her. She couldn't imagine a worse death.

Dor burst into a sprint as she neared her assignment and ignored the pain as she forced her burning legs to move faster. Her back gave a twinge that caused her to gasp, but she didn't slow. She couldn't afford a beating today. Her lashings from the week prior were finally scabbing over and healing.

A bell rang.

"Damn it," she muttered. She'd have to take the shortcut to make it. Her assignment was still another rotation down.

She moved to the brink and sat, hanging her legs over the edge, before rolling onto her belly and shimmying backward. Her stomach dropped just as her toes found the first crevice. Making sure she was secure, Dor began to climb down. A sigh of relief escaped her as her feet finally reached the next landing, but there wasn't time to dawdle. She darted into a rough stone corridor, sweat dampening her brow. Just a little bit farther.

As she swung around a corner, her foot slipped in a puddle of water and her arms pinwheeled. She barely managed not to fall. Dor gagged as something squished between her toes. She huffed out a small breath, her lungs aching as she ran. Mercy, she hated the slime that liked to grow on the damp stone. The texture made her skin crawl. It was in times like this that she wished she had a nice pair of leather shoes. But that was a fanciful idea. Shoes were dangerous in the Pit. If someone didn't kill you for them, then they'd be the end of you anyway. Dor had managed to escape too many life-threatening situations by climbing the stone walls to safety. No shoes were as good as her toes.

Dor darted into the mine and rushed to the tools, snatching up a pickaxe. Spinning on her heel, she almost stumbled into an older woman who scowled at her with narrowed brown eyes.

"Sorry," Dor mumbled and raced to her spot.

Harsh, lofty voices echoed in the space around her as the warriors commanded that they start their work. Her breath came in gasps, and her heart pounded as she heaved her ax up and began her task, adrenaline running through her veins.

"That was close," her best friend muttered from Dor's left.

Dor glanced at Ada and smiled. "Nothing like a rejuvenating jaunt in the morning."

Ada rolled her eyes as she worked, her dirty arms flexing as she swung the ax. "You take too many chances. One of these days, your luck is going to run out."

Dor rolled her shoulder to dislodge the itchy feeling creeping up her back. "I wouldn't call the beating I received last week *lucky*," she said lightly.

Ada paused in her work and glanced up from underneath her lashes, her expression unreadable. "That's not what I meant," she said softly, her moss-green eyes honest. "I don't want to see you hurt again." She touched her heart. "It pains me when you have a punishment, and with the way they've been acting lately..."

Dor's eyes darted to the warriors who scrutinized the miners. Their body language screamed aggression. She nodded. The warriors *had* been more agitated of late.

"I'll be more careful."

Ada gave her a weak smile and returned to work. The two fell into a comfortable silence as they mined. Dor's muscles tensed as the warriors passed them. A warrior's gaze lingered on Dor for longer than necessary, causing the hair at the nape of her neck to rise, spreading a prickling sensation across her body. She released a breath through her teeth as they moved on, thankful they hadn't demanded her to stop and provide them with entertainment.

Dor glanced at her friend who astutely focused on her work, although Dor could tell Ada was tracking the movements of the warriors as they finished their rounds and passed by once again. The stiffness in her friend's shoulders melted away as the warriors rounded the corner and disappeared from sight.

Ada did have a reason to be on alert. Even beneath the dirt and grime, she was a beautiful girl. Her ragged dress and dirt couldn't conceal it. Dor glared at the rock and struck hard with the ax. Her mother spoke of how beauty was revered up on the surface, but in the Pit, it was a curse. Beauty drew attention. Attention that no one wanted.

Attention meant death.

***

Fatigue weighed down on Dor. Their short break at the middle of the day had come and gone, and her back screamed, but she continued to swing her pickaxe even though she was sure blisters were forming on her hands and sweat had clearly soaked everything she wore. Her upper lip curled. That was something she'd come to loathe about the damp pit. It made it impossible to keep the calluses she tried to build up each day. No matter how many days she worked, her hands stayed soft and formed blisters.

"Move faster," an angry voice demanded.

"I'm sorry," a little voice replied.

Dor peeked over her shoulder toward the sound of a tiny, placating voice. A guard hovered over a small boy and pointed toward the cavern wall. Her heart sank as the little boy, who couldn't have been more than eight, hefted up a large pickaxe and swung it, his thin arms shaking. She winced as he lost his balance and fell to his knees. The pickaxe was too big for the boy. She wasn't sure how he'd been swinging it all day.

The warrior stepped closer, his expression promising something terrible. "I *said* pick up your ax and work."

She willed the little boy to get up. "You can do this," she murmured under her breath.

Ada reached out and clutched Dor's arm, her small, dirt-streaked face holding fear for the boy.

The boy dragged himself from the ground, knees bleeding, and tried to pick up his ax. Tears trekked down his face as he barely managed to lift the tool from the floor. He attempted to swing the ax but lost his balance again and ended up back where he started. On his knees before the warrior.

Dor's stomach dropped as the boy stayed on the ground. He didn't cower or beg for mercy. He knew what was coming next. He was the picture of defeat. The warrior yanked the whip from his belt and reached for the boy.

Before she knew what she was doing, Dor tore away from Ada's grasp, dropped her pickaxe, and placed herself between the boy and the warrior.

"Get out of the way," the warrior snarled.

Heart in her throat, she forced herself to answer in a soft, mild way she hoped would calm him, and held up her hands in supplication. "My lord, he's tired and the ax is too big for him. He also hasn't had any food today. If you give him a moment, I'm sure he can finish his shift since it is almost over." She inhaled. "Or I can help him finish it after I complete my assignment."

She trapped a scream inside her mouth as he grabbed her by the throat and roughly dragged her forward.

"You think he should be rewarded for his laziness?"

"No, my lord," she said, her words wheezing out of her as she clawed at his hand. "I think he's worked very diligently today, and it would cost you nothing to show the poor child some mercy as a reward for working so hard."

The guard glared into her face. "You presume to tell me what I should do?"

"I presume nothing," she whispered.

"You presume much," he bit out, spittle spraying her nose and cheeks. "You'll be punished for your insolence once I'm through with the boy."

She closed her eyes so the warrior wouldn't see the hate she felt for the wretched creature holding her. That's what he was: a creature, a beast with no humanity left.

Dor forced back her revulsion and hatred, wrangling her temper. She couldn't lash out. If she did, she wouldn't be able to help the boy. Having been a recipient of lashings for many years now, she knew the boy wouldn't survive what the warrior planned. They were often careless with male children, because they were easier to come by than females.

Dor's mouth dried as she forced her eyes open to stare evenly at the warrior, her decision made. "I'll take his punishment."

He sneered. "You will be receiving a punishment of your own for being insolent."

She nodded, even as a trickle of fear slithered down her spine. "I know, but I'll take his as well."

The other warrior approached, taking in the scene with a smile. "What do we have here?"

"A bit of fun," the warrior holding her said, his expression melting into one of delight. "Michelle, you're going to be able to try out your new whip."

Dor kept her expression blank, letting none of her fear show. The warriors were deadly when they smelled even a trace of fear. Dor sucked in a deep breath as the first warrior released her. He rubbed his hands together in glee, and her stomach rolled.

"Come along," he commanded as he moved toward the whipping post.

She spun and helped the little boy to his feet. Dor handed him to the nearest slave, not even registering the person's face as she whispered to the boy, "Go find your mama."

The boy melted into the cavern's swarm of people amid the darkness.

"Come!"

Dor bit back her snarl and forced her legs to walk toward the whipping post. She glared at the metal ring set high in the stone wall. Why they called it a whipping post, she had no idea. The warriors smirked at her, which caused her to straighten her spine and lift her chin, despite her fear.

She didn't tremble when they tied wide, leather bands around her wrists, nor when they yanked her arms high above her head, causing her to lift onto the tips of her abused toes. Dor pulled in a deep breath and glanced in Ada's direction. Her friend's pale face had lost what little color it had possessed and now looked positively green beneath the layer of grime. Their eyes met, and Ada dipped her chin once in acknowledgment; Dor wasn't alone.

Turning to face the wall, Dor lowered her chin, biting her roughly woven dress and twisting her hands so she could hold on to the leather straps securing her wrists. She inhaled deeply and focused on the stone in front of her as they ripped open the back panel of her dress, exposing the skin of her back to the cool, wet air.

The first lash always surprised her. Her body tensed and jerked as pain radiated from her spine. Even though she expected the pain, it was always worse than she remembered. When the second lash struck, her teeth snapped together, and she pulled in a deep breath through her nose. Tears pricked her eyes. The pain never got easier. After receiving so many punishments, she would have thought it would get easier, but it never did. It was always like the first time.

Tears began to fall down her face, and whimpers slipped from her lips as the warrior continued to lash her, splitting open old wounds and scars on her back. Liquid ran down the back of her legs and pooled on the ground beneath her. Her body sagged as the punishment continued, the warriors laughing. The leather straps bit harshly into her wrists, but she didn't feel them. All she could feel was the fire trying to burn her alive.

Spots dotted her vision, and she smiled as darkness came to claim her. A large paw sank into her hair and yanked back. Her eyes flew open as the guard peered down into her face and licked his lips.

Bile burned her throat.

"Thank you for the pleasure of letting me beat you today. I've always wanted to do that. I had an itch I needed to scratch," he said, his hot, rancid breath wafting across her face. He pressed closer. "I have another itch I'd also like to scratch," he drawled.

Despite the immense pain, the threat of what he was implying had her forcing her legs to stand underneath her. She shifted toward him with a snarl on her face.

"Try it," she whispered, soft and deadly. Many a man had tried it before, but they never survived the encounter.

He stared at her, his smirk faltering briefly before he sneered and yanked her head back to the point she thought he might snap her neck.

"You're not worth it," he spat. "Too disgusting and grimy." A malicious smile. "I don't want used goods anyhow." He released her head and then slapped a hand against her back.

Dor screamed and swung forward into the stone wall. The pain was too much. Darkness blanketed her as the warrior snapped at someone next to her.

"Don't let her down until everyone is finished. Then, she completes her task and the boy's."

Chapter Four

Dor

"Dor."

Dorcus moaned and tried to hold on to the warm darkness that caressed her senses and washed out the world around her.

"Dorcus, you need to wake up."

No. She didn't want to deal with the pain. Something sharp stung her cheek.

"You need to wake up now!"

Dor moaned but forced her eyelids open, water leaking from their corners as she squinted at her best friend. "Why?" she croaked.

Ada pressed closer and scanned Dor's face in concern. "How's your head?"

"Better than my back."

"That's good. Your skull took a bashing."

"My head?" Dor whispered, trying to keep the pain out of her voice. Ada was her closest friend, but growing up in the Pit had taught her many things, one of those being that you should never show weakness. "What's wrong with my head?"

"Many things." Ada quirked a half-hearted smile. "Don't you remember?"

She shook her head, triggering dizziness that caused the room to spin. The last thing Dor recalled was pain. Damned, incessant pain.

Ada slipped in front of her and reached up to untie Dor's hands from above her head.

"The guard slammed you into the wall before he left. You hit your head pretty hard," her friend reiterated.

"I didn't feel a thing. I'm pretty hard-headed."

"That you are. Prepare yourself."

Ada released the rope and caught Dor underneath her arms to avoid touching her back. It was a small mercy, but it didn't stop the pain from ravaging Dor's back. The movement alone agitated her wounds something fierce.

"Devil, take me," Dor growled as the floor seemed to buck and roll beneath her feet.

"Watch your mouth," Ada hissed, dragging Dor farther into the cave. "Words like that have power. You never know who'll appear."

"So superstitious," Dor panted, trying to keep herself from vomiting all over her friend.

"*He* has eyes everywhere."

Dor sobered, if only for a moment. What Ada spoke was true. The warlord had powers beyond anything she could comprehend. The man was a legend. A god. The devil.

Ada accidentally pressed her hand against Dor's left shoulder, causing a searing agony. Dor whined and tried to breathe through the misery.

"I'm sorry," Ada grunted as she moved even deeper into the cave. She carefully deposited Dor on her belly so her back was exposed to the chilly cavern air, then squatted next to her. "You're going to be okay." Ada's gaze drifted to Dor's back, and the skin around her eyes tightened as she frowned.

"That bad?" Dor didn't need to ask. She'd taken beatings before, but this one she felt in her bones.

"It looks worse than it is."

Dor doubted it.

Ada bit her bottom lip. "You need to be more careful."

"A little boy, Ada. What was I supposed to do?" she asked, more tears coursing down her face and collecting in a small hollow of the porous rock beneath her right cheek. "I couldn't leave him to that fate. I couldn't."

"I know," Ada said softly. "They would've killed him. I'm so—" She began to shake as she curled her hands into fists. She stared at them for a beat, then looked at Dor. "Everything about this situation is wrong." She bent and pressed a kiss against Dor's temple. "I'm going to finish up your work and the boy's. Just try to relax, and then I'll get you home."

"Thank you."

"You'd do it for me."

Dor watched Ada heft up the pickaxe and begin to work. Everyone helped each other as much as possible in the Pit. They formed bonds and families, but the help only extended as far as not putting another in danger. Ada was a gem of a friend whom Dor could never repay.

Dor clenched her teeth as the muscles in her back spasmed, and her body throbbed in horrendous pain with every beat of her heart. As Ada worked, the earsplitting sound of metal on stone melted into the background, forming the beat of a melody her mum used to sing to her as a child. Dor began to hum to focus on something other than the pain and drifted off into the music around her.

***

"Swamp apples," Ada cursed.

Dor blinked slowly and focused on the blurry outline of her friend. "I thought we said no cursing," she slurred.

"We've got to get you to your mum. You've lost too much blood."

Dor's eyelids began to droop, and she knew somewhere in her mind that this was a bad thing, but she was just so exhausted.

Ada slipped her hands underneath her armpits once again and panted next to her ear. "This is going to hurt. Help me as much as you can."

Dor keened as her friend hauled her to her feet. Colorful dots expanded across her vision as Ada began to trek from the cave.

"It hurts so much. Just leave me."

Ada growled. "I won't do that. Your mum would have my head. Plus, we can't afford for you to get an infection. You and I both know what happens when someone visits the healers."

Dor winced and forced her shaking legs to bear some of her weight at the word 'healer.' The warlord's healers were the scourge of Scythia. Razor-like smiles and false intentions. Her mum had taught her to fear little in the world, but the healers were one of those terrors to be feared. They were the devils who pretended they were saints. Their elixirs were the bane of many a woman's existence. Yes, they could heal any affliction, but, with that, came a heavy price. A woman either gained the attention of a warrior, or she became an experiment.

Dor fought a shudder as her stomach rolled. Many girls had been exploited since they'd blossomed into womanhood, and Dor didn't want to be next. Bile burned the back of her throat as she thought of what befell Odia, one of her former friends. They'd taken her, bred her, and when the monster of a child was born, they'd ripped the babe from Odia, like she was rubbish, and left her for the dragons.

"Monsters," Dor breathed.

Ada glanced sharply at her as they hobbled toward the entrance of the cavern. "Hush. You're speaking nonsense that will get us both killed. Try to keep silent so we can get you to your mum. We can't afford to attract attention." She glanced pointedly at the guards patrolling a nearby corridor.

Dor forced herself to stand taller, despite her injuries, and hobbled with Ada toward their home. She eyed the guards from beneath the mop of hair that hung over her face. The warriors seemed to be able to sense weakness, so she kept her chin up and lengthened her stride. Once out of sight from the guards, she groaned and leaned heavily on Ada as they followed the circling corridors and stairwells.

The walk seemed to take forever; the hallway began to move.

"I don't think I can make it much further."

Ada glanced at Dor. "I don't know what to do. You can't climb, and I can't carry you, which means we have to walk."

"How much further?" she wheezed.

"One more level."

There was no way she could make it. "We need to take the shortcut."

Ada's eyes rounded. "You can't do it."

"I have to," Dor ground out.

Her friend studied her and blew a piece of hair from her freckle-covered face. "You better not fall."

Dor pressed a smacking kiss against her cheek. "I'll try not to."

They wove through a few more tunnels and finally arrived at the last little lip to reach their home. Dor almost broke down in tears as she stared at the six feet of stone that kept her from her bed. It seemed like thousands of feet when her back was shredded into ribbons.

"You can do this," Ada encouraged. "I'll go first and help you up."

Ada scampered up the side of the rock like a monkey and disappeared from sight within a couple of seconds. Ada's face popped back over the edge, her brown braid dangling as she lay on her stomach and reached for Dor with both hands. "Use your feet as much as you can. I'll do the rest."

Dor nodded and slowly lifted her arms above her head, tears rushing to her eyes as her back pulled and throbbed. She slipped her sweaty hands into Ada's.

"You're almost there," her friend crooned.

Dor pressed her head against the wet, stone wall and took a couple of breaths before tucking her toes into a crevice and pushing her body upward. A shout of pain exploded out of her when Ada tugged her higher. Dor snapped her teeth together, blood filling her mouth as she bit her cheek.

"Just a little further, Dor," Ada grunted.

Cool stone scraped her arms, belly, and shins, but it barely registered with her compared to the searing white-hot pain that burned her back.

"What happened?" a male voice demanded.

Dor glanced up as Jadim leaned over Ada. Sweet, sweet Jadim. If anyone could get her home safe, it would be him. A sloppy smile tugged one side of her lips up. If they had lived in another world, she might have married him.

"I've got you," Jadim crooned as he placed his hands beneath Dor's arms and pulled.

Dor wailed when her agony doubled and an inhuman sound escaped her mouth as he pulled her closer, his fingers pressing into her mutilated skin. *Just kill me.*

"No! Her back!" Ada yelled.

Dor flopped limply in Jadim's grasp, crying.

"I'm so sorry," he mumbled. He pressed her close to his body and sprinted toward her home.

She gagged and then promptly threw up. "Sorry," she bawled as she watched her vomit slide down his chest in revolting rivulets.

"It's nothing, Dor."

The smell of incense surrounded them and overpowered the putrid stench of her vomit. Home. The knot of fear in Dor's chest loosened. She was home. She would be safe.

"What the hell?" her mum shouted. "What happened, Jadim?"

Dor forced her eyes opened as Ada moved around Jadim's tall frame. "She took a beating."

"Place her on the bed, Jadim. Ada, I need you to fetch a numbing cream from the herbalist."

"What should I pay her with?" her friend asked, wringing her hands.

Dor's pregnant mum rummaged in a small, decorated box on the nightstand and pulled out two dainty, black pearl earrings.

"Mum, no," Dor whimpered as Jadim placed her as gently as he could on the bed. Her mother treasured those earrings. They were a gift from Dor's father, Blair.

Her mum placed them in Ada's hands before turning to Dor. She smiled and brushed a strand of hair from Dor's face. "They're just things. My family is *always* the most important thing to me. Do you understand?"

She nodded and focused on her mum's soothing touch.

"If you don't need me, I'm going to follow Ada and make sure she gets to the herbalist. The warriors are in a foul mood today."

"Thank you, Jadim."

A large hand touched the back of her head, and Jadim kissed Dor's hair. "I'll be back."

Her mum watched Jadim leave before heaving herself from the bed, her huge belly straining against the too-small dress. She poured water in a bowl and grabbed clean rags from the table, then returned to the bed, setting the bowl and rags down with care. "How did this happen?"

"There was a little boy," Dor whispered between clenched teeth. "He was so skinny, and he didn't have the right tool. It was made for someone twice his size. He couldn't work anymore." She drew in a slow, shallow breath before continuing. "It was the end of the day, and they wouldn't show one shred of humanity." More tears fell down her cheeks, but, this time, for a different reason. "They would've killed him."

Her mum placed a soft hand on her cheek and wiped away the tears. "You've done a good thing, love. You should be proud."

"I'm not proud. I'm angry. I want them to die." Shame washed over her. Such thoughts were ugly and led down a road she didn't want to travel. Silence hung between them at her voiced treason.

"The right way to live is not always an easy choice, but just remember those who commit atrocities against others will suffer. Such is the way of the world. Injustices will be righted. We just have to be patient."

Her mother's words seemed like a dream. They didn't live in the same world as the other kingdoms. They lived in darkness. In the Pit.

The only things that bred there were rage, pain, and bitterness.

They lived in hell, and the devil ruled them all.

Chapter Five

Sage

She winced as Zachael yelled at Garreth, who sat in a chair at the corner of the room with his head hung low. Sage had never seen the weapons master lose his temper. It was almost as if she could feel his rage pouring from his person, the air heating around them.

"I can't even look at you." Zachael's voice turned ragged. "I helped raise you, boy. How could you do such a thing?"

"I have no excuse for my actions. I accept the consequences."

Hayjen scoffed and crossed his arms, glaring at Garreth. "Well, thank the stars for that. I'd hate to have to hunt your sorry arse down."

Sage pulled her attention from Garreth and eyed her husband. The man hadn't said one word since his Elite had begun his confession. She studied his stony face, looking for one hint of his thoughts.

Nothing.

He shifted slightly and startled her. Tehl hadn't moved from his spot in the opposite corner across from Garreth.

"Your life is – " William bit off his words as Tehl uncoiled himself from his wooden chair and stood to his full imposing height.

Sage shivered, and Zachael's anger paled in comparison to the ice-like rage that overcame her husband's face.

The prince took three steps closer and paused to stare at Garreth, his eyes like chips of frigid blue glass.

"You hurt Sage." A wintery-like chill seemed to whip through the room at his words. "*My* wife. *Your* princess. You deserve death, but that would be too easy." He paused, working his jaw. "She was your friend."

"I'm so sorry," Garreth said. He lifted his head and blinked back tears. "I never meant for anyone to be hurt, but that doesn't change my actions." He swallowed. "All I can do is try to make amends."

Tehl took a step closer. "You think you can make amends for the horrors she suffered? Because from where I am standing, there is *nothing* you could possibly do to make things better. I am tempted to just kill you. Our laws demand your blood for your betrayal, but it doesn't seem right that you'll be free from the sting and rot of guilt, and yet your princess will fight monsters for the rest of her life." His hands curled into massive fists by his side, and a slight tremor moved through his body. "She could have died there!" he thundered.

Sage stepped to his side and hugged his arm, stroking her hands soothingly along his skin. She'd never seen him this worked up before. He turned to look down at her, and she stiffened; his eyes were so cold, it was like falling through a frozen pool. She swallowed down her trepidation. Tehl would never hurt her, and he was hurting himself. He'd been raised with Garreth. His betrayal had cut him deeply.

"I am here. I am alive."

"No thanks to his actions," Tehl growled.

She bit her bottom lip, not agreeing or disagreeing with him. "Rhys was a wicked, vile creature that had no conscience. Garreth made a mistake, but he's not a bad man."

"You're sticking up for him?" her husband snarled. "The man who put you in that hellhole?"

Sage lifted his fist and ran her fingers over his knuckles. "If it hadn't been Garreth, it would have been someone else. Maybe someone with less of a moral code than your Elite. Rhys was determined to get to me, and he had ways to get what he wanted. Don't forget that he worked for you at one time," she said softly.

Tehl's lips thinned at the reminder. "Garreth is a traitor."

"Not by choice."

"He made his choices."

"You're right," she agreed. "But think about the circumstances.

If your child had been the one threatened, how would you have reacted?" Sage pointed at Garreth's dejected form. "Look at him. Doesn't it seem like he's suffered enough? I know self-hate when I see it. I'm sure he hates himself more than you ever could."

"That's debatable," Tehl muttered, eyeing the Elite. "So, you would just let him go without any repercussions? A traitor? What's stopping him from doing it again?"

Sage dropped her husband's hand and faced her former friend. "Do you plan on betraying us again?"

"No," Garreth said, his voice ringing with certainty.

Tehl scoffed. "And you believe we can trust his word?"

"I do," she said, staring at the Elite. "He has nothing left that can be taken from him, but his own life. The Scythians have stolen his future from him. I believe he'll serve us quite diligently."

Zachael scowled and crossed his arms, mirroring her uncle's position. "Once a traitor, always a traitor."

"Since when did you start dealing in absolutes?" Sage demanded, arching a brow at the weapons master. "Your thoughts and speech are cloudy with betrayal, anger, and hurt. Have some bloody compassion and look at the whole situation."

Zachael pursed his lips. "I will try, my lady."

"Good." Her eyes snapped to her brooding uncle. "Do you have anything else to say on the matter, Hayjen?"

He shook his head. "No, I've said my piece."

She finally turned to her silent husband. "And what of you? Will you demand his life?"

"I am a keeper of the law, and the law states that he should hang."

Sage nodded, expecting that reaction. "But you have the capacity to show exceptions when there are extenuating circumstances?"

"Yes," he said tightly.

"He committed his crime against me. Then legally, I am to have a say in his punishment."

"That is accurate," Tehl bit out.

"Will you allow me to sentence this man, as is my right by law?"

Tehl flashed her a glare, but jerkily nodded.

Sage once again lifted his clenched hand and kissed his knuckles. "Thank you, my lord." She squeezed his hand once and addressed Garreth. "Are you ready for your sentence?"

"I am, my lady."

"You have admitted guilt of treason. The laws states that you must hang for such a crime, but as one of your sovereigns, I find this too harsh of a punishment. Therefore, I strip you of your Elite status. You will serve in the second battalion, and your holdings and monies will be distributed to those who are in need."

She turned her attention to Hayjen and Zachael. "Please direct this soldier to his new battalion."

Garreth stood and followed both men from the command tent.

Sage sighed and rubbed at her forehead. It was a just punishment, but she still felt guilty. She couldn't imagine the horror of losing a child.

Her skin prickled at the continued silence, and she faced the brooding man at her back. "Love?"

Tehl held up a hand. "I don't know if I can speak right now. I'm too angry."

"Thank you for letting me decide."

He flashed her a disgusted look. "He deserves so much worse."

"Perhaps, or perhaps not. But what is done is done. We can't go back, as much as we wish we could."

"I can't believe I ever trusted that lying, deceitful – "

"One mistake shouldn't be enough to ruin a lifetime of good deeds and service."

"You're too soft, love."

Sage shrugged. "Maybe, but I refuse to rule with a black and white attitude."

She squeaked when he wrapped her up into a tight hug, his breath ruffling her hair. Sage wrapped her arms around him and held him back.

"Stars, I love you."

Her body froze and the words seemed to echo in her mind. *I love you.* He loved her. He showed her this by his actions daily, but he'd yet to actually say it. Her eyes welled up.

"Do you realize that's the first time you've ever said you love me? And it's because I punished a man. That's twisted."

Tehl pulled back, his brows slanting together. "This isn't the first time."

"I assure you, it is," she whispered. "And I love you, too."

"I tell you I love you all the time," he argued. "I just said it moments ago when I said, 'You're too soft, love'."

Now, it was her turn to frown. "What?"

Her husband cocked his head, his black hair hanging around his face. "When you call someone love, it's because you love them," he said simply.

Sage blinked stupidly at him. "That's just an endearment or pet name."

"No," he murmured softly. "Endearment literally means a word or phrase expressing love or affection."

Warmth bubbled from her chest. He'd been calling her love since before they were married. A tear slipped down her cheek, and she smiled. "You've loved me for that long?"

He clasped her cheeks in his hands. "I think I loved you as soon as I saw you. Well, at least, once I discovered you were a woman."

Laughter bubbled out of her.

Her prince loved her.

All was right in that moment.

Until the warlord ruined it.

Again.

***

"No. We will not meet. It's too dangerous." Tehl commanded.

Sage stared numbly at the piece of parchment lying in the center of the table. It looked so innocent, not like the insidious poison it was.

"Does the warlord always send letters in the middle of the night?" Gav asked, his purple eyes filled with distain.

"This is the first," Lilja answered, leaning on the table.

Sage spared a glance at her aunt. The Sirenidae looked tired, but still beautiful. *It was unfair.* "All he wants is a meeting?" she asked.

"He supposedly wants to discuss peace terms to avoid a war that will bring about a devasting loss of life," William said.

Rafe scoffed as he stepped next to the round table. "If he wanted peace, then he could have fought for it when we were in his own kingdom. No, he doesn't want a peaceful solution. He wants something else."

His amber eyes locked on Sage from across the table and stayed.

She blanched but held his gaze. She knew as well as he what the warlord wanted.

"It's a trick," Raziel, the crown prince of Methi, muttered darkly from beside his brother, "or a trap. He would *never* compromise or retreat. The monster doesn't care about death. He's after something."

Her. He was after her.

Sage tried to speak, but her mouth wouldn't obey her mind.

Her aunt's gaze traveled from the map to Sage's stricken face. "My spies tell me that he is aware that the Methians have allied with us, but he is not afraid of their numbers. He still believes he has the advantage." Her lips pursed. "But he loves to play mind games. We have our Crown Prince and Princess – the Crown's Shield and Rebel's Blade – fighting with us. Our men have a mental advantage of their sovereigns riding into battle with them."

"This isn't about a trap," William said from her right. He reached across the table and lifted the letter toward the lantern light. "This is about unnerving those who are leading." He set the parchment down with a heavy sigh.

A nervous chuckle slipped out of Sage. All of their advisors turned toward her. She stood from her chair and reached for the letter. Her hand shook, and she gritted her teeth.

It was only a piece of paper. She could do this.

Tehl, who'd been pacing behind her, pressed against her left side. She smiled at him gratefully and read out loud a part of the message.

"It is in our best interests that we meet to find a solution that is advantageous for both our peoples. I look forward to meeting with your delegation. It's been far too long." Her throat constricted.

The last sentence was for her.

Sage placed the message back on the table. "I'll say what you all won't. He wants to see me."

"We won't give him the satisfaction," Lilja snarled.

"It's too dangerous," Gav said softly. "He's not capable of rational thought when it comes to Sage."

"In his twisted mind, our refusal will signal that we want war as badly as he does. He doesn't like to be ignored." She blinked repeatedly as a memory resurfaced of the warlord holding her face tight so she couldn't look away from his face. "We need to choose wisely."

"We can't risk it," William added.

Raziel and Rafe both nodded. "We agree."

"It's a mistake to refuse him," Sage whispered, then turned to her aunt. "Lilja?"

The Sirenidae massaged her temples and then straightened. "Sage isn't wrong. There will be consequences for our refusal, but we can't negotiate with a monstrous warlord. His motives are too murky."

"Then it's agreed," Tehl rumbled from her right. "We send a refusal."

"It will be done," Gav replied.

Sage's stomach bottomed out.

She wanted nothing to do with the warlord, but she couldn't help but feel like she'd just failed some sort of test, and that they'd just doomed themselves.

Chapter Six

Jasmine

She'd dreamed about court when she was a young girl.

She'd imagined there'd be decadent dishes of all her favorite things, including chocolate pudding, tartlets that melted on her tongue, and, of course, cake. One could not forget about the cake. She'd dreamed of sparkling crystal, fine young ladies draped in shimmering gowns, and young men in pressed breeches, velvet waistcoats, and boots so shiny she could see her reflection in them. Laughter would tease the air like soft musical bells while elegant couples whirled around the dance floor in a kaleidoscope of silken color.

But that was pure fiction, the dreams of a little forest girl who spent too much time with bows, hunting rabbits in the wild.

Jasmine shifted on her aching feet and glared down at the pale blue slippers pinching her toes. They were beautiful, finer than anything she'd ever worn before, but bloody uncomfortable. All she wanted were her sturdy boots. Well, at the moment, she also wanted to escape the drudgery of court and snuggle with the twins.

"Are you all right, my lady?"

She pasted a smile on her face and glanced to the left, meeting pretty brown eyes. "I'm fine, Gem, thank you."

Gem—Lady Hollisa—frowned at her but nodded slowly. "I don't believe you, but I'll let it drop." Gem took a delicate sip from her glass of wine and fell quiet as she scanned the room.

Jasmine eyed the lady. Gem was her only friend in court since Sage had left to wage war. She was just as much of an outcast as Jas. Gem's family held a modest demesne, but her father had gambled most of their wealth away, and her mother had caused one too many scandals. Gem and Jasmine had bonded over the twins. Gem happened to love children, and Jas loved anyone who loved the twins. Not much was said between the two of them, but it was a relief to have someone guarding her back. And she needed it.

Jasmine glanced around the room, still musing over her childhood dreams. She had it partly right. There were women in shimmering gowns, dashing men, and dancing, but that was where all similarities ended. Court wasn't a fairytale. It was a nightmare.

Women smiled prettily but spoke venom behind each other's backs. Beneath the handsome façade of many men lurked ravenous predators. And if those weren't obstacles in and of themselves, then there was the meticulous etiquette that was imposed on everyone. One wrong action could ruin everything.

But the joke was on everyone. Jasmine was already ruined.

Her eyes connected with Joshua, the foppish blond. He smiled at her from over the rim of his cup. He winked, and it was all she could do not to roll her eyes. Despite her newly announced marriage, he kept on persuing her. His cronies smirked in her direction before laughing among themselves. Shame washed over her as she glanced away. It was her fault. She'd made a name for herself since arriving at the palace, and not a good one. *Whore* was quietly whispered in every circle she came upon. She didn't feel much these days, but she carried the shame, guilt, and anger with her everywhere.

"Out of all the women he could've chosen, he chose *her*?" a soft whisper reached her ears.

"Rumor has it, they were found in a very compromising position before they wed," another voice whispered.

"I see. The poor man. At least a beautiful wife isn't necessary for an heir."

Gem had frozen at her side and now flicked a worried glance in her direction, but Jas ignored it.

The gossipers behind them weren't wrong. No matter how the maids dressed her, she still stuck out among her peers like coal among diamonds. She was rough while they were class.

"No matter." The second voice giggled. "His marriage hasn't

seemed to slow him down one bit."

That wasn't far from the truth, either. Her gaze sought her husband among the gallantry, and it was easy to spot him. His gilded curls were barely tamed back from his face, which was lit like a beacon. Men and women alike surrounded him like bees to honey. Jas eyed the beautiful brunette hanging off his arm, soaking up his every word. The prince smiled down at the lady, his lips turning up in a wicked grin that could charm the pants off a nun. The brunette simpered at him and batted her lashes.

Jasmine watched it all without one ounce of jealousy. Their marriage was one of convenience. Even though she abhorred unfaithfulness with every bone in her body, she didn't care what he did as long as he kept away from her and the twins.

The whispering started up behind her again.

"He even took in her two prior children." A pause. "She's not a widower."

Small gasps exploded, followed by titterings that had her fingers curling into the skirts of her dress. *Vicious vipers.*

"What a gem he is to take in the bastards of a whore."

Gem's eyes widened, and her hand touched Jasmine's bare arm. "Their words mean nothing."

She was right, but a line had been crossed when they started talking about her family. No one attacked the twins and got away with it.

"Don't let your temper get the best of you," Gem cautioned.

Jas smiled and patted her friend's hand as her anger melted some of the ice that encased her. "I suggest you leave so you won't be lumped into what's about to happen." She pulled away from

Gem and spun on her heel, moving toward the group of whispering ladies with the grace she usually reserved for hunting.

Rose, the redheaded demon, lifted her head and smiled sharply at Jasmine as she neared the group. Jas returned the smile and paused by one of Rose's lickspittles.

"My lady," Rose murmured, "to what do we owe this pleasure?"

So that's how they were going to play it.

"You looked so entranced by your conversation, I just had to join the fun."

"We were speaking of the weather," a short ginger-haired girl blurted from her right.

Jasmine scoffed. "Come now, please tell me you can lie better than that?"

The ladies around her blanched, all but Rose who tilted her chin up. "Whatever could you mean?"

Jas leaned in close, like she was going to tell them a secret. "I heard mention of bastards, and I love a good story. Please continue on."

Silence met her statement, along with the shifting of feet and rustles of expensive crinoline.

"How disappointing you all are. I thought one of you would have the guts to say it to my face."

"You're making a scene," Rose murmured. "You should calm yourself. It's not good for someone in your condition, so I've heard."

She barely managed to contain her flinch. No one knew she was with child except for a select few. The harpy was trying to goad her into giving out information. Jas blinked owlishly and scrunched up her brows. "Condition? What ever could you mean?"

Rose smiled thinly. "I must be mistaken."

"That is the least of your mistakes." The twit never should have said something about the twins.

"I beg your pardon?" Rose said.

Jas tsked. "Your mistake was to speak badly of my family." She eyed the women around her – who dropped their eyes to the floor – before settling back on Rose. "You tread on dangerous ground."

"Are you threatening me?" Rose hissed.

"More like a promise. Keep your schemes and games to yourself."

Rose laughed. "There's nothing you can do to touch me, forest trash."

Several startled gasps escaped the ladies in the circle.

Jasmine grinned. "We can take this outside if you'd like."

More gasps.

The redhead tossed a curl over her snowy shoulder, sneering. "So barbaric."

"That's right," Jas purred. "I am a barbaric hunter. Let me tell you a little story about this forest trash. I spent most of my life hunting and tracking. I rarely lost any prey I set my sights on, even if it took days. That sort of dedication takes commitment and patience. You think about that when you are falling asleep tonight, when you enter a dark passage, or when you hear the scuff of a foot upon stone behind you." She smiled; the sight was positively evil if the paling expressions of the women around her were anything to go by. "Harm my family by word or deed, and I will find you. There's nothing that could keep you from me."

A sliver of satisfaction curled in Jas's gut at how Rose's eyes had grown considerably wider.

"I—I'll out you. I outrank you. We'll receive protection."

"Do you think they'll believe you?" Jas asked curiously. "The matrons think I'm a delight, and then there's the matter of my marriage. I may just be forest trash, but I did marry a prince."

The redhead opened her mouth and promptly shut it. Large hands settled on Jasmine's shoulders, surprising her. She kept her expression pleasant and didn't shrug off his hands like she wanted to. Instead, she leaned back against his strong frame, making a point.

"Dear wife, I believe it's time for us to retire for the night."

She nodded and faked a yawn as she spun to face her husband. "I'm absolutely exhausted, my dear. Take me to bed."

Sam's brows rose in surprise, and then he smiled devilishly at the women behind her. "I can't possibly refuse such a wonderful evening."

The ladies curtsied to him as he drew Jas's hand into the crook of his arm. Attention followed them as they exited the dining room. She glanced over her shoulder and caught the nasty sneer on Rose's face. Jas was under no illusion that there wouldn't be consequences. But it felt good to finally push back against the harpies that had made her their target.

War was raging in Aermia, and now she'd started one of her own.

***

Sam led her down the arching hallways that echoed with their footsteps and up two flights of stairs to the royal suites.

"What was that about?" he asked, his tone casual.

Jas pulled her hand from his arm and opened the door to their suites. "Nothing." They'd only been married a grand two weeks, but she'd learned a few things about the man. He was an expert at wiggling information out of people.

"It didn't look like nothing," he said. "It looked like you were about to rip out their throats. It was a little sexy."

Jasmine froze and glared over her shoulder at the insolent man who was leaning against the wall, grinning at her. "I haven't the energy to slap you for all of your innuendos tonight, my lord. Take your presence elsewhere."

"I wasn't the one who announced that we were going to bed."

Her lips twitched. He had her there. "Nonetheless, I'd appreciate it if you'd leave me in peace." She stretched and winced as something pinched in her back. It had been getting worse and worse of late. At times, she'd cramp all day long.

His smile faded, and his gaze dropped to her belly for a moment. "Is it the babe?"

The babe.

Her stomach rebelled, and she dashed for the bathing room, barely making it to the privy. She heaved, careless of her honey curls tumbling onto her face. Hair could be washed, but no one wanted to clean up vomit.

A cool hand pulled her hair from her face and the other rubbed small circles on her lower back. Again, she heaved, the rest of her dinner making another appearance. Tears dripped from the corners of her eyes and snot from her nose.

She wanted to throw off the prince's hand, but it felt too nice against her heated, aching body. Every day, there were new aches and pains as her body stretched to make room for the babe. She'd never hated being a petite woman more in her entire life.

The babe.

A life was growing inside her. One she had no knowledge of creating. She heaved again as more tears began to flow down her cheeks. Mira said it was a blessing that she didn't have any memories of the begetting, but part of her felt empty, robbed, blank. A shudder worked through her.

Ruined.

She wiped at her mouth and panted. Sickness was expected with pregnancy, but this was something more. It was like she was trying to vomit up all her feelings, everything she tried to keep suppressed.

"Are you well?"

No. "I'm fine." Jas batted his hands from her person. "You don't have to stay here."

"You're right, I don't have to." But he made no move to leave. "You need to talk about it."

Jas glared up at the gorgeous man staring down at her with concern. "Because we're so close?"

His lips pressed together as his blue eyes narrowed. "We could be if you let me."

"Along with all the hordes of other women? No, thank you."

"You want to know about—"

She held up a hand. "I don't want to know. It's not my place."

"You're my wife."

"In name only." She stood on shaking legs and waved away the prince as he tried to help her. "I'm fine."

"Your color and retching tell me otherwise. Plus, I know when a woman uses the word 'fine,' she's clearly not."

Jasmine staggered to the huge vanity and eyed her pale complexion in the tall, gilded mirror. She used a deep purple towel to wipe her face. "What a joke," she said. "Those with child are supposed to be radiant. If I'm glowing, it's because I'm green."

She pushed from the vanity and left the room, the prince following on her heels as she bustled into their suite. Well, technically, it was *theirs*, but only Sam slept in the large royal chambers. She slept with the twins in a much more modest room adjacent to the opulent suite.

"You're sure you're all right?" he asked as he hefted a plain-looking, black, wool cloak from a plush, striped chair near the fireplace to her right.

"Definitely." Jasmine eyed the cloak but said nothing. He was probably up to more shenanigans. She didn't ask, and he didn't offer.

"I'll be back to wake the twins."

She pursed her lips, not wanting to agree, but nodded anyway.

"Good. Rest well, Jasmine."

"Happy hunting," she responded.

Sam paused with his hand on the door and studied her over his shoulder. An eternity passed as they stared at one another. It seemed like he was searching for something, but she wasn't sure what. One thing she did notice was that the man was unfairly handsome, beautiful even. Every morning, she woke feeling like death warmed up, but he never looked the worse for wear, despite his late nights out.

He winked at her, pulling Jasmine from her thoughts. “I’ll see you in the morning, beautiful. Give both twins a kiss from me.”

She opened her mouth to retort, but he’d already disappeared through the door.

That was the worst part of the whole arrangement—his involvement with the twins. Jasmine worried her lip as she stared at the closed door to her left. He seemed like a good enough person as a whole, but there was a darker side she’d caught glimpses of that she wasn’t so sure about. It was like he had many versions of himself.

Then there were his escapades. The twins wouldn’t understand now, but they would in the future and it would undoubtedly hurt them.

But those were troubles for another day. Carefully, she turned to the door directly behind her and twisted the knob slowly so it wouldn’t wake the sleepy little monsters in the other room.

Today, being married to the prince proved useful in protecting her family, and she couldn’t find a fault in that.

CHAPTER SEVEN

Dor

Dorcus cracked open her eyes and squinted into the softly lit room. The piddly candle on the old table flickered and cast shadows on the walls of their home as it threatened to sputter out. Guilt washed over her. They could only afford so many candles a month, and they couldn't afford to burn them just because Dor was hurt.

She shifted on her bed and inhaled deeply as pain pulsed through her. Sacred darkness, she hurt. Once settled, she glanced at her mum's slumped form. Her mother slept near the bed in a rickety, old chair that looked like it would collapse at any second, her head hanging so her chin rested on her chest. Dark bruises marred the delicate skin beneath her closed eyes, and a soft snore wheezed from her nose. Dor's eyes dropped to her mum's arms which rested on top of her giant protruding belly. The pose was restful, yet protective. Even in sleep, her mum safeguarded her children.

Dor glanced back at her mum's freckle-covered face and luscious fiery-red hair. Her mum always claimed her hair was what had caught her father's attention, but Dor knew better. Her sire had fallen in love with her mum's fiery disposition. She was what had woken him up after Dor's birth mum died, or so he claimed.

Stars above, she wished he was here. He hadn't visited them in a while, and it pained all of them. She glanced at the carved doorway toward the small room her sisters slept in. It hurt the little ones the most. They didn't understand why their sire didn't live with them. Other slave men had offered to live with them as protection and support, but her mum wouldn't hear any of it, despite their eunuch statuses. She clearly still felt it would be a betrayal to her warrior, even if there wasn't a physical attraction between the slave men and herself.

Dor understood her mum's decision to an extent, but part of her wished there was another adult living with them, especially a male. Their sire's name was a curse and a blessing. Sometimes it brought safety, other times danger. But they did the best they could and kept their heads down.

Her mum's head dipped farther, and her red hair hung around her plump face. Dor smiled. Toward the end of the gestation cycle, her mother's face always rounded out, but even so, she was beautiful. The woman seemed to glow every time a child began growing in her womb. Dor hated to wake her up, but if her mum slid any farther down in her chair, she'd fall right onto the floor.

"Mum," Dor whispered, keeping her voice low so as to not wake her younger sisters.

Her mum jerked and sat up. Her green eyes scanned the room before landing on Dor, then filled with worry as she hefted herself from the chair. She knelt on the bed and brushed a piece of long, dark hair from Dor's face.

"How are you feeling, love?" she asked.

"Okay enough," Dor said softly. "I hurt."

"I know. Let me get you something for the pain."

Dor's back seemed to burn hotter at the mention of pain. "I can get through it."

Her mum ignored her and stood. "It was a blessing you passed out. There was so much blood, and we had to cut away some of the flesh." She shuffled to the side, so Dor stared at her profile.

Her stomach rolled, and saliva flooded her mouth.

Her mother glanced toward where her sisters slept soundly, and Dor followed her gaze. A small flicker of warmth entered her chest as she watched her sisters sleeping, how they wrapped around each other, clutching a roughly woven blanket.

"Ada and Jadim stayed to help. Ada kept the little ones occupied while Jadim and I cleaned you up the best we could."

"Thank you." She swallowed hard. She didn't deserve such a wonderful family. "How are the girls?"

"Scared, but they know how strong you are."

Dor didn't feel strong. She felt weak and stupid. "I'm so sorry for worrying you."

Her mum blanched and clenched her jaw. "It's never easy to watch one's child in pain or to see one's child hurt." She pressed a hand to her chest, just below her collarbone. "It hurts my heart that you've been abused, and it makes me want to rage."

"But you mustn't."

A bitter laugh spilled from her mum's lips. "I know better than most. I wish your father was here. He'd know how to proceed and protect you. I don't know what to do, Dor. How are you supposed to work tomorrow? How can we hide this from the warriors? We don't want to draw more attention."

They couldn't. If she didn't appear for work, the warriors would hunt her down and take her to the healers. A chill ran down Dor's spine. She'd never visit the healers unless dragged there by her hair.

"There isn't a choice," Dor said steadily. "I have to work."

Her mum's eyes glassed over, and she scrubbed at her tears, anger clear in the motion. "Damn hormones. I hate this. No one should live like this. If you can't complete your work tomorrow, they'll kill you."

The words didn't scare Dor. They should have, but when you live with death always hovering in the corner like an unwanted spider, it ceases to inspire proper fear.

Dor glanced toward the girls. But leaving her family *did* frighten her. They needed her, especially with another little one on the way.

"I'll get my work done. I have to. There isn't another option."

She inhaled shallowly as another wave of pain crashed over her. "I can do it," she forced out while reaching her hand to her mum.

Her mother clasped her hand and gave it a squeeze. "I love you, sweetness. You're one of the best things this life has blessed me with."

Tears pricked Dor's eyes. It was she who was beyond lucky. Dor's birth mother had died while in labor, but the first person she could remember seeing was Bel, the woman who had raised her as her own. She stared at their clasped hands, hers a deep olive, her mum's creamy. It didn't matter what blood ran through a person's veins, only that love ran through their heart. And Bel loved Dor like a daughter. Dor *was* Bel's daughter.

"Love you, Mum." She blew her mum a kiss. "We'll get through this."

Her mum nodded and stared blindly at the floor. "I don't know how long I can keep living like this," she said under her breath. "But we have to keep moving forward. It's all we can do."

She patted Dor's hand and sat on the edge of the bed, her expression blank as she stroked her belly.

Dor watched the familiar movement and thought about what it would be like to be in her place. It would be lucky to be chosen as a breeder and be able to provide for your family, but that was the only part that appealed. Dor glanced away from her mother's belly to stare at the wall, fighting the nausea which rose at the idea of warriors touching her. The idea of submitting to one or several of the warriors chilled her to the very bone.

She frowned. Her father wasn't like one of the feral creatures that ruled over them, but he was the exception to the rule. He'd already warned Dor that the relationship between himself and her mum wasn't normal. In fact, in public, they never showed affection for each other since her mum was considered an imperfect. Her lip curled. Dor hated the word, but a very small part of her was thankful she wasn't the Scythian standard of perfect. If she or her sisters had been considered perfect, they wouldn't have been allowed to live with their mum. That thought terrified Dor the most. What if she *did* become a breeder and they stole her child? She knew how she'd feel about that, and she'd die before she'd let a child go.

But that was life in the Pit. Dor was destined to become a broodmare for the monsters that lorded above them. But at least she would be able to bear it because she had her family. Her mind wandered to Jadim. When the time came, she was sure he'd offer his protection and home for her. They could never be anything more than companions because of him being a eunuch, but at least she'd have someone to help raise any children she was allowed to keep.

"Have you any news of Father?" Dor asked, pushing aside her disturbing thoughts.

"He's been busy."

In other words, he'd been causing mischief for the warlord. Dor scowled. Everything wrong in the world was that monster's fault. "It's not supposed to be like this."

Her mum glanced sharply at her before her gaze darted to the doorway covered only by a threadbare blanket. "You need to watch your tongue. Such things have a way of being heard."

Wise advice. "I'm sorry. I just wish things were better."

"They will be." Her mother glanced at Dor's back and then glared at the doorway. "Your father wouldn't have allowed that to happen, and the warriors wouldn't think twice about hurting the commander's daughters."

Dor didn't argue with her. More often than not, it put a target on her back. Warriors seeking to hurt her father went after the imperfect children he'd been known to visit. Or because of her sire's position, the slaves around her looked at her with suspicion, like she was the reason they were languishing in the Pit, like she wasn't one of them when she suffered as they suffered. She wasn't quite a slave and she wasn't quite a Scythian either. She was something in between that had no place in her world. And if that wasn't enough, it was easy to set off the berserker side of the warriors guarding them. The newest warriors were sent into the Pit to learn control. Rage ignited in her gut. It wouldn't do for a warrior to lose control among the court of vipers that lived above them. Oh no, they were sent down to train among the unarmed masses. No matter where Dor turned, danger awaited her.

Her mum sniffed and waddled toward the table in the corner to retrieve a little jar filled with green paste. Once again, Dor brushed her morose thoughts away and focused on her mum's swaying gait.

"I think we've talked enough about my health for one night," Dor said. "How are you feeling?"

"Little bit is going to be in my belly for a while yet," she said, patting her stomach and then lifting the jar from the table. "She'll be here soon enough."

"You think it is a girl?"

"I know it is," her mum answered as she waddled to Dor, and huffed as she sat in the wobbly chair next to the bed that groaned as it bore her weight. "How is your pain?"

Dor swallowed, trying not to think about her mutilated back. "It's as fine as can be."

Her mother clucked and opened the jar. A pungent scent filled the air that Dor wasn't sure she liked.

"I know you, Dorcus. You have a high tolerance for pain and a penchant for ignoring what's best for yourself. You need this to sleep tonight if you're to work tomorrow."

"Did you really sell your earrings?"

Her mum leaned forward and pressed a kiss on her temple. "I did, and it was worth it. Things come and go, sweetness, but the people in our lives are always the most important."

"I hate being unaware of what's going on." Dor rarely took anything for the pain when she was beaten. It was better to be in pain and cognizant of one's surroundings than drugged and vulnerable. Her mind flashed to when she had passed out earlier that day. She was lucky Ada had been there or Dor could've found herself in a whole different position.

"I know, but I'll protect you. Nothing will come through that door without my say so."

Some of the tension in Dor's body released at that. She trusted her mum to protect her. She'd done the best she could all of Dor's life.

"Let's get you to sleep."

Her mum reached for a wooden spoon and placed it between Dor's lips. Dor bit down on the wood and then pressed her chin against the slightly damp bedding. Her mother's first dab on her back caused stars to burst across her vision and her hands to curl into the blanket beneath her.

"I'll be quick. Be strong, Dorcus."

Snot and tears dripped down her face as she hissed curses to keep from wailing and waking the little ones. Her body broke out in sweat, and she began to lose touch with the world around her as her back began to tingle and numb. A sigh of relief gusted from her lungs as her mum finished, and the medicine began to work its magic. Dor spat out the spoon and leaned her salty cheek against the cool bedding.

"Thank you, Mum," she whispered as her eyes slowly closed.

"You're welcome. Sleep well, precious."

"I don't know how I will survive tomorrow," Dor mumbled as sleep tugged at her.

"We will figure it out in the morning. Each day has its own worries."

Her mum capped the jar, stood, and blew out the candle. The bed dipped as her mum crawled in next to her and began playing with her hair, humming a lullaby about love, dragon songs, and a flying girl. Dor tucked her hands beneath her head and let herself drift into oblivion.

Chapter Eight

Sam

Sam stripped off his boots and socks, and winced as a barnacle poked into the arch of his left foot. Lifting the stinging appendage, he glared at the small cut as it began to leak blood.

No matter how careful he was when visiting his spy, he always managed to hurt himself.

He pulled off his jacket, vest and shirt, goosebumps running up and down his bare skin. Sam rubbed his arms and eyed the narrow entrance to the underwater cave in the stone floor. His nose wrinkled as he approached the dark, watery hole. His heart picked up as he strained to see what lay beneath the still surface.

"Wicked hell," he muttered, his whispered curse echoing around the stone cavern.

He hated this part. There weren't many things that scared him, but being trapped in an underwater coffin was one of them.

"Stupid Sirenidae." *Of all the places to meet.*

Granted, the risk of discovery was low, but it was a bloody nightmare getting to the rendezvous. At least, it was for him.

Inhaling deeply, he sat on the stone edge and swung his legs into the chilly water. He hissed. Damn, it was cold. Steeling his nerves, Sam sucked in a huge breath and shuffled off the ledge.

Darkness engulfed him, and he reached forward to grasp the rough, rock wall and push himself downward. His ears popped, and his lungs burned uncomfortably as the soles of his feet touched the sand. He squinted into the darkness and ran his hand around the tunnel wall ahead of him.

Some of his panic drained away as the plants on the walls began to glow; neon pinks, blues, and greens radiated light into the watery corridor. Sam pushed off the wall behind him and swam ahead, his legs propelling him through the space in a span of four heartbeats. The mouth of the tunnel widened, and Sam swam toward the dancing surface.

As his head broke the pool's surface, he sucked in a huge breath, his lungs bellowing like he'd just trained for hours.

"Running from something?" a sensuous female asked, her voice full of amusement.

Sam treaded water and spun in a circle until he located the source of the voice. His eyes narrowed on the Sirenidae, who was lounging on the smooth rock near the pool, like a lady presiding over her court.

"What are you doing here, Mer? I was expecting Oria." He pulled himself to the edge of the pool, which resembled a sparkling jewel due to all the bioluminescent plants. Water spilled from his body, and he plopped down on the rock next to her as he blinked saltwater from his irritated eyes. They never hurt while he was swimming, but once he left the water, they burned like the devil.

Mer straightened, her long, flowing, silver hair slithering around her like silk. "Not even a proper hello?"

Sam smiled at her and leaned closer to kiss her cool, pale cheek, thankful she was dry. The first time they'd met, he almost accosted her because of the Lure. He shook his head to dispel the sweet scent that haunted his memories. "I'm sorry. I'm a bit out of sorts after my swim."

The Sirenidae nodded in sympathy. "I live in the sea, and swimming through the tunnels still unnerves me sometimes."

He shook his head, displacing some of the water from his hair, and then slicked several golden strands from his face. "I'm surprised to see you, Mer. I honestly didn't expect to meet with you for at least another week. I thought we had agreed not to meet often because of the danger?"

The smile on her full, pink lips slid away as she turned to face him fully, crossing her long, pale legs. Her magenta eyes, so similar to Lilja's, locked on him. "I had no other choice."

His stomach soured. He had a feeling she wouldn't have good

news to share with him. "What's happened?"

"Oria is dead."

"How?" he asked, shocked.

She pursed her lips and glanced away. "They spotted her before she could retreat from the cove. They hunted her down like an animal." Her voice wavered. "She barely made it back to me before she passed." Mer cleared her throat and turned back to him, tears shimmering in her eyes. One lone tear slipped free, and she touched the droplet as it moved down her cheek. She stared at her damp fingers for a second. "When we weep in the sea, the ocean sweeps away our pains like they were never there—I like that I can see the evidence of my pain."

Sam stared at her but kept silent, knowing it was better to let her get it all out.

Her jaw tightened, and she met his gaze, her eyes like hardened jewels. "She died in my arms."

"I know it's not enough, but I'm sorry for your loss." And he was. He liked Oria. She was quiet, to the point, and brilliant. Once she'd seen something, she could remember the details perfectly.

"She knew the risks of her journey."

"It doesn't make it any easier," Sam said softly.

Mer sucked in her lips and nodded. "True."

He watched the Sirenidae slowly compose herself as she tipped her head back to stare at the blue glowworms that shone like stars in the ceiling of her wet cave. Sam hated that she was in pain, and it bothered him that he still had to ask her questions after she'd lost a friend, but information was of the utmost importance.

Without it, thousands would die.

"Mer..." he said carefully.

She held her hand up. "I didn't come here to cry on you." She swallowed and dropped her head to clash gazes with him. "Oria reported to me what she'd seen."

The bleak expression on her face chilled Sam more than the water he'd just exited. "And?"

"The Scythians are getting ready to deploy their fleet of warships."

"How soon?"

"Three weeks."

"Bloody hell," he barked, standing. The seaweed on the rocks squished between his toes. Three weeks. Twenty-one days. Stars above. So little time. His mind spun as he paced. They needed to have their fleet of ships sent out immediately. He turned to face Mer. "I need to get back to Sanee, so I can pass this on. Is there anything else you need to tell me?"

"The sea is restless."

Code for the Sirenidae people. "Do you fear an uprising?" Sam asked frankly.

"No." Mer shook her head. "But there are those who will stand with you when the time comes."

Sam froze, shock temporarily locking his muscles. "Has the king changed his mind?"

"No."

Worry wormed its way into his chest. "Are you in danger?"

The Sirenidae chuckled darkly. "The *world* is in danger. None of the four kingdoms, nor the sea, is safe from war now. If we do not fight, then we've already lost."

"Are you being careful?" His one meeting with the Sirenidae king hadn't painted the man as the most forgiving person he'd ever met.

"As careful as I can be." Mer's smile was sad as she gazed at him. "I refuse to stand by and let the world burn. My aunt was right in leaving. There will be consequences for my actions, no doubt, but it's not a sacrifice unless it's a sacrifice."

"I'm not asking this of you," Sam whispered. The Sirenidae assistance would make a difference, but he knew what she was planning was betrayal. "You'll be branded a traitor."

She shrugged. "It's possible, and I'm prepared for that outcome. No one really wins in war."

Truer words were never spoken.

Sam took two steps forward and wrapped his arms around Mer, hugging her. "If you need me for anything, just send word, and I'll come."

She eased back out of his embrace. "I'll hold you to that. Who knows? Maybe I'll end up at your doorstep asking for shelter when this is all through."

"I hope not," he said softly, stepping back and easing himself into the pool once again. "Be careful. Lilja would have my head if she knew you were coming to meet me."

A smirk touched Mer's mouth. "My aunt has eyes everywhere. I wouldn't be surprised if she already knows about this meeting." Her expression melted into seriousness. "I'll have my warriors scout the waters. As soon as the Scythians set sail, you shall know about it."

"Thank you." He wished he had better words to express his sincere appreciation. "I'll see you soon."

"Until then," she whispered.

Sam offered her one more smile before he dove beneath the surface.

The tide of the war might have changed.

CHAPTER NINE

Dor

Devil take, but Dor hated mornings. The cave's lighting never seemed to change, making it even more difficult to rise at the dawn of a new day.

Dor laid her head on the table and stared absently at the measly blanket that served as the curtain for their door while she waited for her back to stop throbbing. Her eyes were puffy from crying and lack of sleep, but at least her mum had cleaned the wounds and given her something for the pain before her sisters had awoken. She didn't want them to see how much pain she was in.

She closed her eyes and tried to imagine what it would be like to experience the warmth of the sun on her skin, to see trees towering over her, to feel the wind on her face. As little feet padded from the other small room, she cracked a smile and opened one eye.

"Trying to sneak up on me again, Lailana?"

Lailana squeaked and stomped around Dor. The four-year-old pushed back her black curls and squinted up at Dor with huge green eyes.

"How did you hear me?" she demanded, her chubby cheeks flushing.

Dor touched her ears. "I have powerful hearing."

Lailana sucked on her bottom lip, her gaze sliding to Dor's bare back. She winced and pointed. "That owie must hurt a lot."

"Not as much as it did before Mum cared for me," Dor answered truthfully.

"Did the mean man hurt you?"

Dor sucked in her cheeks, trying to figure out how to explain what happened. It did no good to lie to any of her sisters about the circumstances in which they lived, but she also didn't want Lailana to lose all of her innocence so young.

"I wasn't as obedient yesterday as I should have been."

"But Mum says you're a good girl who helps others."

"Even good girls make mistakes, and this is what happens when I don't do what I'm supposed to. There are consequences to every decision we make, wee one."

"That's not fair."

"Life isn't always fair, you're right, but we do the best we can."

Lailana stared at Dor's back for a few more seconds, her forehead wrinkling, brows slashing together. "I don't want an owie like that."

"Hopefully you won't ever have to experience it."

Her sister nodded and then glanced at the empty table. "Breakfast?"

Dor pulled her sister into a loose hug and kissed the unruly curls on the top of her head. "Is food all you think about?"

Lailana's stomach growled in answer to Dor's question. Lailana giggled, and, to Dor, it was the best sound in the world.

"I don't only think about food, sissy," Lailana protested.

"What else do you think about?" Dor asked with a smile.

"Dragons and sweeties."

"You would," she laughed.

"Father always brings me a treat." Her little face clouded over. "Where is Papa? I miss him."

Dor's stomach sank, but she was saved from answering as their mum pushed through the cloth door.

"This little one is hungry," Dor said, stroking her sister's curls. "Her belly won't stop shouting at me."

Her mum smiled and opened her arms as Lailana skipped over, gave her a hug, and then plopped a kiss on her belly.

"Ez?" her mum called. "Time to get up, love, or you're going to miss breakfast."

"I'm up," Ez mumbled, as she stumbled out of their darkened room.

Even at the age of ten, Dor's middle sister was a beauty. Short, dark wine-colored hair, green-hazel eyes, and pale skin. A year earlier, a warrior had taken a particular interest in Ez, and Dor and her mother had taken to cutting the girl's hair to avoid wandering, perverted eyes. The only thing that made Dor feel better about the whole situation was that her sire had made that warrior disappear permanently.

"How'd you sleep?" Dor asked.

"Just lovely," her sister replied, her tone tired and bitter. Ez stopped to Dor's right and winced as she took in the nightmare that was Dor's back. "That's going to take a while to heal. Do you need anything, sissy?"

Her middle sister had a prickly temperament, but she was more caring than many people Dor knew. "Mum took care of me. Why don't all of you go and get breakfast?"

"Are you coming?" Ez asked.

Dor placed a hand on her upset stomach, pain and anxiety causing it to roll. "No, I don't think I could eat a bite." With the work she had to accomplish today and the pain she was in, she would likely throw up anything she ate. "I'll be sure to eat dinner tonight."

"Jadim will be here in a bit to help you get to your assignment." Her mum placed her hands on her lower back and stretched, her face a mask of discomfort.

"How are you doing today?" Dor asked, eyeing her mum.

Her mum made a silly face that caused Lailana to giggle and everyone's countenance to brighten. "As good as expected. Now let's go and eat."

Her sisters followed their mum and blew Dor a series of kisses as they disappeared out of the door. Dor slowly straightened and glanced at her feet, wiggling her toes. Once again, she was thankful for not having shoes. She couldn't imagine the pain and effort it would've taken to get them on. She sighed, and forced herself to stand in their quiet home. There wasn't much in the room. A bed stood to the right of the entrance, a small nightstand next to it. There were three wooden chairs that circled the beat-up table and a rocking chair in the corner that had seen better days. It may have looked like meager lodgings, but it was still Dor's home, and the little sketches on the walls brought a smile to her face.

Dor slipped out of their cave and slowly began the trek down to her assignment, her muscles and back stiff. Pulling in a deep breath, she sighed. Not many people scurried about the Pit—a rarity—but that would change in a matter of minutes. No one missed breakfast. It was the one meal they were guaranteed. Dor took her time enjoying the quiet reprieve that she normally wasn't afforded. She loved her family dearly, but sometimes she longed to sneak away to a quiet cave just to be able to hear her own thoughts.

A hand wrapped around her elbow as she moved around a corner, causing her to stumble. She hissed as the wounds in her back pulled, then glared at the person who'd grabbed her. Ada frowned and squeezed Dor's elbow once before stepping back.

"I'm sorry, I didn't mean to scare you. You looked as if you were about to keel over."

"I'm fine," Dor replied.

Ada blinked and leaned comically to the side. "You were almost walking sideways." She straightened, pulled a piece of meat from her pocket, and slipped it into Dor's hand. "For your friend."

Dor tucked the meat away and glanced around the empty hallway before whispering a soft, "Thank you."

"Are you slipping to your spot?"

"Not until I've finished my assignment."

Ada nodded. "Can you even work?"

Dor smiled and strode toward her destination. "Mum numbed my back pretty well. I'm almost as good as new."

Her friend snorted. "I'll believe that when I see it." A pause. "I'll help you as much as I can."

Dor's heart warmed, and she carefully threw an arm around Ada and hugged her. "I love you."

"The same," Ada said, keeping her eyes down as they moved past stoic warriors who surveyed the area dispassionately.

They made their way into a smaller, stone corridor that smelled of damp rock, decaying leaves, and mold. Dor's nose wrinkled, and she breathed through her mouth to try to avoid the scent. She'd grown up in the Pit, yet, she'd never gotten used to the stench in certain areas.

"Don't be such a baby," Ada remarked as they arrived at their cave.

Dor pulled a face and glanced toward the whipping post. Dried blood covered the floor and the leather straps that had held her up. She blanched and hustled past the post to keep from heaving. Sweat broke out on her body as she retreated farther into the cavern and leaned her face against the cool rock.

Ada moved next to her and placed two sets of tools on the ground. "I retrieved yours."

Dor swallowed hard and used her open-backed shirt to wipe her face. "Thank you."

Workers filed in and moved to their designated work stations, all of them eyeing Dor's back as they set up. Dor scratched her arms and tried to ignore the feeling of many eyes on her. She held her breath as a mean-looking set of warriors moved through the group and signaled for them to start work. Thankfully, they paid her no attention, and her breath whooshed out. Thank the stars it wasn't the warriors from the prior day. At least, in this way, she was lucky.

***

Dor's arms shook, and her whole body broke out in a cold sweat. She'd only been working for a few hours and yet it felt like days had passed. Her back screamed with every movement she made, and wetness she suspected was blood trickled down her back.

"You need to take a break," Ada huffed as she swung her pickaxe.

"If I slow down any more, I won't be able to pick it up again."

"You'll kill yourself."

"Many things could kill me, but this isn't one of them."

"What if—"

Ada cut off abruptly and looked behind Dor. Dor forced herself to work harder and peeked out of the corners of her eyes to see what her friend was staring at. A man had materialized beside Dor and stared at her.

"Are you Dorcus?" he asked, his voice as quiet as the night.

Chills ran up and down Dor's spine as she forced herself to work harder. "I am."

He stepped closer and tugged the pickaxe from her hand.

Dor gaped at him and then glared at the man. "There are many tools. I'm sure you can find your own. Please kindly return mine so I can get back to work before either of us gets in trouble."

He flicked a glance around the cavern and then stepped closer to whisper in her ear. "You helped a little boy yesterday?"

Dor nodded and tipped her head back so she could meet his gaze. "Anyone would have."

He shook his head, his long hair falling into his eyes. "Not everyone." His gaze slid to her shoulder. "That was my little brother you saved yesterday. My family and I would like to pay back our debt. I shall work in your place today."

"I can't let you do that. There's no debt to pay. He is just a child, and children need protection."

The tall, young man nodded and squared his shoulders. "I understand, but I've heard eyewitness accounts of your beatings. If that warrior had touched my brother, he would have surely died. This is not something we can forget." His fingers curled possessively around the ax. "You're not well. Leave, and I'll finish this."

"And what of your own work?"

"I work during the night, so this is my resting time. No one is looking for me."

"And what of the other workers?" She glanced around the cave, noting the interested looks sent her way. Would they report her? It would be better to work in pain than receive another punishment. Surely, she wouldn't make it through another lashing.

"They won't say a word. They respect you for your sacrifice."

Her back spasmed, and pain lanced her spine. "I can't possibly accept your offer. It's too dangerous."

"I wouldn't put you in danger," Ada said softly to her left. "I spent most of the night making arrangements. You don't know him, but you can trust me."

Dor stared at her friend. "You helped arrange this?"

Ada nodded. "Let the man work, and you go to your spot for the rest of the day."

Dor glanced between the stranger and her friend, feeling like she would cry. "Thank you."

"It's the least we can do," the young man said. He lifted his chin. "Now leave before the guards return."

Dor kissed Ada on the cheek and crept to the end of the cavern to escape through the back passageway. Every step away from her post instilled more tension in her body as she waited for someone to call her out, but not a word was said.

Only the sound of metal striking stone accompanied her as she escaped working for the first time in her life.

CHAPTER TEN

The Warlord

He waved away the messenger and checked the seal for tampering.

Nothing. It was completely intact.

How boring.

He'd been suspicious of the messenger for some time now. He sighed. No executions today.

Zane slid a fine dagger across the seal and opened the letter hungrily. His expression hardened, and the voices inside him began to hiss their displeasure.

She's ours. They're keeping her from us. She should weep with gratitude and crawl to our feet begging for forgiveness.

He carefully placed the opened letter on his desk and inhaled deeply. The darker part of himself longed to crumple the letter or throw his desk through the wall of his tent. But those were baser feelings he'd mastered years ago, and he refused to lower himself to such beast-like behavior.

He pivoted on his heel and leaned a hip against his desk as he planned his next move. Their refusal didn't bother him. It was that she'd let them refuse him.

His jaw clenched.

His consort knew how much he hated to be ignored. A thought occurred to him. She knew him and understood him better than anyone other than his sister. Maybe this was a game?

A wicked smile curled his lips.

Zane loved games, always had. If she wanted to play, who was he to say no? It would make his victory all the more sweet.

"Blair!" he commanded.

Soft steps approached, and his commander entered the tent, then bowed so deeply his braids almost touched the leren fur covering the floor. "Yes, my lord?"

Zane pushed off the desk and eyed the map of Aermia pinned to the wall of his tent. "Burn the first southern village."

"It will be done."

"Leave the people."

"Yes, my lord."

"Very good," Zane murmured. "Dismissed."

He watched as his second in command backed out of the tent.

Blair had been very devoted over the years, but he had his flaws. Zane's lips pursed. It would be a shame when the time came to execute the man. But it had to be done. If a warrior was left in power too long, it led to two outcomes: they either became too familiar with him, or they began to have doubts. Both options were dangerous.

The warlord reached a finger out and touched the black crown piece that represented his consort and her army.

"Soon, fiery one."

Soon, the voices chanted.

Sage would come to them.

It was only a matter of time.

CHAPTER ELEVEN

Dor

Dor carefully moved down the corridor toward the dull light and peeked around the corner, her heart picking up speed as guards patrolled the area.

Just act normal, Dorcus. You can do this. Don't let them see your fear.

She heaved a relieved breath as she maneuvered into the main hallway that circled the Pit in an endless spiral and joined the few workers heading toward their destinations below. At the thought of climbing all the way back up to her home, her whole body ached. But there was nothing else for it. She couldn't rest at home, so downward into hell it was.

Sweat beaded on her brow, and her breathing became labored as the path turned into steep stairs. Descending them was the worst part. Fear zipped through her veins at the thought of falling. She'd seen it happen before. Once a person slipped, there was no stopping their momentum. It only led to death.

She jerked as the woman next to her wrapped a firm hand around her left elbow and pulled her toward the inner wall, away from the edge. Dor glanced at her, askance. The woman smiled tiredly, deep lines marring the skin of what once might have been a beautiful face.

"You're making me nervous with all of your shambling about. Can't have you dying."

Dor nodded. "Thank you."

"It's no place to be daydreaming."

Thoroughly chastised, Dor thanked the old woman and continued her descent in silence. She ignored the heavy breathing of the workers around her, and focused on putting one foot in front of the other. As the group approached another set of guards, Dor tried to walk as naturally as she could and kept her head down to avoid attracting attention. The back of her neck prickled, and she glanced over her shoulder and locked eyes with a young warrior who seemed to scrutinize her. She whipped around, her pulse galloping, and prayed he wouldn't stop her. Each step she descended seemed to take hours as she waited for the warrior to call out. It was only when she'd moved down three more levels that she relaxed a little, her back screaming at the abuse. One worker after another disappeared into caves and crevices until it was just Dor.

Chills ran up her arms as the air heated and the light darkened to almost nothing. Her nose wrinkled at the cloying odor of brimstone and musk, and something dead. She eyed the gloomy surroundings and ran her left hand along the wall until her fingers caught on a star-shaped groove at about hip height. Then, she began counting. Fifty stairs until she would reach her destination. Dor blinked repeatedly as if it would help her eyes adjust to the almost-darkness that cocooned her like a cloud of smoke.

Forty-eight, forty-nine, fifty.

Her left hand ran along the wall and into a crevice that was only a handspan taller than her. With care, she edged sideways into the crevice and squeezed through its tight opening while trying to avoid scraping her back. Dor counted six steps and then reached her hands above her head as she entered a cool open space. She held in a deep breath and then released it. There was something about small spaces that always terrified her, and the older she became, the tighter the entrance to her secret spot became. It was only with memorization and the special breathing techniques her mum had taught which allowed Dor to still visit.

She blinked in the darkness, knowing it wouldn't magically become brighter. She placed one foot in front of the other and ran her hands along the ceiling as she traveled deeper into the narrow cavern. Realistically, she could have closed her eyes for all the good they did her, but she couldn't quite do it. For some odd reason, it made her feel safer if her eyes were open.

Her fingers brushed along the downward-sloped cavern ceiling, and her breath hitched as the tunnel tapered into a tiny passageway made of stone. Her heart pounded when at last she dropped to her hands and knees and began crawling forward into the small space. Rock scraped her shoulders after several moments, and she paused, her whole frame quaking. The stone felt like it was closing in on all sides. A sob escaped her as she imagined the stone suffocating her.

Dor shook her head to dispel the image. "Just a little farther," she panted. "You can do this." But her body didn't want to move. "Move it, Dorcus."

She drew in a deep breath and closed her eyes, to count her breaths like her mum had taught her. Once she was sufficiently calm, she began moving again through the tunnel she knew by heart. Hands and knees soaked from the small puddles she crawled through, she picked up her pace as the oppressive stone threatened to swallow her.

"Thank the stars," she gasped as the tunnel abruptly opened up and she spilled from the narrow channel into a small, round cave.

Dor knelt on the ground and placed her hands on the tops of her thighs, head bowed, and pulled in deep breaths. No matter how many times she went through the tunnel, each time was just as hard as the first. She didn't mind being in the caverns, but there was something terrifying about being surrounded by unforgivable stone that could easily take her life.

Once she'd caught her breath, she glanced around the space, barely able to see the spherical outline of the cave. When she'd first discovered this cave, she was only six years of age. Even now, she didn't know what had scared her mum so badly, but when her mum told her to run and hide, she did. She'd run and stumbled blindly until she couldn't crawl anymore. That's when she'd met her scaly friend.

Dor scooted forward and squinted at the wall until she discovered the rock she was searching for. Soft light slipped around the cracks as she wedged her fingers around it and tugged. Stone grated against stone until the plate-sized rock pulled free. Weak light flooded the small cavern, and Dor held an arm up and blinked. Her breaths caught as they did every time.

The cave sparkled. Every inch reflected light in the dark stone like thousands of tiny stars. It was beautiful. It was a piece of magic she held close to her heart. Even in the Pit, there was beauty.

A soft click caused her to smile, and she bent forward to peek through the opening to the other side. She whistled a soft tune and waited with bated breath for her friend. Her smile grew as scales scraped against stone and heavy footsteps neared her spot. The first time she'd heard such a sound, she'd been terrified, but not now. Now, she couldn't wait for what stood on the other side.

Dor carefully pushed her arm through the opening, and held her hand out as an enormous, scaled muzzle gently pressed against her palm. Heat infused her hand as the dragon nuzzled her in a happy hello.

"Hello, Illya."

Dor giggled when the dragon clicked a familiar *hello,* and a dry, rough tongue licked her arm. She playfully shook her hand out and then stroked the dragon's snout, marveling at the experience. It had been twelve years since she'd first met Illya, and each time she was able to visit him was like something out of a storybook.

Dor pulled back and leaned down, placing her chin on the edge of the stone. "How has your week been?"

Illya pulled back and hunkered down so Dor could see one silver feline-looking eye that reflected like rainbows in just the right light. His black scales caught the faint light and reflected colors like slicked oil. Dor's breath caught. He was the most magnificent creature she'd ever beheld. A sense of awe settled over her as she stared at the little of him she could see.

"You are the most beautiful thing I've ever beheld."

The dragon huffed, seeming to understand her. Over the years, she'd come to know Illya well. His mannerisms, likes, and dislikes. Some days, she'd prefer his company over that of the other humans she lived with.

He turned his face, as if preening.

Dor rolled her eyes. "Don't think too much of yourself, you vain beast." She scanned what she could see of his face and frowned as she noticed a new wound on his neck. The scales had been torn from him and his flesh had been cut open. A small growl escaped her. It sickened her what the healers did to the dragons. Their endless experiments made her want to kick something. "What did they do to you this week?" she whispered.

Illya blinked at her slowly, like he could understand every word from her mouth, and leaned closer as she reached a hand out to trace the scales under his eye, as if needing the soothing touch as much as she did. It was uncanny at times how he understood her moods better than she did.

Nothing that you could prevent.

Her dragon's clicks, hisses, and soft purrs had seemed to form the words that had blossomed in her mind, and she shook her head at her active imagination. Dragons didn't talk, and prisoners didn't have dragons. She pulled her hand back, earning a hiss of displeasure.

"Just wait, you'll enjoy my surprise." Dor wriggled her eyebrows at Illya. "I've brought something special for you, but I'll only give it to you if you promise to sing for me."

Illya hissed and pressed his snout against the gap and puffed air into her cavern. Her hair blew back from her face in a rush, and she grinned at the mischievous dragon.

"Okay, okay," she laughed as she pulled the small treat from her pocket and held it out to him. "I'm sorry it's not much. Next time, I'll do better."

He gently took the dried meat from her hand, conscious of his huge, razor-sharp teeth. It amazed her how he could be so gentle with such massive teeth—teeth he could tear her arm off with should he want. He gobbled down the treat with an enthusiasm that both buoyed and broke Dor's heart. Part of her was happy she could bring him something he enjoyed; the other part of her was broken-hearted he was so hungry. Illya hummed a satisfied sound in the back of his throat, and then sniffed her hand for more treats.

She smiled sadly and shook her head. "I'm sorry I don't have more for you this week. It's been a nightmare. I'll do better next week, I promise."

Dor stroked his scales above his eye and traced the long, jagged scar that caused his scales to grow up like spikes. Her heart squeezed. She still remembered when he'd received that one. She had been only eleven years, and she'd cried, thinking her dragon was dying. Even then, when he was in so much pain, Illya had snuggled as close as he could to impart comfort to her.

"It's not right how they treat you," she murmured.

Dragons were the worst kept secret in the Pit. Everyone knew they existed, but no one dared approach one of the beasts lest they be eaten. The healers starved the beasts and gave them elixirs to keep them calm while they experimented on them.

Her jaw clenched.

One of the only meals the dragons received were human traitors. It sickened her, but she understood what hunger could do to a person, let alone an animal. She couldn't fault Illya for any meals he had eaten. If she could get him and her family out, she would. Sometimes, in her space, she'd imagine them flying away and never coming back. But those were just childish dreams. There wasn't any escape for any of them, despite how much she wished it.

"I turn eighteen years in six days," she said. The words tasted sour upon her tongue. "Only six days until they come for me."

Disgust and burning hatred lit and began to simmer in her belly. Dreams weren't the only thing she indulged in with her dragon. She also released words and feelings that would get her killed if she ever repeated them in the hearing distance of another person.

"I hate them," she hissed. "I hate them so much. Sometimes I think about doing terrible things. Like... rebelling." Her last word was so soft, it was almost as if she never said it. But as soon as the word was released, a well of feeling rushed forward in her. "Everything is wrong about this place. No one deserves to live as a prisoner just because of the kingdom they were born in. No woman deserves to be bred like an animal. I'm sick of being judged because of how I look." She cursed and glanced at her hands. "Just because we're different doesn't mean we're inferior." Her skin prickled as she spoke the treason that had rooted deeply in her heart. "Who gave the warlord the right to leash human beings and declare them disposable because of their genes?"

A tear dripped down her cheek. "I hate him." Her hand shook as she reached toward Illya and stroked his frill on the crown of his head as he pressed as close to her as possible. "I hate being forced to live here. I hate the injustice. I hate being powerless."

That's what bothered her the most. She was powerless to stop the pain and suffering around her. She was powerless to fight the fate that had been placed before her.

Another tear fell.

"I'll be a mother soon." Her dragon nuzzled her fist, and she forced herself to open her hand and keep stroking his scales. "Maybe you'll be able to get to know my children." She swiped at her watery eyes with her right forearm, hating that she didn't get a say in what happened to her own children. The unknown was the most frightening. Would the warrior let her keep the children and raise them? Would he take the child and discard her like rubbish?

I will love your young.

Dor froze and blinked, staring at the dragon who eyed her quietly. She barked out a laugh. "I'm hearing things and laughing at my mind. It must be all the stress." And the pain.

She winced and cautiously stretched her back, the healing wounds pulsing with heat. Swiping at her gritty eyes once more, she got comfortable, pillowing her head on her arm as she stroked Illya's muzzle. "If you don't mind, I might rest a little bit, and, when I wake, I'll tell you a story."

Her dragon hummed and rested his head on his claw-tipped paws.

When she'd first met Illya, she'd been terrified and had started spouting stories to keep the dragon from eating her. She wouldn't step that near to him, and neither would he, but after that first visit, she'd found herself coming back. It took many months for them to trust each other, but Dor won him over by telling him stories. Some true, some nonsensical.

Her eyes slowly closed, and, as she drifted off to sleep, a deep voice crooned.

I'll watch over you.

CHAPTER TWELVE

Tehl

"Bloody hell!" William gasped, staring at the immense fiilee to his right, causing Tehl to hide his smile.

The older man gaped, his long beard quivering as his mouth bobbed in awe—and a good dose of fright, Tehl suspected.

"That's Skye," Tehl said, as the fiilee crept closer, sniffing the ground beneath his paws. His lips twitched. Nali had no doubt relieved herself in the spot, marking her territory, and the immense creature was clearly not thrilled.

"She's beautiful, no?" Raziel, the crown prince of Methi, said as he strode into the meadow.

Tehl glanced behind the Methian prince, hoping to spot his wife. The troublesome woman could scarcely leave the beasts alone. Every time he turned his back, she'd disappear from their camp to go and train with the beasts.

The first time he'd caught her flying on the back of one, Tehl's heart had practically leapt out of his chest. Once he'd calmed himself down, he'd then noticed the man riding behind her, pressed fully against her. That had stirred up feelings he'd rarely experienced.

Jealousy.

He knew what curves and beauty lay beneath her clothes, and it rankled him that another man was wrapped around *his* wife and could obviously feel her shape. When they'd landed, Sage had a skip in her step as she rushed toward him. Her green eyes had sparkled like emeralds and color had turned her cheeks a pretty pink that he wanted to taste.

Tehl honestly couldn't remember what she'd said to him. For one thing, she was speaking faster than his mind could comprehend, and he was a bit distracted. She pecked him on his mouth and then ran down the path toward camp like a wild fae thing he had no chance of catching.

"She's fiery," Raziel had commented.

Turning back to face the Methian prince, he had been relieved to notice the man wasn't watching his wife, but had been attending to his beast.

"I have no designs on your wife." Raziel's golden eyes had met his for a moment. "I like mine a little less jaded."

Tehl's hackles had risen at the insult. Raziel had taken one look at his face and held his hands up in surrender.

"It's not meant as an insult." A shrug. "I like my friends jaded and sarcastic, so she's perfect for that role. And you, my friend, have it bad," Raziel goaded.

"Have what?"

"You love your mate, as you rightly should. One day, I hope to find the same thing. You are a lucky man. Any person can choose a spouse, but those who have a love match are to be envied." Raziel had blown some of his wine-colored hair from his face and smiled wolfishly. "Plus, they always produce the strongest kits."

Now, Tehl wasn't an ignorant man, nor was he overly shy, but something about the Methian prince's words had made him want to blush. Instead, he'd smiled in pride. He and Sage *would* have amazing children.

"Tehl?"

He blinked and stared at William's lined face. "Yes?"

"Daydreaming?"

"Something like that."

Raziel gave William a knowing smile and gestured toward Skye. "Would you like to meet her properly?"

A boyish smile illuminated the general's face as he stared in wonder at the fiilee. "I don't think there's anything I've ever wanted more, other than to bed my wife," William said with glee.

The Methian crown prince released a booming laugh and slapped William on the back. "Well, I can't grant your other wish, but this is, at least, in my power." He glanced at Tehl. "One of my men is bringing the spymaster for a visit. He should be here within the hour."

Sam. Well, that was a piece of good news. They'd been at the war camp for several weeks, and, so far, all of it had been for nothing. The Scythians hadn't crossed the border. They'd made their presence known by their massive fires at night and the war songs and drums that never ceased to stop. Tehl had yet to figure out their aim. His best guess was they were trying to manipulate their psyche and intimidate them.

A shadow passed over Tehl and swung around the meadow. He tipped his head back and watched a pure-white fiilee glide to the ground. His brother grinned and waved. Tehl had to smile back. He wasn't sure if the reason Sam was so giddy was because of the flight, or the extremely attractive Methian woman holding him.

She slid off the fiilee and offered a hand up to Sam like he was a lady. His brother was too far away for Tehl to hear the words, but whatever he had said to the normally stoic warrior had the woman blushing. He rolled his eyes at his brother's antics, knowing Sam just couldn't help himself.

Sam climbed down from the fiilee and took the woman's hand and kissed it, further turning the woman into another admirer, Tehl was sure. The bastard.

Sam abandoned his happy victim and almost pranced across the meadow, a wicked smile on his face.

Stars above, Tehl had missed his brother. Things had been much too serious without his sense of warped humor to break the ice. He took a few steps and embraced him.

Sam pulled back, grinning. "Missed me? I'm flattered. It's only been a few weeks."

"Not long enough," Tehl muttered with a straight face.

His brother snorted. "I see the dry humor is alive and well."

He shook his head at Sam. The man wasn't wrong. "What news do you have?"

Sam's face melted into an expression much too serious for Tehl's liking. "I think you'll need to sit down for this one."

***

His blasted brother was right. If he hadn't been sitting, he'd have fallen down.

"Do the punches ever stop coming?"

"Not with the warlord," Sage said darkly. She leaned heavily against the circular, wooden table that stood in the center of the room. His wife stared blankly at the massive leather map that lay on the tabletop.

Raziel paced behind Sage and Lilja along the tent wall, his hair almost brushing the ceiling. Tehl had thought he was tall, but the damn man was a bloody giant. Did they breed massive humans in Methi?

"Tehl?"

He blinked slowly and turned toward Lilja as she pointed at the map. "Yes?"

The Sirenidae stood from her chair, her burnt-orange dress whispering around her bare legs. Tehl wondered how she could stand the cold with so few garments on. He pulled his jacket closer and stood to get a better look at the spot she was pointing to on the map. She placed a small pin at the mouth of Sanee's bay.

"If the Scythians get anywhere near the bay, we'll lose Sanee," Lilja declared.

"We can't lose Sanee," Tehl muttered. It was unthinkable to lose the capital. "Do you think this is a ploy to get us to remove our army?"

Lilja shrugged a snowy shoulder. "I can't presume to know the mind of the warlord. This could be a trap, it could be a legitimate maneuver, or he could just be trying to bluff us. General?"

William's mustache moved from side to side as he wiggled his lips, his eyes glued to the map like it held the secrets to the world. "It would be smart to pin us in on both sides, but I don't think he has enough men to pull off such a venture. Sage?"

"I don't know." Frustration colored her tone as she glared down at the map. "I didn't exactly see much of his stronghold. We were led through the jungle and then down into a cave-like hole area."

"The Pit," Lilja supplied.

"The Pit," Sage continued, "was massive, but I think it only held laborers." She pushed back from the table and crossed her arms. "I wish I had more information, but that's all I know."

Tehl frowned. Sage wasn't the only one who'd been in Scythia. "Where's Blaise?"

"She's out on scouting duty. She'll return this evening," Raziel supplied.

"And how do you know that?" Lilja questioned.

The Methian prince smiled, his golden eyes dancing. "My brother is also on duty."

Tehl smothered his smile. Rafe had assigned himself to every one of Blaise's duties, and the Scythian woman hated it. Just a week ago, Tehl had watched Blaise pull a blade on Rafe and almost take off the tip of his nose. What had been even better was the look on Rafe's face once he realized she'd pulled one over on him. She'd held not one blade, but two, and had also cut a good chunk of hair from his head.

"She's our best bet." Tehl turned to Sam. "But Jasmine has invaluable information. You'll speak to her?"

Sam frowned, but quickly smoothed his expression. "I'll speak to her and pass on any prudent information." He turned his attention on Lilja. "What of Blair?"

"Blair's been silent."

That settled like a rock in Tehl's stomach. Blair was playing a dangerous game. He didn't exactly trust the Scythian, but Lilja did, and that was enough for him. Anyone Lilja held in esteem was an ally worth having.

"Any word from the rest of the Sirenidae?" Sage asked Lilja.

Lilja shook her head. "It's been quiet in the seas." She pinned Sam with her magenta gaze. "How did you come by this information?" she asked curiously.

Sam smiled casually. "Spies."

Lilja smirked, a picture of amusement and sexuality. "And who is your spy? Or better yet, *what* is your spy?"

Sam grinned. "You know I can't tell you."

She laughed. "I have my suspicions."

"And that's all they are. *Suspicions*."

William rolled his eyes and clapped his hands. "You young'uns and your games," he said gruffly, but with affection.

Lilja glided to his side and pressed a kiss against his whiskered cheek. "You flatterer."

"Let's reconvene this evening," Tehl said. "We'll be able to get a better idea of our enemy's numbers then."

Raziel nodded and strode from the tent with a nod at Sage and Tehl. Lilja looped an arm through William's and strolled out of the tent, leaving Tehl with Sam and Sage.

"What a nightmare," Sage breathed.

Tehl watched her in concern. She'd lost some of her color at the news of the armada the Scythians were readying.

She ran her hands through her dark brown hair. "I hate surprises."

"I love a good surprise," his brother piped in. "Especially when it involves a naked female."

Sage rolled her eyes, but a small smile touched her mouth, removing some of the grim lines that were bracketing her lips. She'd been much too serious since arriving at the camp. The circumstances were glum, but, still, she'd lost a little bit of the sassiness Tehl loved.

She walked over to Sam and hugged him. "How's Jasmine?"

"She's doing well."

"That's all I get?" Sage asked, stepping back.

Tehl full-on grinned as he stepped closer and wrapped an arm around his wife's waist, content with how she leaned into him. Stars above, they were in the least romantic setting, but he still couldn't keep his hands off his wife.

Sam watched the two of them, a twinkle in his blue eyes. "She told me if I didn't tell you to visit soon, she'd track you down herself."

Sage smiled. "That sounds more like her." She squeezed Tehl and moved out of his arms toward the tent flap to their right. "I'll let you two catch up."

Both men watched her disappear outside and then faced each other. Sam shifted from foot to foot in an uncharacteristic show of unease and nervousness.

Tehl cocked his head and arched a brow. "I thought Zachael beat that out of you."

Sam shrugged. "It rarely happens."

Tehl brushed by his brother and snagged a canteen from atop his cloak. He pulled the stopper out and took a huge swig. If his brother was nervous, then he had truly awful news.

He held out the canteen to his brother and was shocked when Sam took two gulps. That wasn't a good sign. His brother rarely drank spirits, and when he did… it was always because something terrible had happened. Whatever his brother had to say now would likely be worse than what he'd already dropped on them.

"Don't keep me on my toes. Just give it to me straight," Tehl ordered. He hated the suspense. "Tell me what's wrong."

"Jasmine's pregnant." Sam winced at his blunt words.

Tehl blinked slowly, trying to comprehend the two small words. Jasmine was with child? His brows pulled together as he counted the days since Sam and Jasmine had wed. It had only been a few weeks – how could he possibly know that soon...

He glared at his brother. "You did not. Tell me you did not do something so dishonorable."

Sam glared back. "Thanks for not jumping to conclusions!"

"As if you gave me any other options! What am I supposed to think? You have a history that I've tried to ignore, but at least you've married the girl." If he hadn't... well, they'd be having a very different conversation at the moment.

"The child is not mine."

Swamp apples. He'd seen how Jasmine had been acting promiscuously after the woman had escaped, but he'd hoped she'd had more sense than that. He didn't think her the devious type to trap a man into marriage. "Did you know before you wed?" he outright asked. It was better to be blunt than to miscommunicate.

"I did."

Tehl studied his brother. "Would the man who ruined her not do the honorable thing?"

The muscle in Sam's jaw ticked as he swallowed. "Tehl, she's *well* along. It won't be much longer until the babe arrives."

The blood drained from Tehl's face as he realized what his brother was telling him. If she was that far along with child, that meant she was in Scythia when the babe was conceived. "Wicked hell, *no.*" It couldn't be true.

Sam's hands clenched and unclenched. "It seems not all have the control of their master."

Tehl sat heavily on the chair behind him. That poor girl. What she must have suffered. Did Sage know? "Who else knows about this?"

"Both healers, myself, and now you."

So, Sage didn't know. The news would kill her. "Why tell me?"

"I don't know what to do for my wife. She's struggling. I think," Sam paused, "I think she needs Sage."

"You know what you're asking of me? This will be a great weight of guilt my wife will have to carry."

"She'll be angrier if you keep it from her," Sam pointed out.

True, but not the point.

Tehl scowled at his brother. "I wouldn't have to keep anything from her if you'd kept this to yourself." He stared at his calloused hands. How was he supposed to tell Sage? "Does Jasmine know you're here?"

"Yes, but she doesn't know I've spoken to you about this. If it were up to her, she'd keep pretending like nothing is wrong at all. But she can barely hide the swell of her belly now. Palace gossips say they think she's just fat." Sam grimaced. "If she won't speak to Mira or I about it, I think she'll speak to Sage."

"You think ambushing your wife is the answer?"

Sam threw his hands up. "I don't know what else to do. She's wrapped an impenetrable wall around herself that I can't get through. The only time I see her soften is with the twins," he growled, frustration clear in every word.

Tehl watched his brother closely. "Do you want to get close to her?"

"Well, I married her, didn't I?" he scoffed. "I was trying to do the right thing. She'd suffered much to help Sage, and she didn't deserve what would happen to her once it was known she was with child. At least this way, she'll have the protection of our name and the love of our family." A pause. "So will the child."

Pride and tenderness bloomed in Tehl's chest. His brother had his faults, but Tehl had always known he was a good man. "You're going to be a father," he whispered. He stood and embraced his brother. "Congrats."

Sam hugged him and slapped him on the back. "I don't know what I'm doing."

"No one does." Tehl pulled back, grinning. "Despite how the babe came about, it's still a blessing. I'll send Sage home for a visit shortly." He sobered. "Maybe she'll actually sleep."

Sam stared at him, askance. "She's not sleeping?"

"The nightmares are getting worse. She actually handed me her weapons to keep me safe. One night, she almost slit my throat."

His brother's expression morphed into something deadly and blood thirsty. "The monsters that caused our women pain *will* suffer."

Tehl mirrored his brother's smile. "That they will."

CHAPTER THIRTEEN

Sam

He rounded the last tent and strode toward his horse. His white war horse gleamed in the darkness and didn't startle as he approached. There was something cozy about the night. Most were terrified of the darkness, of what it concealed, but Sam thought of it as more of a warm blanket of protection.

Sam brushed his hand along Moonlight's flank and checked his saddle. He could never be too careful. No one wanted to die because of negligence.

"Leaving so soon?" a husky, sensual voice called.

He straightened and craned his neck to smile over his shoulder.

Lilja stepped from the forest that bordered the war camp and sauntered toward him, all grace.

"I was wondering when you would come find me."

She smiled coyly and brushed a silvery-white lock of hair from her shoulder. "And what gave you the impression that I wanted to speak with you?"

Sam laughed softly and turned to face Lilja. "Like calls to like, love."

"That it does."

She sat daintily on a tall round rock and crossed her long pale legs that the slitted skirt just couldn't keep contained.

Sam groaned and ran a hand down his face. In his mind, he knew she was old enough to be his mother, but damn him, if the woman wasn't alluring.

"Do you really run around the camp in that getup? It's amazing you haven't been accosted."

Lilja laughed. "They've all seen me spar."

"That makes sense."

He considered himself capable with many weapons, but in a fight with the Sirenidae? She'd win, hands down. The woman was death wrapped in a beautiful package.

"What do you want with me?" he said tiredly. "It's been a long day."

"I suspect it has," Lilja replied softly. "I'm intrigued as to how you obtained the information about the Scythian fleet."

Sam arched a brow. He wasn't going to give her information for free. "You're fishing and you know it."

"Fish. What an interesting word to use. I've been in the caves that house the Scythian ships, and it would be impossible for anyone to get inside conventionally. They would have to be excellent swimmers," she enunciated and pinned him with a look.

He kept his expression placid. How in the hell did she know? "What are you getting at?"

"Don't play coy. You have a Sirenidae spy."

"Anything is possible."

Lilja brushed imaginary lint off of her skirt. "You should know that keeping company with you is very dangerous for your spy, and I'm not speaking of their missions. I'm speaking of what will happen to them if the king finds out about their extracurricular activities. Death would be a kindness."

Sam held back a shiver at her somber warning. "I assure you that I care for all of my spies."

The Sirenidae stood and shook out her dress. "I'm aware, which is why I'm imparting this to you." She took a step closer, her magenta gaze intense. "I may not be permitted to permanently reside in the sea any longer, but it does not mean I am ignorant of what happens in its depths. Tell my niece I love her, and to be safe."

He kept his mask in place and marveled at the woman standing before him. He'd spoken to no one about his newest recruit, and yet, Lilja knew. "I'd very much like to spend a day in your mind," he murmured.

"I just bet you would." She stepped closer and adjusted his coat. "You should also know that rebellion is brewing in Scythia."

It was years of practice that kept him from jerking at her words. "You have proof?"

"Someone I trust very much. I suspect when the time comes, we may have more help than we anticipated from the enemy side."

His mind spun. That would change things. "Would you please keep me informed of the situation?"

She nodded. "If anything changes, you'll be one of the first to know."

"Aermia is lucky to have you," Sam said, meaning his words. Information could make or break a war. It was the difference between defeat and victory. "If you ever find you want a job..."

Lilja barked out a laugh and hugged him. "I'm much too old for spying and trickery."

Sam snorted. "Who's lying now?"

"When this is all over, I plan on growing fat on my ship with my delectable husband."

"Debauchery," Sam joked.

"Only if one is not married... speaking of which, how is your new wife?"

"As good as can be expected when married to a rake and scoundrel. She hates me."

"How delightfully honest," Lilja remarked. "Maybe give her a reason not to. Show her the real Sam."

It sounded easy. But in truth, it was impossible. His scandalous behavior perpetuated his world class reputation as a rake and flirt. While everyone focused on his perceived debauchery, they never looked any closer at what was really going on. And it worked for him. Well, up until now.

"I don't know if I can," he said honestly. "I feel like I don't know him anymore."

"That is something I understand. I've played many parts during my life. It was only once I met Hayjen that he helped me discover myself. Jasmine and her children could be that for you. Don't give up before you've even started. That's the coward's and fool's way out."

Sam pressed a kiss to Lilja's cheek and then stepped back. "I'll think about what you said." He slipped his foot into the stirrup and slung his right leg over his horse. "Take care."

Lilja waved and smiled, flashing her white teeth. "You do the same. You might want to have a conversation with Gem when you arrive home. I believe she has something she wants to tell you."

Sam opened his mouth to ask what she meant, but the Sirenidae melted back into the forest. He chuckled and shook his head.

"Bloody woman," he whispered and then pressed his heels into the sides of his horse. "Home!"

Chapter Fourteen

Dor

Dor woke with a start, sweat dripping down her back. Where was she?

She quickly blinked, trying to get her bearings. Her breath caught as she admired the gemstone-walls of the cave. Illya's cave. She was safe.

Dor relaxed and glanced toward the small opening. Her hand rested on Ilya's snout as the dragon slumbered. How much time had passed? She squinted into the dragon's room—though she could not decipher the time of day, the amount of pain plaguing her bare back that was currently plastered to the rough stone behind her told her much time had passed.

"This is going to hurt," she whispered to herself. Illya lazily cracked one silver eyelid and stared at her while she panted and prepared herself for the onslaught of pain. "If I pass out, wake me, Illya."

Her fingers clutched at the uneven stone to ground herself as she sat up. Her gasp echoed in her cave, and a growl escaped her as she sat up, her raw flesh clinging to the stone behind her. Water flooded her eyes, and white light flashed across her vision as she pulled away completely. Warm liquid dripped down her back as she gulped in the heated air her dragon blew into the small space. She was going to pass out.

A series of concerned clicks, growls, and hums rumbled from her dragon as he pressed closer to the wall between them.

"I'm okay," she puffed as she leaned forward with a groan. Dor lifted her hair to make sure no strands had pressed into any of her gashes. Sweat dotted her brow as agony pulsed through her injuries. Stars above, she hated lashings. It was one of the cruelest forms of punishment. If it were up to her, she'd burn every blasted whip in the Pit.

Illya whined, and Dor reached through the opening to run her hand along the length of his scarred, midnight snout. "It's just a little kink in my back. I shifted in my sleep and slept the wrong way."

He inhaled deeply. *I smell blood.*

She was going insane. Maybe from the blood loss. Dor rubbed the right side of her face. "I was whipped yesterday," she admitted.

"A little boy's life was in danger. I couldn't stand by and do nothing."

A true leader.

She snorted at her active imagination. She was a leader of nothing and no one. The Pit didn't breed heroes and saviors. It bred monsters and madness – she just happened to be one of the lesser monsters.

Pushing onto her knees, Dor pressed her face into the small rock opening and waited for Illya to press closer. Her eyes watered as he exhaled hot air into her face. "That was not necessary," she muttered as she brushed a kiss against the tip of his snout. As if the dragon couldn't help himself, he breathed on her again. It seemed like he enjoyed marking her by whatever means possible.

Dor pulled back and caressed his face, feeling a sense of loss at the prospect of leaving. This was the worst part. It felt like she was abandoning him. Each time she visited, there was a possibility he wouldn't answer her call. She couldn't imagine life without him. He'd become the best part of her life.

"I wish I could free you." The words were fanciful, filled with longing, truth, and hopelessness. Freedom wasn't in their future, but at least they had this time together.

You will free us all.

She ignored the unbidden thought as Illya stared her down like he was trying to tell her something.

"I have to go," she said, forcing a smile. "Thank you for sharing this afternoon with me and letting me rest here, but I need to return to my family."

Her dragon pushed harder against her hand and briefly curled his tongue around her wrist in his goodbye. Absently, she wondered if Illya longed for her company like she did for his. Maybe he was just biding his time with her, but it felt like something more. Inside, she knew he was inexplicably hers and she was his.

Dor massaged underneath his chin and pulled away. If she didn't go now, she wouldn't leave. Glancing over her shoulder, the hair on her arms rose as she stared at the small black hole she'd have to crawl through. A shudder worked through her body as she turned back to Illya. "I'll come back and visit you tomorrow, if possible. I'll try to bring a bigger treat for you."

Illya sniffed and clicked a soft, crooning sound. *I'll await your visit, precious one.*

Her eyes widened as she swore the words formed in her mind. "Illya, there's something wrong with my mind," she whispered. Her mum had always encouraged imagination, but at the age of eighteen years it was time she grew up, and yet, every time she visited, she imagined her dragon spoke to her. Which was impossible. Animals didn't speak. She eyed the dragon. Well... dragons weren't really animals. They were myths.

She shook her head at her fantastical thoughts. "Until we meet again," she whispered as she heaved the huge rock from the floor and inhaled deeply before shoving it back into place. Her pulse pounded as the stars around her winked out and inky darkness cloaked the space with its smothering presence. She sucked in a steadying breath and forced her legs to move away from her dragon. Time seemed to stretch as she made her way out of the secret spot.

Dull light spilled through the narrow crevice as the tunnel widened, and she was able to climb onto her feet. Her back protested the movements, but she didn't stop as she kept focused on the light. Almost there. She rotated sideways and shuffled through the crack, biting her bottom lip to keep from crying out when a sharp stone jabbed her back.

She paused, holding her breath, and scanned the staircase. Nothing stirred, but her skin prickled nonetheless. It felt like a million insects were crawling over her body. It was almost impossible to see at this level, she reminded herself. No one was watching her. She slipped onto the smooth, dry pathway and began the long trek up the winding staircase. It was one of the few places in the Pit that stayed dry. Dor stared at the black stone beneath her feet. The only explanation for this that she could figure was that the dragons released so much heat in their breaths that the surrounding area stayed dry. Which meant—she scanned the area—Illya couldn't be the only one.

Her legs wobbled, and Dor stumbled. She latched onto the wall to her right as she caught her breath, staring at the drop. That was the second time today. She needed to be more careful. She heaved a breath and glanced above and immediately wished she hadn't. The pathway seemed to spiral on forever.

Her legs burned as she forced herself to start climbing. The longer she tarried here, the more worried her mum would be.

Guilt pricked her. Worrying was the last thing her mum needed to be doing in her condition. The babe was due soon.

The steep stairway ended and melded with the sloping pathway that circled the Pit like a giant, coiled snake. The air cooled, as did Dor's sweat. Her stomach sank as she eyed the lanterns flickering around the Pit. They glowed a sickly green color. Night had officially come. Her mum would be worried.

Dor forced her legs to move faster and eyed the slaves that descended toward her. At least the night workers would cover her arrival. There was safety in numbers. She noted three guards loitering by an intersection of corridors to the main path. She tucked her chin and kept her head down as she approached them. They seemed too relaxed to be on duty. That always spelled trouble. It meant they were visiting for recreational purposes.

She held her breath as she passed the warriors, and thanked the stars that they were too occupied with bawdy jokes to notice her. That was until she caught a low whistle and murmured words.

"Long legs, but look at that back. That one screams trouble. Not worth it."

Her shoulders pulled up toward her ears as she hunched forward and practically ran away from the men. For once in her life, she was thankful for the beating if it meant it kept warriors from looking too closely at her.

She rounded a corner and plowed straight into a wide chest. A scream caught in her throat as two calloused hands wrapped around her biceps. Her gaze flew to the man holding her, and she almost sobbed in relief.

Jadim.

He stared down at her with arresting blue-green eyes, his lips pinched. He glanced over her shoulder and then directed her down a maze of hallways.

"Where have you been?" he hissed.

"Out." His jaw clenched in a familiar way. They'd been friends since childhood, and he'd always done that. She used to see how many times a day she could get him to clench his jaw. "Ada told you where I was?"

"She said you were safe, but that was hours ago. She's been so worried."

Dor shook his grip off and then placed her hand in his as they continued walking down the dark stone corridors. She shivered at the sickly green light that seemed to move and writhe around them. Devil, take it, but she hated the night lanterns.

"I didn't mean to worry anyone. I fell asleep." She straightened and winced as her back twinged. "My guess is that my body is trying to heal so I slept longer than I intended to."

Jadim's square jaw loosened, and he glanced at her through a thick fringe of lashes. Dor almost stumbled at the look. Sometimes she couldn't help but notice how devastatingly handsome he was. It was a shame what the healers had done to him.

"Don't look at me like that."

She forced her gaze away from his face, hating that she was mooning over a man she could never have. The healers had made sure of that, and her reactions only made it worse for him.

Ashamed, she squeezed his hand once. "I'm sorry."

"It's not your fault," he said softly, squeezing her hand back. "In fact," he paused, glancing around before slowing to a stop.

Dor arched a brow in question.

He wet his plush lips and stared down at her, his expression serious. "In six days, the healers will come for you."

Her stomach dropped and rolled at the reminder. "What of it?" She glared at the ground, hating how her voice wobbled, how fear showed its ugly face. Only six days until the last of her freedom would be ripped away, and she'd become just another broodmare for the Scythian court.

He dropped her hand and crooked a finger under her chin, forcing her to look up at his handsome angular face. "It is what it is, but you're not alone."

"I know," she croaked.

"Chances for perfect offspring are low," he murmured, telling her what she already knew. "So you'll be raising babes in the Pit."

Dor shrugged a shoulder. "It's not much different than what I've done with both of my sisters." But her stomach quivered at the thought of having her own child. "Chances are it will take time for a babe to catch in my womb."

Jadim stepped closer and clasped her face between his hands. "It only takes once, Dor."

She shuddered at the possibility of a child within the next year. She wasn't ready for a child, but wouldn't it be better to be only taken once? She didn't know. "I'm scared," she admitted.

"I know, but you won't be alone." He leaned forward and kissed her forehead. "I'll help raise the babes, if you'll have me."

She froze and stared blankly at his chest. "You wish to bond with me?" Her voice cracked.

He pulled back and brushed his thumb along her left cheek. "I do. I'll care for you and any children of ours."

She swallowed her tears and stared up at the selfless man before her. He would care for them, and help raise children that weren't his own? "What could you possibly gain out of this union? How could I accept such a gift?"

He wiped away a tear that dripped down her cheek. "I would gain a wonderful, capable wife who happens to be one of my best friends." He glanced away, his throat working, before staring down at her. "You know how I long for children."

Dor swallowed back the ugly sobs that threatened to break free. What the healers had done to Jadim was possibly one of their most heinous crimes. In a bid to control the slave population and to ensure imperfection wasn't passed to other children, the healers sterilized all the males. None of the men could have children or even accomplish the act of love making. They'd turned every male slave into a eunuch, and it sickened her.

"I do."

He stared down at her and slowly leaned closer to press a soft kiss against her lips. Her skin tingled, and she wrapped her hands around his wrists and leaned against him. Slowly, Jadim pulled away and brushed his nose against hers.

"Will you accept me?"

Dor swallowed and stared at the wonderful man who held his

breath while awaiting her answer. A small part of her didn't want to accept. It felt like she was taking advantage of someone she loved. But the reasonable part of her mind knew she couldn't raise wee ones on her own. Jadim would treat whatever babes she birthed as his own, and he would be a wonderful father. Plus, she loved him. He was one of her best friends, and she could see herself growing old with him. And there was the tiny part of her that she liked to pretend didn't exist which had loved the boy standing in front of her for years, despite knowing what their future could only hold.

"I accept you," she said reverently.

He smiled and pressed another kiss to her lips that was all too quick, but Dorcus knew it was for the best. It was better not to court disaster and disappointment, for both of them.

"Thank you," he breathed, his eyes sparkling. He hugged her close, mindful of her exposed back and then stepped backward, taking her hand in his. "We should speak to your mum."

Dor nodded, staring at the man who began to direct them both toward her home. She had a nagging feeling that what she had just agreed to would lead to heartache and pain for both of them, but she'd had no choice. And really, there wasn't anyone else she'd ever want to grow old with. She had loved Jadim for as long as she could remember. She squashed that thought and concentrated on the pain throbbing across her back. If she let herself dream of the impossible, the agony and disappointment for both of them would be unimaginable.

She was lucky, but she didn't feel it. It felt like she was being denied the most important relationship of her life. Their bond felt like a cheap imitation of what a marriage should be.

Stars above, she was ungrateful and greedy. She mentally slapped herself and thought about everything she was gaining, not what she would lose in six days.

Everything would turn out all right. She had to believe that, or she'd disappear down a black hole she'd never be able to crawl out from. She had an amazing family and now a mate who would support her despite how others would use her.

That had to be enough. If it wasn't, she wouldn't survive much longer.

Chapter Fifteen

Sam

Sometimes he was so bloody tired.

Sitting on his desk was a never-ending stream of information to sift through, and women to calm. Most men thought women were irrational creatures prone to hysteria and bouts of fancy. But Sam knew better. They were smart, cunning, creative, and stealthy. If he had a choice in whether to remove the world of men or women, he would burn the male population. Plus, women were a delight to look upon. He was the first to admit he loved them. But at the moment, he wanted to tape one woman's mouth shut.

He set his documents aside and surveyed one of his lovely spies who was doing her best impression of sucking on a lemon. "Would you repeat that?"

Her nose crinkled as if she smelled something rotten. "You weren't listening?"

Of course, he was listening. It was his job to listen, but if she intended to irritate him with her petty complaints, then surely he'd needle her back just a bit. "I dropped off when you began to prattle on about hair colors, but I'm focused now. I had a bit of a busy night, so please forgive me."

Marilyn's expression softened a touch. "I heard what you did for those girls yesterday. That was well done."

Sam smiled weakly. He wished he could've done more. Hopefully, the mother and her young daughter would enjoy their simple life in the country, away from the monster who had made them his personal punching bags.

"As was the man's punishment," Marilyn said with a feral smile. "Maybe he'll see my brother in hell."

Sam's smile mirrored Marilyn's. There would be no tears for the man who'd suffer for the rest of his life in the mines or die, or for Marilyn's brother who'd taken it upon himself to hurt children. Sam was still unsure where that man's bones had ended up.

"I did my best. Now—" He rapped his knuckles on his desk, eyeing Marilyn's hair covering. "What's happened?"

His spy's right eye twitched as she pulled the veil and embroidered cloth band from her head. Her hair was not her normal blonde with silver streaks, but bright orange. "I believe some of the girls thought it would be amusing to pull a prank."

His lips twitched. "I see."

She puffed out an annoyed breath. "It seems I was not to be the original recipient, but I am the victim, nonetheless. How, my lord, am I supposed to serve my lady with hair the color of carrots?"

He coughed and kept his laughter held back, as he knew it would set her off in a fiery tirade. Marilyn may be an older woman, but, in all her years, she still hadn't learned to control her temper. It was ironic. Her hair now matched her temper.

"Is there a way to get it out?" he asked smoothly, not one tremor of humor in his voice.

"If there is, I don't know of it." She harrumphed.

"I'm sorry about your beautiful hair. I'll reach out discreetly to one of my contacts to see if they can find something to help. And, as for the girls, I will personally speak with them." He stood and walked around his desk, taking Marilyn's hands in his own. "For now, go to the garment room and pick a new fabric for a new veil."

She smiled at him, her wrinkles becoming more pronounced. "I thank you, my lord."

Sam patted the top of her right hand. A woman never complained about new clothes. Unless it was Sage, or his wife Jasmine, who refused to wear anything he put in her closet. It drove him crazy that she wouldn't accept his gifts. Even thinking about it now put him on edge. He hid his frown and smiled at one of his oldest spies. "My pleasure. I'll speak more with you at the end of the week."

She nodded and left the room, the door clicking shut quietly behind her. Sam shook his head and sat once again at his desk.

Marilyn could be as mean as a dragon at times, but she was one of his most loyal and experienced spies, and tough as nails. His spies weren't machines; they were human beings. So, he did his best to be as understanding as he could.

He sorted all the documents on his desk and piled all the important ones in a stack in front of him. Sam began decoding each message. Absorbed in his work for hours, he didn't notice how the candle had burned low and how dark his hidden office had become until it was very late.

Sam straightened, rolled his shoulders, and stretched. Stars above, did he long for his bed.

Someone knocked timidly on his door. There were very few of his girls that knocked that way. "Come in," he called.

He set down his letter and smiled as Lady Hollisa, or Gem as her friends called her, stuck her head into the room, her large brown eyes blinking at him owlishly.

"May I come in?" she asked.

"You know the answer to that." But he stood and swept his hand out in an invitation. Gem was proper through and through, and skittish as hell, so he tried to make her feel as comfortable as he could.

She tiptoed in and hovered in front of the doorway, wringing her hands. "You've been missed during your absence," she said, her voice soft.

"Thank you, Gem. How are you?"

"I'm doing well."

"And your mother?"

Gem pulled a face. "Causing mischief as usual. I'm surprised my parents haven't killed each other yet."

Sam smiled. That was why he loved Gem. She was honest. She made a wonderful spy. Her title afforded her certain liberties and allowed her into social circles most of his spies could not gain access to. It helped that her mother was a bed-hopper and her father a gambler. It also made her invisible.

Sam knew most people ignored Gem because of her family's scandal, which clung to her like a foul odor, but they couldn't downright dismiss her because of her family's title. But Sam had noticed her. They'd even become friends before he'd offered her a position as one of his spies. She'd accepted, and, to his surprise, she'd admitted to having a perfect memory. If she saw or heard something, she was able to recall it perfectly. It was a bloody gift for them both. Sam was able to gather reliable information, and she was able to earn coin without her father's knowledge.

"You've been gone two weeks."

A statement. Very typical of Gem. She rarely asked a question outright. She skirted the issue until her converser revealed themselves without remembering what she'd primarily hinted at. It was brilliant.

"Yes?" He crossed his arms and arched a brow at her. "What do you want to know, Gem? You know, if it's within my power to tell you, I will."

"It's not that," she said softly, bunching her pale pink skirt in her hands.

"What is it, dear?"

A small blush touched her cheeks at his endearment. "I hate spying on Jasmine."

So that was what she was after. "You're not necessarily spying *on* her – you're protecting her."

Gem scowled. "Don't split hairs. I've lived in court for almost as long as you have. It feels wrong to report to you. She's my friend."

Sam pursed his lips. That was one of his biggest rules: you couldn't be friends with your mark. Once feelings were involved, it always became messy and dangerous. But, in the case of Jasmine, he knew his wife would need friends in court, ones that wouldn't stab her in the back. So, he'd assigned Gem to her, and it pleased him immensely that the two had got on as well as they did.

"You want her to be safe and successful here, right?" Sam drawled.

"I do, but I don't want to betray her confidence."

"I'm her husband. By law, I'm privy to everything that involves my wife. Legally, you're doing no wrong."

Gem glared at him, and placed her hands on her narrow hips. "I'm speaking morally. And, despite how you pretend, I know you understand my meaning." She straightened, looking as ferocious as a kitten. "I came here to tell you that I'll continue spying for you, but I refuse to give you any information as to her thoughts and feelings. Jasmine is broken enough, and I refuse to cause more harm."

He blinked. Gem had a spine of steel, but he rarely glimpsed it. Part of him was happy she loved his wife so much and was willing to stick up for her. The other part was irritated, because Jasmine was impossible to read most of the time. He had a talent for coaxing, charming, and soothing women, but everything he did seemed to push his wife farther away.

"I respect that," he forced himself to say.

"Good," Gem exhaled, relief clear upon her face.

"May I ask what brought about this change of heart?"

"Jasmine's a good person, and she's shouldering so much. I love children, but I couldn't imagine raising twins at my age."

"She's not alone," Sam said.

Gem raised both eyebrows. "And just when have *you* been around, my lord?"

Sam scowled. "When I'm here, I do my best."

"Well, I don't think it's helping."

"And why is that?"

"Because she believes you're out galivanting with half the female court, and she's planning on moving into the country with the children."

Sam kept his expression blank. Jasmine was leaving? "My wife is trying to escape me?" he asked calmly. His hands clenched, and, suddenly, he felt too hot under his collar. He wanted to throw something.

Gem blanched. "Damn, you just can't help yourself," she accused.

"What did I do?"

"You needled me, and I played right into your hands. You wanted information on Jasmine, and, like an idiot, I just handed it right over."

He had wanted information on his wife's activities, but he wasn't interrogating Gem. "It wasn't on purpose."

Gem studied him and shook her head. "I believe you, but—" She pointed a finger at him. "Keep your mouth shut." She scanned the room and met his gaze. "The only reason I'm telling you this is so you won't do something rash and muck up your marriage even more than it already is."

"How have I mucked it up already?" he cried. "I've done everything in my power to make sure she and the twins are cared for."

"Sure, you've cared for their physical needs, but what about their mental and emotional ones? Wicked hell, your wife is *happy* believing you're out with other women." Gem's gaze bored into his. "You need to be honest with her, Sam, before it's too late."

"When is she planning on leaving?" Saying the words a loud make him slightly ill.

"During your next trip to the war camp. She seems determined to leave within the next three weeks."

"So, I have three weeks to woo my wife. I can do that." He could. His parents fell in love in two. He'd spent his whole life around women.

"But that's not the reason for my visit."

"There's more?"

She sat daintily on the chair in front of his desk. "She's been disappearing for two hours every day."

Every muscle in his body locked up. "Have you tailed her?"

"She gives me the slip every time."

His brain scrambled for answers. How in the blazes did a pregnant woman give Gem the slip? His pursed his lips in thought. "And what does she look like when she returns?"

Gem swallowed. "Tumbled."

Sam slowly stood from his chair, placed his hands on his worn, wooden desk, and leaned forward. "Like the wind blew her around, or are you insinuating that *my* wife is unfaithful?"

"I would never insinuate anything like that."

He eyed her. "You're close with her, so you must know what condition she's in?"

Gem blinked. "Yes."

"You also know that she's been a target for some of the more vicious back-biters and that some of the men have set their eyes upon her?"

Gem nodded, her lips pressed firmly together.

"I want to protect her, and I can't do that if you're not honest with me."

She sucked her lip in and released it, scowling and stabbed a finger toward him. "I'm just sharing what I've seen, and don't think I don't know what you're doing. Stupid, manipulative man," she mumbled and then continued. "There are many explanations for what she might be doing. Don't jump to conclusions."

Sam scoffed as she repeated what he had taught her over three years ago. "But usually the most obvious conclusions are the right ones. Humans rarely change their habits." He hung his head. "I can't believe this."

"Can't you?"

He lifted his head to glare at Gem. "I'm sure you'd like to tell me."

She tilted her chin in a haughty way and stared down her button nose at him. "You've established an entire persona of being a world-class rake and scoundrel. Your wife believes you have multiple mistresses and visit different women every night. So, why are your delicate sensibilities so offended? This is of your own making."

Sam straightened. "That is too far."

"That is the truth of it, my lord," Gem said gently. "I don't believe it is of her character to do such a thing, if that helps."

It didn't. He knew the self-destructive path she'd been walking down before they married. He inhaled deeply and went to the calm, logical part of himself he liked to use when figuring out a problem. He'd been absent enough. It was high time he found out what Jasmine was up to.

He smiled at Gem. "You're right. I think I should pay my wife a visit."

His friend blinked at him and then pushed up from her chair. "Don't do anything you'll regret."

"I don't have regrets."

But he did have a wife to spy on.

Jasmine might have been able to give Gem the slip, but she'd never been stalked by the best.

Sam moved to the wall and lifted a worn black cloak from the hook and clasped it over his chest, before pulling the hood over his golden hair. Today, she'd have the pleasure of meeting the spymaster.

He moved to the door and opened it for Gem. She took his hint and scurried to the door, pausing in the threshold. She placed one hand over his, the other holding the door, and squeezed.

"I wish you luck."

"Thank you, but I don't need luck when I'm hunting."

Chapter Sixteen

Jasmine

Stars above, she hurt.

Jasmine glanced over her shoulder at the lush, dark-green woods with longing. This was always her least favorite part of the day. As she turned around to face Sanee and the massive hill that led to the castle, part of her soul shriveled inside her chest.

By all accounts, it was a beautiful sight to behold. Tiny, cobbled streets wound in curving paths that were lined with faded, quaint, but well-kept homes. Her gaze latched on to the great stone structure that was her new home. The sunset haloed the castle and washed the white stone with a pink so soft it looked like a maiden blushing. If it wasn't for the menacing wall that surrounded the palace, the castle would almost look harmless and welcoming.

Her jaw clenched as she hiked farther into town. Little did the dreamers like her former self know that the palace held vipers and intrigue that no one wanted to be part of. She stumbled as she stubbed her toe on a loose cobble, and barely caught herself against the plain wall of an apothecary. As her eyes watered with pain, she had to admit that living in the palace wasn't all doom and gloom. She'd met some amazing people, and Tehl and Sage were making changes for the better.

Jasmine turned left and opened the back door to the apothecary. Carefully, she clicked the door shut and set her belongings on the floor.

"Jas, is that you?" Vienna yelled.

She rolled her eyes. The old woman only had one volume. Loud.

"It's me," she called back while peeling her leather trousers down her legs that were loosely tied over her protruding belly. Quickly, she yanked her tunic off and pulled a simple muslin dress over her head. A small growl escaped her as she tried to lace the back herself.

"Why didn't you call for me?" Vienna demanded as she bustled into the room, her gray hair a fuzzy halo around her wrinkled face. She batted Jasmine's hands away and laced up her gown.

Jasmine placed her hands on her hips and scowled down at the bump that wasn't as easy to hide anymore. "Who invented dresses like these? It's ridiculous."

Vienna snorted, her scent of thyme and lilac swirling around Jasmine as the old woman released her and began rummaging around the room. "Men. I think they like us to be dependent on them. Aha!" She pulled a small bottle from a heavy wooden shelf and held it out to Jasmine. "For the marks."

"How did you know?" Jasmine asked, not hesitating to take the gift.

Vienna quirked a smile. "It is my occupation to help everyone I can, and if that wasn't enough, I've birthed six babes myself. You'd be shocked to see my skin. It looks like a leren took a liking to me."

Jasmine winced. Good hell, she hoped hers wasn't *that* bad. She wasn't a particularly vain creature, but she didn't want to look like something had mauled her. "Thank you. I appreciate it."

"It's nothing, my girl." Vienna waved her off and then gestured to the game bag. "It's nothing compared to what you bring me." She licked her lips. "What did you trap this time?"

Jasmine grinned. "I've brought you four nice-sized rabbits and a haunch of venison."

Vienna's beady eyes widened. "Tell me you did not drag a deer around in the woods?"

"No. I did not. Luckily, my aim was true and the beast didn't travel very far. As for this—" She pointed at the chunk of meat. "It wasn't too heavy for me to carry. I'm pregnant, not an invalid. Women have been caring for their families for ages while they've been with child."

The old woman harrumphed but took the meat. "Would you like to stay for dinner?"

Jasmine hid her look of pity for the woman. Vienna was as tough as nails, but she was lonely. She'd lost her entire family to the sickness that swept through the kingdom. "I would love to, but I must get back. But, if you're up for a visit, I'll bring the twins in two days. They've been dying to play with that green muck you've been experimenting with."

"Slime," Vienna said with a twinkle in her blue-grey eyes.

Jas shuddered, thinking of the wet sludgy texture. "Children find the oddest things to be interested in."

"You can't tell me you weren't enthused about mud, muck, and bugs when you were a child."

"Touché," Jasmine said with a smile. She placed her bow and quiver in the back corner of the room and wrapped her bloodied clothing in a sack. Skinning and cleaning meat was always a dirty job.

"Goodness me, child. You cannot take those back with you. Hand them over."

She rolled her eyes, but did as she was bade. They argued every night about this, but Vienna always won. "I feel like I am taking advantage."

"Nonsense. You provide me with food and good company. It is I who is in your debt. I'm the lucky one who gets to entertain royalty."

Jas snorted. "I'm not royalty, no more than you are."

Vienna tossed the soiled clothing on the square wooden table, and studied Jasmine in a way that was far too knowing. "I've been on this earth for a long time, my girl. Many things have come and gone, but there is one fact that is always true. We're only hindered by ourselves. You have more power than you believe. Open your eyes, and you might be surprised by the influence you have."

Jasmine kept her mouth shut and nodded. She didn't necessarily agree with the old woman, but Vienna had more experience than herself. "I will give it some thought."

"Good, now, get back home. I'll see you tomorrow."

Jasmine slipped on her boots once again and snatched up her other small game bag, tucked the bottle into a pouch at her waist, and retrieved her cane. She glanced longingly at her bow, hating that she had to leave it behind, but it was way too cumbersome and suspicious to lug around. "Goodnight, Vienna."

"Goodnight, child," the old women said, following her into the dark alley. "Be safe. There have been more crimes in this area since the army has moved out."

"I'll be cautious." The fingers of her right hand tightened around the cane. She may be without her bow, but she wasn't without a weapon. She waved goodbye and trotted onto the busier street ahead.

With care, she moved through several streets without so much as one person looking her way. But a scratchy feeling had begun spreading between her shoulder blades a few alleys back. Someone was following her.

Awareness crept along the nape of Jasmine's neck until the fine hairs stood on end. This was the part she hated the most. Lately, she had the feeling of being watched whenever she went on her weekly visit to the woods and then the apothecary. So far, there had been no evidence to justify her feelings—no glimpse of a person behind her, no sound of footsteps—but she knew what it was like to stalk prey. And, during these moments, she knew she'd become someone's target.

Carrying her leathered game bag in her left hand and her hickory cane in the other, Jasmine continued to walk at a brisk pace, her back and feet aching with every step. But she wouldn't let the pain distract her. Her gaze took in every detail of the buildings around her, and she cursed as she realized, in her haste, she'd taken a wrong turn toward the docks. That was not a place to be careless.

"Stupid," she breathed. Jasmine glanced at her belly and then scanned the area for familiar sights. She exhaled in relief as she figured out where she was—only two blocks away from the main road where there'd be more lanterns and guards. Chastising herself, she picked up her speed and veered left. She needed to pay more attention. Lapses in attention could mean the difference between life and death for a lone woman.

As she passed near a drainage ditch, noxious fumes wafted upward and made her eyes water. Swamp apples, that was disgusting. She instinctively covered her lips with the left sleeve of her dress, but it didn't help. She caught the gleam of a man's gaze and quickly dropped her arm to breathe out her mouth. Sticking out in this area of Sanee wasn't a good idea, and any resident who lived around here would be used to the God-awful stench. Why would anyone live here when they had the choice to live in the country? That was something she'd never understand.

A chill ran through her body that had nothing to do with the fall weather. The road was eerily quiet. Most of the dilapidated buildings had been abandoned, but held flickering lights of pickpockets, drunkards, and ladies of the night who were squatting in the buildings' entrances. The glow from the broken lamps on either end of the street scarcely cut through the fog that began to creep up from the bay, slinking over and around homes like an insidious nightmare.

We'll get through this little bit. Just a block more until we reach safety.

But her pace faltered as new figures emerged from the weak light. A momentary surge of relief washed over her as she identified the trio of off-duty soldiers. They laughed loudly as they advanced in her direction, clearly well into their spirits, on their way to being truly drunk. They wouldn't be any help to her

Jasmine crossed to the other side of the street, keeping to the shadows, hoping they were too inebriated to notice her. She glanced in their direction and caught the eye of the tallest soldier. *Damn it. Too late.*

The tall one smiled lazily and swerved in her direction.

"Here's a bit of luck," he exclaimed. He slapped hands with his companion to his right as they strode in her direction. "I've been hankering for a bit of sport."

Distaste threatened to wrinkle her nose, but she kept her expression cool and picked up her speed, her heart hammering in her chest. "I'm sure you'll find your amusement just down the road," she said stiffly, while her grip tightened on the crooked handle of her cane.

The men were obviously worse for the drink. Stars above, she hated drunks. Her uncle had a taste for spirits, and it never failed to bring out the worst in him. Even thinking about it, Jasmine could swear she could smell her uncle's foul whiskey breath. She didn't doubt that the soldiers had been loitering at the tavern all day. Everyone knew it was a death sentence to go into battle against Scythia, so the men were trying to soak up as many amusements as they could before they were called upon.

If only their tastes were a little less sinister.

Her heartbeat escalated as their long legs caught up with her. "Allow me to pass, gentlemen," she said crisply, crossing the street once again. She was thankful for the speech lessons she'd been given. Maybe if they realized she wasn't some light skirt, they'd leave her alone.

They moved to block her totally.

"Talks like a lady," observed the youngest of the trio. He was red-headed, his hair springing up in unkempt rusty coils.

"She *is* a lady," remarked the tallest, hulking, hatchet-faced man—the one she'd caught the attention of. "I've never had a lady before. I bet she's looking for some fun if she's out for a stroll on such a night." He regarded Jasmine with a yellow-toothed leer and waved his hand toward the moldy, wooden wall of a home that shouldn't have still been standing. "Go stand next to the wall and lift your skirts. I'm in the mood for a little play that's upright."

"You're mistaken," Jasmine said sharply, attempting to walk around them. They barred her way, and her pulse whooshed in her ears as she glared at the men. "I'm not a prostitute. However, there is a fine brothel just down the road where you can find such service from what I hear. Now, let me pass."

"But I don't want to pay for it," the large man said nastily. "I want it free with a pretty little thing, and I want it *now*."

For a brief moment, she thought about screaming. But what good would that do? It would probably just call more predators in. And it was hardly the first occasion Jasmine had been insulted or threatened. That was one of the reasons why her father had trained her with a bow and staff. Sometimes, men took it upon themselves to take what they wanted, despite the refusal. She didn't want to fight them. She was exhausted after her long hunt in the woods, and, frankly, she was hungry. A certain sort of numbness trickled through her veins as she decided on her next action. If she did nothing, chances were they'd be so rough they'd hurt her, but if she fought, she might be able to get away unscathed. The key word being *might*.

Her jaw set as her fingers curled even tighter around her cane. Men were such pigs. They thought they could take and take and take. Tonight, they would take nothing from her. They were bullies and nothing more. She'd looked into the black eyes of true evil. These men had nothing on the warlord.

"As soldiers in His Majesty's service," she said acidly, "has it occurred to you that your sacred duty is to protect a woman's honor instead of violating it?"

To her distaste, the question elicited hardy chuckles instead of shame.

"Needs to be taken down a peg, if you ask me," commented the third man, a stout coarse-looking fellow with a pockmarked face and dark eyes that robbed the words from her tongue.

He looked like… She shook her head. She couldn't think about him.

Jasmine blinked as the younger one rubbed the fabric of his crotch in a crude gesture.

"She can ride my peg."

Terror threatened to swamp her, but she shoved it down deep. Fear would get her hurt or killed. "I don't see much of anything."

The young one glared and crossed his arms as his two companions cackled.

The hatchet-faced man grinned at Jasmine with easy menace as he wiped the corners of his eyes. "Over to the wall, my fine lady. Don't be causing a scene." He pulled a serrated blade from his belt and held it up to display its wicked edge. "Just do as we say, and it'll be over before you know it."

Jasmine's stomach flipped unpleasantly, and her legs quivered. "Drawing a weapon while off-duty is against the law," she observed coldly. "Added to the offenses of public drunkenness and rape, you will earn yourselves a flogging you'll never forget and at least ten years in prison." She didn't know that for sure, but their punishment would be hell if Sage caught wind of it.

The hatchet-faced man bared his yellow teeth. "Maybe I'll cut out your tongue, so you won't tell anyone," he stated.

Jasmine didn't doubt for one second that he would. As the daughter of a former soldier, she knew that pulling out a knife meant he would most likely use it. Her mum had been a healer, and once she'd seen a woman who'd managed to get over the Scythian wall so cut up that Jas had barely been able to tell where one cut had ended and another began. When the woman had healed, she explained that a man had wanted to give her something to remember him by.

"Calm yourself," the young man said to the hatchet-faced man. He brushed his copper curls from his freckled face. "There's no need to terrify the poor girl." Turning to Jasmine, he added, "Let us do what we want." He paused. "It will be easier if you don't fight."

Bile burned the back of her throat. There was no way she wasn't fighting. Taking hold of the strings of her surging fear and anger, Jasmine recalled her father's advice about distracting your opponent.

Keep your distance, and avoid being flanked. Use speech as a distraction.

"Why force an unwilling woman?" she asked carefully and set her game bag down on the dirty street. "If it's the lack of coin, I'll give you each enough to visit a brothel." Carefully, she slipped her hand into the outer back pocket of the bag and closed her fingers around her skinning blade. Deftly she concealed it from their view as she stood, the familiar elk-horn handle resting in her palm.

In her peripheral vision, Jasmine saw the hatchet-faced man with the bayonet knife circling around her. At the same time, the stout man began to close the distance between them.

"Thank you for the offer. I'm sure we will take your coin once we make use of you."

Jasmine adjusted her grip on the skinning blade, resting her thumb on the flat side of the handle. Gently, she applied the tip of her index finger along the blade. She may be little, but like Hell would she let them anywhere near herself or the babe.

Make use of this.

Drawing back her arm, she released the blade in a slinging motion, stabbing her wrist straight to ensure the wickedly sharp dagger aimed true. A feral grin curled her lips as the knife sunk into his cheek. He roared with astonished fury, stopping in his tracks. Jasmine pivoted around the soldier with the bayonet knife, whipping her cane in a horizontal hard strike. Then, she smashed it against his right wrist. Taken by surprise, he cried out in pain and dropped his knife.

Jasmine followed the blow with a backhand strike against his left side and heard a vomit-inducing crack, then jabbed the tip of the cane at his groin to make sure he wasn't getting up. He'd doubled over, and she used the handle to strike him over the head.

He crashed to the ground like a marionette with its strings cut. *Good riddance.*

Jasmine snatched up the bayonet knife and spun toward the other two soldiers.

In the next moment, she froze in surprise, her chest rising and falling rapidly, her heart threatening to explode.

The street was silent.

And both men were sprawled on the ground.

What in wicked hell?

Was this a trick? Were they playing dead to lure her in?

Her hands began to shake as quivery energy worked its way through her, and her body began to slow and recognize that the emergency was over. She bent over and puked, her body shaking, but she never took her gaze off the men.

Slowly, she stood and wiped her mouth with the back of her left hand. She ventured closer to look at the fallen men, taking care to stay out of arm's reach. Her skinning blade had left a bloody wound in the larger one's cheek, but that wouldn't have knocked him out. She eyed the red mark on his temple. That wasn't from her. Even if she'd jumped, she wouldn't have been able to hit him on the head.

Her attention darted to the younger soldier whose face was a swollen, bruised mess, and his nose was streaming. It looked broken to her.

"What the devil?" Jasmine murmured, looking up and down the silent, foggy street.

She had that feeling again, the prickly awareness that someone was there. She rolled her eyes and straightened, clasping her cane and bayonet knife in each hand. Obviously, there was someone else here. The other two soldiers hadn't knocked themselves out.

"Come out and show yourself," she said sharply. She clenched her jaw as her voice wobbled on the last word. Heat pressed against the back of her eyes.

Stupid hormones.

She cleared her throat and tried again. "There's no need to hide like a rat at the back of the pantry. I know you have been following me. Come out."

A masculine voice came from directly behind her, nearly causing her to jump out of her boots. "My, my, my, what kind of mischief have you been getting yourself into, my dear?"

Jasmine turned in a quick circle, her gaze chasing over a flicker of movement in one of the darkened doorways. It was unnerving how the tone dripped sin and depravity. Despite herself, she couldn't help but shiver. "Enough of the games."

A stranger emerged from the shadows, the darkness forming into the shape of a man in a fine but worn black hooded cloak. He paused a few feet away and lifted back his hood, revealing blond hair that fell in waves around his face and deep, piercing blue eyes she'd know anywhere.

Jasmine's jaw slackened. "It's you!" she exclaimed. This was not good.

Her husband, the prince of Aermia, smiled wickedly at her. "Hello, my love. Have you missed me?" he crooned at her.

Chapter Seventeen

Sam

His wife was bloody insane.

Certifiably insane.

And it was quite possible he'd committed murder tonight, and that he'd now chain her to his bed.

Well, that was a little dark, but the circumstances warranted it. If he hadn't found her when he had, he dreaded to think what might've happened. Sam forced his hands to stay loose and relaxed, instead of curling into fists like he wanted to. He glared at the soldiers littered across the ground, and something feral threatened to break loose inside him. He might even reach out for

Rafe's expertise in making vile men disappear...

The idea had merit.

If he hadn't found her in time... Hell, he knew exactly what those low-lives would have done. What really rankled him was that they were Aermia's own men.

Filthy garbage.

Sam pulled his eyes from the carnage sprawled across the darkened street to stare at the bane of his problems this evening.

Jasmine stood, gaping at him, her cane clutched tightly to her heavy chest, her pants the only sound to cut through the swirling fog. He scanned her from head to toe, looking for injuries. No blood. But that didn't mean there weren't injuries. She had wounds that she hid from the world, and this would just make them worse. With his spies, he'd seen what happened when one didn't face their trauma. And Jasmine? She was the queen of avoidance and ice.

"Are you all right?"

She blinked, and her whole demeanor changed. His scared wife melted away, and an imperious charlatan took her place. "What are *you* doing here?"

That was the question of the evening. What were either of them doing down here? What was his wife doing down in the dock district, attacking men with a skill he didn't know she possessed? His gaze moved a fraction to the hand she held against her belly, and his rage ignited once more. This time at Jasmine. How could she be so careless? He planned on asking her this, but what came out of his mouth was so much worse.

"Are you stupid?" The question hung in the air, and he wanted to scoop the words right back into his mouth. What did he think he was going to get out of her by being an arse?

Her lips thinned, and a storm began to brew in her ocean-blue eyes.

Devil take it, a storm of his own making was about to erupt.

Chapter Eighteen

Mira

Mira watched as her father bustled around the infirmary, mumbling to himself. He lifted a handful of loose herbs and sniffed it heavily; his coppery eyes squinted in concentration behind spectacles that sat precariously on the bridge of his nose.

"What is that?" she asked, folding a set of homespun sheets and setting them on the cot in front of her.

"Something special," he answered before carefully wrapping the plant in a leather square and then placing it gingerly in his travel bag.

Her lips pinched as she stared at his full pack, and the smallest bit of envy made her frown at the pile of sheets she still had to fold. Mira understood why Jacob was needed at the war camp: he was *the* Healer for the royal family, and most of the royal family was stationed around the battlefield. She loved the infirmary, she truly did, but she wanted to be able to help with more than scrapes and headaches. One of the only things that kept her sane was her work near the docks. Many people could not afford the services of a healer, so when she had spare time, she visited the poorer folk and did what she could to help.

"What are you thinking, my girl? Your silence unnerves me, and I can practically smell your anxiety and fear."

She peered up at him from beneath her lashes, another sheet clutched in her hands. She'd never thought of her father as being old. He had too much energy and never seemed to slow down, but, in the last few months, time and stress had taken a toll on him. Deep lines bracketed his eyes and mouth, his hair was almost snow-white, and his skin had taken on a translucent quality. He wasn't sick—she knew this, because she'd badgered him to allow her to check him once a week.

No, her papa was aging, and she *hated* it.

"I'm worried for you."

He nodded, his metallic eyes boring into her as if he could see all of the fears she tried to hide from him. "I'm not going to die, my girl. I'll be home soon."

Heat filled her eyes, and she turned her attention back to the crumpled sheets between her fingers. Jacob was all she had. They might not have shared blood, but he was her papa in every way.

And a life without him? She couldn't imagine it.

A soft rustle filled her ears as he approached and lay a hand over hers. "Come here, darling."

Mira dropped the sheet and pivoted into her father's waiting arms. The tears she'd been holding back now ran down her cheeks as she cried her fear for him into his clean, linen shirt. Her papa hugged her close and pressed his cheek to the crown of her head, rocking her back and forth.

"It'll be all right. It's not like I'm going to be fighting. I'll be helping those who need it." He released her and cupped her damp cheeks. "I know you're worried, but I promise to be careful. I have many years left in me. I'm not dead yet," he said bluntly, his copper eyes twinkling.

She laughed, her smile watery. "I can't help but worry."

"I know, I know," he murmured and dropped a kiss onto her forehead. "I'll be back before you know it."

Nodding, she tilted her right cheek into his hand and then stepped back, wiping the tears from her face. Mira swallowed down her worries and put on a brave face. She didn't want him leaving with the memory of her weeping for him.

"So, what else do you have to pack?" she asked.

He waved a hand at the table covered in tinctures, herbs, and poultices. "I need all of that."

She huffed and affectionately kissed his whiskered cheek as she eyed the bag that looked like someone had thrown dirty laundry into it. "You may be a brilliant healer, but you don't know how to pack a damn thing."

He chuckled and followed Mira to the table as she began rearranging the mess that was his travel bag.

"That's what I have you for, my girl."

"I shall forever go down in history as the girl who could only pack a medicine bag," she said sarcastically, then smiled. She'd learned many skills from her papa over the years, but organization had not been one of them; that had come by naturally and out of necessity, since Jacob was horrible at organizing or labeling anything.

She peeked at him from the corner of her eye as he sniffed an unlabeled bottle, his copper eyes intent on the purple-pink flowers inside. For as long as she'd known him, he'd had an uncanny way with scents, more so than any other person she'd come across. Sometimes, it was like he truly could smell her emotions. As a child, it had driven her nuts, but now she was just curious. Jacob was an eccentric man, but how he reacted to certain situations in life wasn't what she would call normal.

Or even *human*.

The Healer had raised her to use her mind and the power of deduction, and every logical conclusion she came to said he wasn't like her. She didn't know exactly *what* he was or *where* he was from, but he wasn't Aermian. However, she kept her suspicions to herself. Her papa was a wonderful father, an amazing healer, and a devoted servant to the Crown. Nothing else really mattered.

She took the bottle of fully-submerged magenta flowers from her father's fingers and wrapped it, then carefully stowed the herbs in the bag.

"Done," she said as brightly as she could and closed the bag.

"Thank you, Mira."

She stared at the leather satchel as trepidation churned in her belly. "You'll be careful?"

"I will, darling. I promise."

Mira faced him and narrowed her eyes at her papa. He was an honest man, but sometimes his idea of being careful wasn't the same as hers. "You need to sleep."

"I will do my best."

"And you'll call for me if you need me?"

He watched her, his expression grave. "I will, but I hope that will not be the case. I want you as far away from the war as possible. It's no place for a lady."

She stiffened. "Many have said that being a healer with you is no place for a lady. Well, I was born in the streets, so I'm not a lady."

He smiled at her softly and took her left hand in his. "I didn't mean that you couldn't handle it. I just want to protect you from the ugliness of war. It changes a person, Mira. And you have an empathetic, kind heart. I don't want that to change."

Mira swallowed down her ire and pulled him into another hug, relishing his rosemary-and-smoke scent that was completely unique to him. "I love you, Papa. Be safe."

"I love you, too, darling." He kissed her on the cheek and grabbed his bag from the table. "Say a prayer for us, and don't get into too much mischief while I'm gone," her papa called as he shuffled from the infirmary.

"I'll try not to," she said.

Her papa barked out a chuckle as he waved one last time and disappeared through the infirmary door.

Her heart clenched, and Mira glanced around the room blankly. She rubbed at her arms as if the chamber had chilled slightly with the departure of her father. Stars above, she hated being alone.

"You're not alone," she muttered to herself. *Get to work and stop moping.*

Mira sighed and moved back to finish the laundry. As she was folding the last towel, a faint howl caught her attention. She frowned and looked toward the door as the wail grew louder. An old woman burst through the door, carrying a small, squalling child.

"Lady healer, please tell me you can help me with this child?" The old woman panted as she plopped down onto a cot. She brushed a lock of shockingly red hair from the child's face and crooned softly. "Isa, love, this healer is going to make it all better."

The little girl sniffed and clutched her hand to her chest. "It hurts, Nanny."

"I know, child."

"What happened?" Mira asked, abandoning her laundry and kneeling in front of the pair.

"A d-d-doggy bit me," the little one cried.

"I see," Mira said gravely. She held her hand out to the child. "May I see it? I promise to help make it better, but I can't do that until I look at it."

The little girl cautiously held out her bandaged hand.

"What's your name?" Mira asked as she unbound the bloody linen, hoping to ease the little one by means of conversation.

"Isa."

"What a lovely name. My name is Mira." She pursed her lips as she got an eyeful of the bite. There were several deep punctures and one tear, but none looked like she needed to stitch them. She sighed. Stitching children was the worst. It killed her to watch the little ones cry and wiggle away as she tried to help them.

"Do you like mint?" Mira questioned as she pushed from the ground and went to her workstation to wash her hands.

"Y-yes," Isa whimpered.

"Well," Mira said, grabbing a pot of hot water. She poured the steaming liquid into a bowl, then added lemon juice and basil oil into it. "You're in luck." She tossed a cloth into the bowl and snatched a sprig of mint from a jar. She strode back to Isa and knelt once again, holding out the mint. "Here you go, little one."

Isa loosened her hand from her nanny's blouse and took the mint with a small smile. "Thank you."

"You're welcome, but I need you to do something for me." Mira held Isa's unique purple gaze and blinked. She'd only seen eyes like that once before. Was this Gav's child? She brushed the thought away and focused on Isa. "I need you to be brave. This will hurt, but if I don't clean it properly, you can get very sick and even lose your hand."

The nanny glared down at Mira, disapproval dripping from her. Mira arched a brow at the elderly woman before meeting Isa's stunning gaze again. She wasn't going to lie to the child.

"Lose my hand?"

"Yes, Isa. Infection is very dangerous. A little pain is worth being able to do all the fun things we can with our hands, don't you think?"

Isa nodded, her wild hair bouncing around her face.

Mira reached for the cloth, and the child stiffened and bit her lower lip. "It's okay to cry, Isa," she said gently before beginning to wash her wound.

She went as quickly as she could, and, all the while, the little one wept, but Isa didn't scream or throw a fit. Only twice did Isa pull her hand away. The tension in Mira's shoulders melted away once it was done, and she rose to get the honey and bandages for the wound.

"I want my papa," Isa croaked.

"I know, love," the nanny murmured.

Mira faced the pair and smiled as the little girl's eyelids drooped and then closed.

"The mint always does wonders," she said as she moved back to Isa's side and dropped to her knees. "My father found a way to coat them in a honey and whiskey combination. Helps dull the pain."

"Thank you," the older woman said. She huffed as she adjusted Isa's body against her own frail one.

"It was no problem," Mira responded while slathering honey over the bite, and then wrapped the bandage around the wound. She tied the linen into a knot and stood, gathering her supplies from the floor. "I'm sure she'll be as right as rain in a few days, but visit me tomorrow just to make sure an infection hasn't set in. Dogs can be nasty carriers of disease."

The nanny frowned. "I can't keep her away from them. Any time there's a stray animal about, it finds its way into her arms."

Mira smiled as she dumped the tainted liquid into the large sink near her table. "Animals can sense kindness. She must have much of it in her heart." She dried her hands with a towel and then spun to face her guests.

"That she does. Just like her mother." The old woman groaned as she tried to stand, but didn't manage it.

Mira bustled to her side and placed her hand on the woman's elbow to help her up. The older woman smiled at her gratefully and strolled to the door, Isa limp in her arms.

"Thank you again, lady healer."

"It was nothing," Mira replied as they disappeared through the door. She smiled and turned back to what was left of the linens.

Perhaps she wouldn't be so lonely after all. Even though Isa was in pain, the little one had eyed the infirmary in wonder. Mira wouldn't be surprised if Isa visited her sooner than they'd planned.

Chapter Nineteen

Jasmine

The joints of Jasmine's fingers began to ache, and she forced herself to loosen her grip on the cane. Sam sauntered forward, his black cloak brushing worn, scuffed boots. She cocked her head. For someone who was royalty, he sure did dress drably. Odd. Maybe he was visiting a woman?

Jasmine shook her head and threw back her shoulders, trying to calm her inner panic.

Her husband paused and scowled at one of the soldiers. He slowly lifted his gaze, and what she saw made her want to run and hide.

Pure, unadulterated rage.

Her lips thinned as he stalked closer. Even in plain clothing and angry, he was an unfair specimen of beauty. Like an avenging angel.

"Are you stupid?"

His words lashed out like a whip, striking her. If she hadn't had her feet firmly planted, Jas was sure she would've stumbled back from the vehemence in his tone.

'Stupid' echoed in her mind. Stars above, she *hated* that word. It was a special sort of slur, one that men in her small village loved to burden their women with to make them feel small and worthless.

"Excuse me?" she hissed.

Sam paused and held up his hands. "That's not how I meant it."

"Then how did you mean it?" she spat. "Because, where I come from, those are fighting words."

"I was worried. The words just came out. I'm sorry."

Jasmine chuckled, the sound hollow in her own ears. He sounded apologetic, but living with the prince had taught her a few things. He was honey-tongued and could sway almost any woman. An expert performer. Others might not be able to see through his masks, but she saw him for what he was: a fraud. Which made it that much worse that he'd seen her at her worst, and the good times just kept coming. He always seemed to be there when her life was falling apart. Speaking of which...

"How did you find me?"

"I happened to be out for a nightly stroll."

Right. She glanced down the road. Faint, bawdy music floated through the dark of the night. Men only walked this path for two things: drink and wenches. She turned back to Sam, revolted by either diversion he might seeking.

"Are you following me?" she demanded.

Subtle amusement flickered across Sam's face, but his tone was serious. "I would never. In fact, I've just arrived from the battle front."

"Then why are you here?" She winced. Jasmine did not want to know. Why couldn't she keep her mouth shut?

"I happened to be passing nearby, and the sound of a scuffle piqued my interest. I'm sure you can imagine my shock when I discovered my wife, my very *pregnant* wife, in the center of a brawl with unsavory characters." His tone dripped disapproval and something else she couldn't quite put her finger on. "It would be a shame if anything happened to you," he whispered the last part.

Her gaze dropped to the men and she swallowed hard. The outcome could have been very different tonight, but on the other hand—she eyed her cane—she might have been able to care for herself.

"I need no protection," she informed him. "Furthermore, if I did, you're not the one I would come to for it." She owed him too much as it was.

Sam gave her an inscrutable glance before going to the soldier she had bashed with her cane. The unconscious man was sprawled on his side. After using his booted foot to roll him onto his belly, the prince pulled a length of cord from inside his cloak and bound the man's hands behind his back. "You do have skill."

She smashed the small flicker of pride that lit inside her chest. She didn't need a man to validate her worth.

"As you just saw," Jasmine continued, "I had no guilt or difficulty in taking out the bastard, and I would've defeated the other two on my own."

"No, you wouldn't have," he said flatly.

Jasmine felt the simmer of irritation. "My father was a soldier. I've been trained in the art of cane-fighting, as well as with a bow. I know how to take down multiple opponents, if need be." *Thank you, Papa.* His training had served her and her babe well.

"You made a mistake," Sam said, his blue eyes glittering as he stood from his crouch.

She'd made many mistakes, but Jasmine was curious as to which one he was referring to. "What mistake?"

As Sam held out his hand for the knife, Jasmine gave it to him reluctantly. He slid it into his leather sheath he'd taken from the soldier and hooked it on his own belt as he replied, "After you knocked the knife from his hand, you should have kicked it away. Instead, you bent to pick it up, turning your back on the others. They would've reached you if I hadn't intervened."

She shuddered, the scene playing out in her mind, and retreated a step back as the youngest man began to moan.

Sam glanced at the bloody soldier who'd continued to groan and stir. The prince stepped closer and smiled at the man. "If you move at all, I'll castrate you like a pig and throw your balls into the sea." His pleasant tone caused ripples of unease to skate along Jasmine's nerves. His tone of forced casualness was all the more chilling.

The soldier stilled, his breathing shallow and panicked.

Good. He deserved to be as frightened as he had made Jasmine.

Sam returned his attention to Jasmine. "Fighting with a retired man of arms isn't the same as fighting on the street."

Like he knew so much about being on the street. Just because he wore a pretender's clothes, it didn't mean he knew what it was like to live in an impoverished area. Jasmine knew. Just like she knew she should have paid better attention tonight. Vienna had warned her.

"Men like those," Sam continued, flicking a contemptuous glance at the soldiers, "don't wait politely for you to fight them in turn. They rush simultaneously, and, as soon as one of them came within reach, your cane would've been useless."

"Not exactly," Jasmine argued. "I would've jabbed him at that point and felled him with a hard strike." That's the way she imagined it anyway. When her child's life was on the line, she was fairly certain she could do almost anything.

Sam moved closer to her, stopping within an arm's length. His shrewd, blue gaze slid over her, and Jasmine held her ground and his gaze. Turbulence swirled in his eyes, and, for a brief second, his right eye twitched.

"Try it with me," he invited softly, his gaze locked on hers, vying for her to accept his challenge.

Jasmine blinked, momentarily surprised. "You want me to hit

you with my cane, now?" She kept the excitement out of her voice. She'd wanted to smack him for quite some time.

Sam gave a slight nod.

"Isn't it a crime to strike royalty?" They couldn't send her to prison now that she was married to the man, could they?

"It is, and you won't."

So arrogant.

He grinned, and she scowled at his dimples. It was bloody unfair to flash those things. No wonder hordes of women followed him around like lost puppies or bitches in heat.

She eyed the way he stepped closer. He trained for hours a day and had a muscular, fluid, limber way of moving that, even when standing, conveyed a sense of explosive power. At least she wouldn't feel bad for striking him. He was trained, after all.

"I wouldn't want to hurt you," she said, prolonging her hesitation.

His grin melted into a sinful smirk. "Who knows? Maybe I'll like—" he whispered just as she surprised him with an aggressive thrust of the cane.

As fast as she was, however, Sam's reaction was lightning-swift. He dodged the cane, turning sideways so the tip barely grazed his ribs, grasped the length of the staff, and levered Jasmine forward. Her toe caught on a cobblestone as her momentum pulled her forward. She lost her footing and released the cane, wrapping her arms around her belly. A strong hand closed around her arm, and his free hand caught the staff easily, as if vesting people of their weapons was child's play.

Her hands trembled, and she stared blankly at the moss-covered stone wall ahead of her as she found herself firmly held against Sam's body, the knit of muscle and bone as unyielding as steel. A feeling of helplessness washed over her. She'd known he was battle-trained, but *that* was something else. He moved with feline grace. Like an assassin. Just who in Hell was the man she had married? Was there no escape from men with secrets? Phoenix's face flashed through her mind, and she shut her eyes to dispel his image and the knowledge of what they'd done.

No. She opened her eyes and forced herself to inhale deep breaths. It was unfair to compare Sam to the Scythian men who'd taken everything from her. The prince might keep things from her, but he'd never hurt her. *Yet.*

Fatigue crashed over her, and each of her limbs seemed impossibly heavy. Trying to piece together what happened in Scythia, combined with the attack and two hours of hunting, was catching up with her. Mira had warned her not to overdo it, but there was too much to be done to sit around. It was in the quiet stillness that the nightmares, guilt, and pain threatened to drown her.

Vaguely, she became aware of Sam's arm loosening and his hand slipping across the swell of her belly. She stared down at his tan hand, resting on her body like it belonged there. Tears threatened to fall, but she willed them back. When was the last time someone had held her? Perhaps it was the reckless velocity of her pulse that accounted for the strange feeling that came over her, but she found herself *leaning* into him until his warm chest was plastered against her back. What was wrong with her? She should move, but she didn't. In that moment, the world disappeared and she felt safe. Part of her realized this was ridiculous. They were in an unsafe part of Sanee, and yet... being held by Sam made her feel safer than she had in a long time.

"How's the wee one?" Sam asked, his voice soft and hypnotic.

Jasmine closed her eyes, conscious of only the faint scent of mint on his breath, and the measured rise and fall of his chest. It was bizarre to say the least, but she could have fallen asleep right there.

The spell was broken by his soft chuckle, the sound rippling gently along her spine. "Making yourself comfortable, are we?"

Mortification slammed into her. Jasmine's cheeks flushed, and her eyes began to pool. What in the blazes was she thinking? She tried to wrench free from him, but he kept his hand in place, holding her against him.

"Don't laugh at me," she said fiercely, hating that her emotions were so unpredictable because of the babe.

Astonishment washed over her when she felt him kiss the top of her head.

"I wasn't laughing at you. I only laughed because you caught me off guard. Not many have that ability." He squeezed her once and released her, handing Jasmine back her cane. His gaze was soft as he looked down at her and brushed a stray strand of hair from her cheek. "I don't wish to fight with you, and now is not the time." He glanced over his shoulder at the unconscious men and then back to her. "We can be friends, if you'll allow it. Life will be miserable if we don't come to some understanding."

Slowly, Jasmine lowered the cane and scrutinized his expression. He seemed sincere. "You'd like to be my friend?"

He flashed white teeth in a smile so bright and genuine, she was sure sugar was pouring from his veins. "I do."

"Why?" They didn't need to be friends.

He cocked his head. "We're bound for life. I don't want to spend our time together as enemies."

She pursed her lips, not convinced. If she had her way, she'd be in the country with the twins in just a few weeks. "You have many friends."

"Friends and confidants are two very different things. I've guarded your secrets, and I hope to trust you with mine." He sighed. "But if that doesn't convince you, think of the twins." A pause. "Think of the babe. Children thrive when they have a set of parents raising them. While it can be done alone, why should it be if there is a choice?"

Why, indeed? "So, we'll just be friends?" She had a feeling she would regret this.

"Friendship," Sam said with a smile.

It would be nice to have more friends. She'd been terribly lonely since Sage had left. The twins were Jasmine's heart and soul, but there were times the darkness seemed just a little too heavy to carry on her own.

"I'll be your friend, but nothing more," she warned.

"I'm asking nothing more from you."

There wasn't anything dangerous about a friend. "Okay," she

said softly.

Her husband grinned, delight clear on his face. "Excellent. Well, the first order of business, dear wife, is to get you to bed."

Her eyes narrowed at him.

Sam waved her off and pulled a small whistle from the inside of his cloak. He blew three times and then put it away. He snatched her game bag up with what was left of her venison, tossed it over his shoulder, looped her arm through his, and began to lead her away from the soldiers.

"Aren't you going to do something about them?" she asked.

"Someone will pick them up shortly. Don't worry yourself."

"They'll be punished?"

Sam bared his teeth in a smile that was anything but nice. "They won't ever hurt anyone again."

Chapter Twenty

Dor

Dorcus wiggled her shoulder and glanced quickly out of the side of her eyes at the warrior monitoring her end of the cave. Ten days had passed since her brutal beating, and her back still ached, but at least the pain had lessened. She rolled her neck and quickly hefted her pickaxe and swung it as the guard's attention turned her way. The resounding clang of metal against stone vibrated through her, and she clenched her teeth as it rattled her bones. The warriors had become more volatile in the last few days, and she would take blisters and sore muscles rather than gaining the attention of the men prowling the cave, looking for a fight.

Footsteps echoed and splashed through puddles, growing louder as they moved in her direction. Sweat beaded on her upper lip, and she swung even harder. Maybe if she focused harder on her work, they'd pass her by.

"You think with the warlord gone you can slack off?" a deep voice growled, causing the hair on her dirty, bruised arms to stand on end.

No. She shook her head but dared not answer or slow her work. Silence would be key. Let the warrior have his say, and then he'd leave her in peace. She smothered a gasp and flinched as a huge hand ran down her spine and hovered just above her butt before kneading the flesh.

"You'd be a pretty thing if you weren't such an abomination."

Humiliation washed over her as she did nothing to stop his groping. It was just a touch. She could bear it if it meant survival. And as for his words... well, she'd heard worse over the years. Living in the Pit had forced her to grow thick skin at a young age. If she objected, things would become infinitely worse.

Just breathe, Dor, breathe.

A gasp exploded from her as his hand roughly grabbed the back of her neck, fisting her hair. He yanked her backward, and her bare feet scraped against the porous rock floor as she stumbled, barely clinging to her tool. Panic rose up as she glanced at Ada who locked eyes with her. Dor lifted her chin toward the wall and mouthed *keep working.* She hissed as he yanked on her hair again, pulling her even closer to his massive frame.

"You'd be lucky to entertain someone like myself."

Tears burned in her eyes, and, with her left hand, she reached back and clung to his muscular arm as he lifted her higher, onto her toes. She choked back her cries, and tried to calm her panic. She couldn't panic. It was a rare thing, but every once in a long while, a warrior would lose control and go into a berserker rage. Fear and pain were almost aphrodisiacs to them. Her mum had warned her to hide if she ever noticed the signs. She'd only seen it twice in her lifetime, and she'd never forget the bellows of fury as the warriors destroyed the out-of-control monster.

She glanced from the corners of her eyes, looking for the other warrior, but he wasn't visible. Her stomach tumbled. If she roused his inner demon, there would be no savior for her. The other warrior wouldn't get to her in time before this warrior tore her apart and killed other innocent laborers. A spark of anger lit in her belly as the people around her kept working, all of them glancing at her from the corners of their eyes. She understood why they did nothing, but part of her wanted them to fight for her.

The warrior's other hand slipped around her body and groped roughly at her chest. She bit the inside of her cheeks as he grunted in surprise as he found the ample treasures he sought. Damned breasts.

"And what do we have here?" he purred as his hand roved down her belly, moving south.

"Stop!" she commanded, her words a snarl. As soon as the words escaped her, she wanted to pull them back inside her mouth. *Stupid! Stupid!*

He froze his assault, his hand tightening minutely. "You

presume to give *me* orders?" the warrior whispered harshly, his hot breath fanning across her neck and right ear.

Dor winced and barely hung on to her pickaxe as he shook her roughly, her teeth rattling. She could get through the pain, but she needed to keep calm.

"I think you need a lesson in humility, and your sire won't be here to save you this time. Plus, from what I've heard, you're ripe for the picking."

She closed her eyes, fighting panic. Her sire. Blair. One of the warlord's favorites, and she'd come of age. No one would object to this warrior claiming her. Her vision swam.

"That's right, little bird. You're all mine."

He released her hair and slapped her on the arse so hard that she stumbled forward, left hand slamming into stone wall. The cave dipped, and the back of her scalp burned from where he had most likely yanked hair from her head. The bastard.

The warrior laughed, the sound sinister as it echoed around them, accompanied by the sharp tempo of the others working the stone. Dor cradled her right arm against her chest, the ax loosely clasped between her fingers as she hung her head to stare at the floor. Her tears dropped silently to the ground. It seemed wrong that her tears fell so quietly because each one was a cry for help.

Why me? Someone help me! Why can't I fight back? Stop crying. Fight back.

Dor sniffed and blinked away her tears. They would help nothing. She had known this day would come, but she'd hoped it wouldn't be so horrendous. She bit the inside of her cheek as the warrior kicked her legs apart and shoved her head down as he leaned over and whispered in her ear:

"I'll bet you'll be as good as your whore mother."

Ten words.

That's all it took to change her life.

Ten words.

Without a conscious thought, her hand clenched around the wooden handle of the pickaxe, and she swung it up over her shoulder. A sickening thud reached her ears, and the warrior slumped against her. Dor crashed into the wall, her breath exploding from her lungs as the warrior gurgled.

"Die for this..." the warrior slurred.

Dor wriggled out from under his weight, and twisted around to stare wide-eyed as he dropped to the floor face-first. She scrambled backward and gaped at the collapsed warrior, her pickaxe lodged in his back.

"Stars above," she whispered. What had she done? She was a dead woman now. There was nowhere she'd be able to hide to get away from this. The warrior knew who she was. Even Illya's cave wouldn't protect her. If they didn't punish her, they'd punish her family.

Trembles wracked her body as the workers stopped their mining to stare. She jumped when the warrior at her feet moaned, turned his face toward her, and opened his pain-filled eyes to glare at Dor.

"You're dead."

A shiver worked down her spine as she stepped away from

him, trying to figure out where to go from there. Ada grabbed her hand and pulled Dor into a hug.

"Are you okay?" her friend asked.

"No. What have I done, Ada? What have I done?" Dor cried. "I'm dead."

Galen, a tall, thin slave, stepped from his post and paused at her side, others crowding closer. He stared silently at the bleeding warrior and then pinned Dor with his gaze. "You need to leave."

Dor shook her head but couldn't make her feet move. Her eyes were glued to the injured warrior trying to push himself onto his knees. Her breath whooshed out of her as another worker lifted his pickaxe. Horror washed over her as other laborers moved closer and fell on the warrior. Galen spun her around and wrapped his arm around her shoulder to move her away from the hideous murder scene.

"You can't be here. You need to run. Now."

"I don't know where to go," she murmured through numb lips.

"Find your mum."

"That's the first place they'll look for me." She squinted at the man she barely knew. "Why are you helping me?"

His dark gaze roved over her face. "Because it's the right thing to do."

She laughed, the sound hollow. Being born in the Pit gave one a sick sense of morality.

Galen nodded at Ada. "Get her out of here."

Ada clasped Dor's hand and tugged her toward the back entrance. Dor lurched after her, stumbling and tripping over her own normally graceful feet.

"We have to run, Dor," Ada whispered. "Don't look back."

Dor wiped the tears from her face and moved as quickly as she could, hardly noticing their surroundings as they raced toward her family's home. A shiver rocked her body as she clung to the shadows, saying little prayers each time they passed a warrior. She felt like she had her crime tattooed across her forehead. She'd sentenced a man to death. A dull ringing filled her ears as she replayed what had happened. It had all transpired so fast. She hadn't really understood what was happening until she'd been standing over the monster's bleeding body.

Bile burned the back of her throat. It was the silence that bothered her the most. There were always background noises of some sort, especially with violence. But, as a warrior was murdered in cold blood, no one had said a damn thing. There had been no screaming or sounds of a struggle, just absolute, suffocating silence. Another shiver worked through Dor, and she rubbed her arms to dispel the chills, coming to one conclusion: she'd rather hear her enemies coming for her. Dor could fight the enemies she knew were there. It was the silent ones that were the deadliest.

Silence was the sound of danger.

And of death.

Ada jerked her arm, yanking Dor into her home.

Dor's mum blinked at her and stood, holding her burgeoning belly. "What's wrong?" she asked, her tone sharp.

Dor tried to respond, but her numb lips wouldn't form the

words. The confession caught in the back of her throat and she choked.

Ada squeezed her hand and spoke in a rush. "There was an accident today."

"What kind of accident?"

"A warrior is dead."

Her mum's expression eerily blanked. "How long ago did this happen?"

"Minutes ago."

"Witnesses?"

"Many, but they protected her."

"It won't be enough," her mum muttered, her face hardening.

"I killed him," Dor whispered, the words bitter on her tongue.

Her mum darted toward the bed and glanced at Ada. "Help me move this."

Ada released Dor's hand and helped move the bed. Her mum carefully dropped to her knees and pried a loose rock from the floor. "Watch the entrance, Ada."

Dor stood like a statue as her friend disappeared outside the front door, and she stared at her mum as she leaned down and lifted weapons out of the secret cache. What in the hell? Why did her mum have weapons? She blinked and forced herself to step toward her mum.

"Mum, what are you doing? We can't have those. They won't protect us, and, if the warriors discover those in our home, no one will survive." Other workers had died for less.

Her mum returned the rock to its place, collected the daggers, and deftly leapt to her feet despite her huge, pregnant belly. Swiftly, she tugged her skirt up and hid two daggers, before placing a sheathed blade between her ample breasts. She approached Dor and jerked her chin.

Dor placed a hand over the offered thigh holster and blade in her mother's pale hand. "We can't."

"Lift your skirt," her mum demanded.

"This will just put us in more danger." She met her mum's gaze. "This is my mess. I'll figure something out, but you can't put yourself in danger. Think of the girls and the babe."

Her mum cupped her cheek with her free hand. "Love, I *am* thinking of the girls, all my girls. Your sisters are safe, and it's time for us to leave. Put this on so we can leave. Everything will be okay, but you have to trust me. Can you do that? Even if there are things you don't understand?"

"Yes," Dor said immediately. Her mum had always taken care of them and kept her word.

"Do you remember how to put this on?"

Dor nodded as she took the dagger and sheath from her mother. Years before, her sire had shown her how to wield a dagger. It had always been so exciting when he visited and would train Dor and her sisters with his own weapons. "Did Father leave these for you?"

"He would never leave us unprotected in his absence."

So, in other words, yes.

Ada swung inside. "A commotion is starting up on the lower levels."

"We need to leave now," her mum said. She glanced around the room and shoved the mattress back in place, and then she swept away the evidence of their activities.

Dor blinked. "What about Jadim?" They'd been bound two days prior, and surely he'd be looking for her?

"He knows what to do in this instance. He'll be safe. He'll meet us." Turning in place, her mother held out her hands to both girls. Ada and Dor both stepped forward to take one of her mum's hands. Her mum's serious hazel eyes moved over both girls. "There will be violence, so stick close to my side. Don't stray for a moment."

The hair along Dor's arms rose. "What's happening?"

"The people are rebelling."

She sucked in a breath. Rebellion. She'd dreamed of that for years, but that was all they were. Dreams. The people couldn't possibly win, and everyone would suffer. The warlord's response would be swift and brutal.

"Both of you know how to protect yourselves. If it comes to it, you protect yourself at all costs and keep moving. You don't stop, no matter what you see. If you do, it could cost you your life."

Dor glanced at Ada in surprise. Dor had been trained by her father in secret, but she couldn't imagine her sweet friend fighting. Ada nodded, a feral glint in her eyes that Dor had never seen before.

Her mum pressed a kiss against her forehead and then on Ada's. "History will change today." She stepped back and tied part of her dress up so the skirts wouldn't trip her up, then tucked her braid into the back of her dress. Her mother lifted her chin, and power slid over her like a mask.

Dor stared at her mum. She'd always been a force to be reckoned with, but she hid behind a demure façade most of the time. Even with child, her mother looked like a dangerous warrior. A dragoness.

"Love you both. Keep close."

With those words, her mum strode for the door, not glancing behind her. Dor rolled her shoulders and followed with Ada hot on her heels. She shoved all her questions and feelings down deep and focused on the rising clamor of thousands of voices. Focus was key if she was going to survive what was waiting. She'd heard stories about the last revolt. It occurred ten years before her birth, and, still, the people whispered in fear of the atrocities committed.

Her mum glanced over her shoulder, her eyes turning more green than brown. "Not one sound," she whispered as they moved off the main path and into one of the darkened corridors.

Her mum ghosted down the hall silently, and both girls followed, Dor's gaze stuck on her mother. The woman moved like a wraith, her steps silent and fluid. She'd never seen this side of her mum. Who was she?

Dor shook her head and concentrated on slowing her breathing as they slipped past the junction of stone hallways. The curved ceiling dripped cool water on her head as they slunk down the hallway. A woman screamed, and the sound echoed around them. Down the right hallway, a warrior fell on a man and woman, his roar enough to terrify Dor into freezing. Dor's jaw clenched as she compelled her legs to move, leaving the couple to the violence of the raging warrior.

Her mum ran ahead and paused, holding her hand up. Ada stopped, and Dor followed suit, trying to blend in with the wall. Ada's muscles locked as someone sprinted down an adjacent hallway, their boots thumping against the stone. Her mum crouched and slid the dagger from her sheath.

The blood in Dor's veins froze as an immense warrior rounded the corner. His gaze narrowed on Ada, and that was his downfall. Dor's mum struck like a viper. She swung her leg, tripping the warrior. He stumbled as she leapt, and, in one smooth jump, she launched over his back, sank her hand into his hair, tipping his head back, and slid the dagger into the flesh of his neck. He collapsed on the ground, face-first, with Dor's mum perched on his back. She straightened and wiped her blade on his tunic, then tucked away her dagger.

"Let's move."

Dor stared at the dead warrior as she moved past the body. "Who the hell are you?" she whispered, staring at her mum's back.

The way she'd moved was unlike anything she'd ever seen. She'd never seen a warrior defeated that quickly. They had every advantage over the laborers. It dumbfounded her to see a petite, pregnant woman down a warrior in close quarters.

"Do you think your father would ever leave his girls without protection?" her mum whispered as they wound through a labyrinth of tunnels.

Honestly, Dor had never given it much thought. Her sire had

made sure to instruct his girls to defend themselves from the moment they could master a weapon, as he did with their mother, but he'd never taught Dor anything like that. Her mum had never given any indication that she could fight like a warrior. Hell, wasn't it just yesterday she was shuffling about their home like an invalid, complaining about her back?

Her mum peeked around a corner and waved them forward. They followed the hallway until it dead-ended.

"Dor," her mum called softly. "Open this door."

She squinted at the wall. There wasn't a door. "I don't see anything."

Her mum huffed a breath and jerked her chin toward a small crack in the stone. "Press your fingers in the crack, and then use your shoulder." Her face tightened, and she inhaled deeply, clenching her jaw.

Dor eyed her mum and gingerly slid her fingers into the crack, feeling around until they caught hold of something metal. Her brow furrowed as she pressed on the metal lip, and the stone wall groaned.

"Wicked hell," Dor breathed as she leaned all her weight against the stone. The stone groaned again and began to move inward, revealing a hidden stairway. Ada slipped through the hidden doorway and up a few steps to make room for Dor and her mum.

"Damnation," her mum cursed.

Dor turned toward her mum and swore a black oath. Translucent liquid gushed down her mum's leg and pooled on the ground. The women stared at each other, knowing what would come.

"Of all the blasted times," her mum growled.

"How long til the babe makes her presence known?" Ada asked.

"Each one comes faster than the last," her mum gritted out as she slipped into the passage, and Dor closed the stone door behind them, cutting them completely off from any light. Water dripped around them, and her mum's breathing deepened as her hand latched onto Dor's and squeezed.

"Can you make it?" Ada asked from the darkness.

"I have to," her mum grunted, her hand squeezing Dor's until she thought her fingers would fall off.

A match struck, and Ada's face became visible. "Lantern?"

Her mum grimaced and jerked her chin up the staircase. "It's about twenty paces up."

Ada spun on her heel and powered up the stairs, disappearing around the corner.

Dor sighed in relief as her mum's grip loosened, despite how her heart galloped in her chest. "I'll be here every moment. If you need to stop, tell me."

Her mum nodded and glared at the door behind them. "The timing couldn't be worse."

"We'll get through this." They had to.

Her mother smiled, dropped Dor's hand, and began trudging up the stairs. "We need to keep moving."

"Where does this lead?" Dor asked, brushing her hands along the walls, the stairway brightening as they joined Ada.

"The surface."

Dor almost stumbled. The *surface.* How long had she desired to see the world above? She shook her head. It was too good to be true. "That sounds deadly."

"It is, but we'll have help."

"Help?"

Her mum nodded. "Yes, there are people on our side."

Dor bristled. Other people? Could they be trusted? For so long, it had only been Dor and her family. And now she was to trust strangers?

Her mum glanced over her shoulder and stared down at Dor, half her face in shadow. "Change is part of life. Choices will have to be made, love. Don't shy away from the unknown. Trust me and your instincts."

That couldn't be any vaguer.

"Will they help protect us?"

"Yes, they will. To the best of their ability."

"Who? Will Father be among them?"

"No. One of his companions."

Another warrior was helping them? Apparently, miracles happened in the Pit.

A miracle in Hell? Dor snorted. It seemed too good to be true.

CHAPTER TWENTY-ONE

Sage

"What is he waiting for?" William asked, his white brows furrowed. He shook his head and stared harder at the huge map dominating the table in the middle of the war tent.

"He's playing with us," Zachael growled, pushing away from the table, his steps agitated.

Sage eyed the group of weary men around her. They were tired already, and it had only been a month. Tehl had expected a proper war, but she'd known otherwise. The warlord had no honor, and he'd do whatever he had to. He could've marched in and met them head on, but he hadn't. He played with them, trying to entice them into entering his jungles, but no one was stupid enough to take his bait.

It was frustrating, yes, but it also worked in their favor.

It gave them more time to prepare. Every day they gained was to their advantage.

As soon as Tehl had sent warning, the Methian army had mobilized. But moving thousands of men took time, especially when they were traveling through the mountains. Their feline counterparts had made it much sooner with their riders, but their number was a drop in the ocean compared to the Methian army hiking their way through the mountain range that separated Aermia and Methi. But they did what they could.

They sent their men in waves to train with the Methi riders and fiilee in private, while the rest held the front line, not that there was much to hold. When they'd arrived the first day, Sage's breath had been knocked from her lungs at the sight of the Scythian warriors lined up along the Mort Wall. Chills had run up and down her arms, and a sense of numbness had settled over her when her eyes had landed on the warlord. His dark gaze had been pinned on her as he gave her a slow, intimate smile.

The pained, broken girl inside her wanted to run and hide, but she had forced that part down and drew on the rage that always teemed just beneath the surface and gave him her own cold smile in return. She wasn't the girl he knew. He'd created a dangerous creature when he'd kept her a prisoner. One he wasn't prepared for.

His smile had grown, and, without a sound, his warrior army

had melted back into the jungle. One moment they were there, the next they were gone, vanished like smoke in the wind. That's what chilled her the most.

How could they fight an army they couldn't hear or see?

Sage blinked back the memory and leaned against the table, her leather breastplate creaking. She'd taken to wearing one at both Rafe's and Tehl's insistences. A volley of enemy arrows had almost ended her life. They hadn't been aiming at her, but if she hadn't been paying attention, that incident could've ended much differently.

Focusing back on the map, she squinted at the small pieces depicting the Aermian and Methian armies, as well as their enemy's movements. She reached out and brushed the black piece that represented the warlord. "There's a pattern, we just haven't found it."

"We've been looking for a month. If there is, I can't find it," Gav said, running a hand through his hair, his raven locks disheveled.

"It's here." She knew the warlord. Nothing was chance. Again, she scanned the worn, leather map. The clue was there, she just needed to find it.

"It's late," a deep voice rumbled, causing goosebumps to run up her arms.

She glanced at her husband. Tehl stood to her left, his legs braced apart, his powerful arms crossed. Dark stubble shadowed his square jawline, and the color of his sapphire eyes seemed to intensify as he stared at the map in concentration. It seemed wrong to call him beautiful, as he was too rugged for such a pretty word. There was a new edge to Tehl that he'd not had before she escaped Scythia. One that was wholly appealing in a dark, sinful way.

He sighed and straightened. "We all need sleep. We'll reconvene with the Methian queen tomorrow morning, as well as with Lilja. Hopefully, Lilja will have some news from her spy."

Sage hid her smile as he caught her interested, blatant stare, and his eyes widened just a fraction. It amused her that he was still a little uncomfortable with attention so publicly, and he acted surprised every time she showed any carnal interest in him whatsoever. Her smile deepened.

Not that he didn't like it.

He'd shown her how much he loved how she'd shed most of her modesty and reveled in it. Well, at least, in private, he did. That's where they differed. He kept his affections mostly private, and she... well, didn't. Some of her humor dropped away at the thought. It hadn't always been that way. Living in Scythia hadn't given her much of a choice in the matter.

A smile flavored with bitterness and irony tipped up the corners of her mouth.

If only the warlord knew what she was doing with the lack of modesty he'd forced upon her.

"Dismissed," Tehl commanded.

Sage barely noticed as their advisors filed out. Her eyes focused on the only black piece marring the map. It seemed, no matter what, she couldn't escape the warlord.

Heat suffused her back like a warm blanket, and Tehl leaned

into her, his lips skating leisurely along the left side of her neck.

"What occupies your mind, wife?" he murmured against her skin, between kisses.

He tilted her head to the right to give him better access, her skin beginning to tingle as he grasped her hips with his rough hands.

"Madness," she whispered, the faint rhythm of drums reaching her ears. She wished the incessant drumming would stop. But it hadn't in all the time they'd been at the war camp.

Just another tactic the warlord was using to unnerve their men.

It bothered her. Sometimes, she'd disappear into the woods and place her hands over her ears, so all she could hear were her own breaths.

"Mad brilliance more like," Tehl said, smiling. His lips burned their impression into her skin.

She snorted and shook her head.

"Come to bed," he coaxed, his tone lowering.

The hair rose on her arms as he caressed her sides and pressed his hips against the back of hers in an unabashed invitation.

How she longed to accept, but how could she possibly accept when her mind was filled with the warlord? It would pervert what they had.

Sage captured his roving right hand and kissed his fingers before biting the fleshy pad of his thumb.

A groan rumbled against her back, and she smiled before tipping her head backward and staring up at Tehl. "I'd love to, but I need a little quiet moment to myself." His expression fell, and she was quick to continue. "A few minutes." She wrinkled her nose and sniffed loudly. "Plus, I believe you need to bathe. You smell like a wet, dirty horse."

A gleam entered his gaze, and, before she could protest, his arms wrapped around her, and he rubbed his sweaty self all over her.

"No," she screeched, trying to fend him off.

He laughed, and Sage stumbled forward and spun around, glaring at him.

"What was that for?"

He grinned, the look utterly heart-melting and boyish. "Now I'm not the only one who needs to bathe."

That devil.

Tehl pecked her on the cheek, swept by her and out of the tent, issuing commands about a bathing tub for his wife.

She rolled her eyes and snatched her sword off the pale wooden chair near the entrance of the tent. If he was going to make the men haul pail after pail of water for a bath for her, she'd better train hard enough that she needed one. Sage chuckled. The sneak would blame it on her, but he was the one with a weakness for baths.

***

Sage nodded to the men as she strode through the camp and held her heavy braid off her neck as sweat dripped down her spine. Time at the camp had taught her one very important fact: she was out of shape.

Every day, she trained as hard if not harder than the men. She needed to make up for the time she'd lost in Scythia. It had been difficult; she'd practiced when she could, but it wasn't the same as being in the ring with an opponent, let alone with armor. That was what was the worst. The extra pounds of weight she was trying to work with.

Dropping her hair, she tossed back the tent flap, passed through the war room, and pushed aside the second flap leading to their personal quarters. Sage discovered her husband lounging in a large, crude metal tub. Scented oil perfumed the air, and her cooling skin warmed with the veil of aromatic steam. Her eyes rounded at the size and depth of the tub. It had to have taken forever to heat the water and laboriously fill it.

Tehl leaned back with one long leg propped up at the far end of the tub, a glass of spirits clasped lazily in one hand. His inky blue-black hair was handsomely swept back from his face. She blinked at all his exposed, tanned skin, a small flush touching her cheeks. Stars above, her husband was handsome.

His deep voice cut through the haze. "I was wondering when you were going to appear. I was waiting to let you get in first, but the water was beginning to cool, so I climbed in. How was your bout?"

Sage smiled and walked toward him while unbuckling her leather breastplate. "I did well. I'm sure I can do better." Carefully, she set the breastplate and her sword on the bed to her right before kneeling beside the tub so their faces were level. "How is your bath?

"Hot." His gaze caressed her face, while his forefinger traced the curve of her cheek. "Who did you spar with?"

She pursed her lips and answered honestly, even though she knew he wouldn't like the answer. "Garreth."

Tehl's gaze cooled, and his lips thinned. "With the traitor?"

She tilted her face into his hand. "No one is perfect. And he never meant me any harm."

"And yet you were hurt nonetheless." He glanced away, his chiseled jaw clenching. "By all accounts, he should be hung. His life is forfeit for his actions."

"True, and yet he still lives," she said softly. "Your mercy couldn't have been bestowed on someone worthier. He's served with you for a long time, Tehl. You grew up together, as children. If it had been someone else, the punishment would've come much easier. It always hurts more when betrayal comes from those we love, but at least we can forgive."

Tehl's sharp, blue eyes snapped back to her. "I haven't forgiven him. I just haven't killed him. Yet."

Sage closed her eyes briefly and reached for the glass in his other hand. She downed what little was left and set the cup on the floor. "Children change everything."

Tehl's gaze softened. "That is true, which is why he lives."

"I understand." And she did. If it had been for any other reason, she might have taken it upon herself to rid the world of him. But she understood sacrifice when it was done for loved ones.

A comfortable silence settled between them.

Two long, wet fingers hooked the top of her linen shirt and tugged her closer to the side of the bathtub. Tehl's eyes were a deep, velvety blue, like the sky in the darkest hours of night. "I find

I am unable to properly clean myself, and I require your services."

A smile curved her lips. "What services?" she asked, playing along.

"I need a bath maid." He caught one of her hands and drew it down into the water. "For my hard-to-reach places."

Sage arched a brow at him and stifled a chuckle at his terrible flirting. She tugged at her wrist and feigned shock. "My lord, I'm sure you can reach *that* by yourself. You go too far!"

"My love," he said, nuzzling the crook of her neck. "Why do you think I married you?"

"For my excellent sword skills," she deadpanned.

Tehl released a huff of laughter against her skin. "That should have been my line."

She giggled, a happy buoyancy bubbling in her chest. She schooled her expression and tried to sound severe as his wet hands roved over her curves in lazy abandon. "You, sir, need to watch your hands or you're going to ruin my clothing."

"Not if you remove it." He gave her a positively wicked smile.

Smiling wryly, Sage pulled away and stood. There were many surprises being married to Tehl, but one of the most delightful of them was that he never held back his pleasure in her form. Every time she undressed for him, especially if clothing had many fastenings, he watched, completely riveted like she was the most gorgeous creature to ever be born. It made her feel like a goddess.

Her husband slid a little lower in the water, his gaze roving over her in a way that caused her belly to flip in anticipation and her skin to heat.

"Tell me about your day," he murmured.

"Well, I trained with another Methi warrior today." She smiled as she unlaced the top of her shirt, remembering the small fiilee and his mistress. "Nali seemed to take to the runt. She cuddled right up to him and played nice." Sage scowled at the row of tiny buttons running along the front of her shirt. Buttons were the worst. She stripped the shirt off and tossed it into the corner. One problem solved.

Tehl's gaze dipped to her steel corset, and a small smile touched his lush mouth. The blasted thing was uncomfortable, but it added more protection. It was miserable to wear, but the look on her husband's face when she took it off was worth it. She blinked as she realized Tehl had spoken.

"What did you say?" she asked, reaching back to loosen the laces.

"I asked if you could undress any faster."

Sage huffed in exasperation. "I challenge you to get out of a steel-and-leather corset faster than me." She stiffened and instantly wished she could retract her words. That hadn't sounded like a retort, but a challenge. And, if there was anything she'd learned, it was that Ramses men loved a good challenge.

"I'll give you thirty seconds before I cut it off of you."

She froze, her fingers tangling in the laces. "You wouldn't!"

The crown prince's eyes glinted with devilish mirth. "It's hiding your skin from me. No piece of clothing is more alluring than your naked skin," he said with a bald look. "I want to see what is mine."

"Yours? That's awfully presumptuous," she said as she picked up her speed.

"Fifteen seconds left, by the way."

"How can you even tell how much time has passed?" she huffed as she untied a stubborn knot.

"I'm counting by heartbeats."

Her stomach flipped. "Well, that's not a completely accurate form of time-keeping." She glanced down anxiously at her corset and threw her hands up in the air. The stupid thing was stuck. "The ties are knotted. There's no way I can get out of it without help," she mumbled with a sigh.

She heard his smoky laugh and a sluice of water. He stood, and streams of water ran over the sleek, muscled contours of his body. She stumbled when he pulled her into his steaming embrace. Sage placed her hand on his naked chest and shivered when he leaned down to whisper in her ear.

"My poor little wife. You misunderstand me. Let me be blunt. I have no plans of helping you out of it. Cutting it from your body will serve me just fine. If you'll recall, I'm excellent with my blade."

Laughter spilled from her lips. "How long have you waited to say that?"

"I've waited weeks for the perfect situation."

CHAPTER TWENTY-TWO

Dor

The darkened stairway seemed never-ending, and their journey was only broken up by the frequent stops her mum required in order to breathe through the birthing pains. The timing between pains and stretches of stairs began to shorten. Dor kept her gaze glued to her mum's back, afraid that she might stumble and fall. An image of her mum tumbling down the staircase flashed through Dor's mind, but she shoved the thought away. She didn't want to dwell on how long one would fall if they slipped.

Her mum wavered to the left and placed a hand against the wall, her groan barely audible. Dor had been present the last two times her mum had given birth and understood the kind of agony her brave mother must be battling. It was a marvel she could walk at all.

"Are you all right?" she couldn't help but ask. She'd uttered that question more than ten times already, but she had to ask it once more. Just watching her mum trudge up the stairs was causing Dor pain.

Her mum waved away her question, but Dor saw her jaw was clenched. "I'm fine," she gritted out through bared teeth.

"Like hell you are," Ada muttered from ahead, pausing for Dor and her mother to catch up.

"Don't curse," her mum bit out despite the labor pains. She pulled in one more deep breath and nodded for Ada to continue.

Ada turned back toward the stairs and lifted the lantern higher. Dor tipped her head back and wished she'd kept her gaze on her mum or the floor. The stairs above them spiraled into oblivion, like a gloomy, twisted version of inside a shell.

Her mind shifted to Illya. What would become of her dragon? The thought of him being caged in a stone hell for all of eternity made her step falter. How could she leave him?

You can't help him if you're dead.

"I'll come back for you," Dor promised with a whisper. She'd do everything within her power to free him.

Wicked hell.

Dor's legs seemed to quiver in rebellion as they continued to move up the stairs. Step after step was torture. She stopped counting the steps once they reached the seven-hundredth stair. A complaint was on the tip of her tongue, but she swallowed it back. If her pregnant and in-labor mum could make the horrendous journey, then she could, too. With renewed conviction, she forced her shaky legs up the steps ahead of her.

Dor jerked and glanced above when Ada yipped in happiness.

Thank the stars.

Ada cleared a platform that led to three different hallways and branched away from the staircase. Dor bent over to inhale deep breaths. Ada did the same but kept the lantern high enough that it still illuminated the stairway.

"Dragon's fire," her mum wheezed as she stumbled onto the platform and leaned against the wall. Her green eyes closed, and she clutched her belly, her face tightening with discomfort. "This babe will be the death of me."

Gooseflesh erupted up and down Dor's arms at her mum's grim words, made a little worse by a sudden slight breeze whistling through the hallways, causing a hollow, wailing screech to echo around them. It was something from a nightmare. Dor was sure the sound would haunt her for the rest of her nights. A tingle ran down her spine as she stared into the darkened hallway to her left. The jagged stone opening looked like a giant maw ready to devour them.

"Let's leave this place," Dor found herself saying as she wet her lips. "I feel this is a bad place down to the marrow of my bones." Dor glanced at her mum. "Which way do we travel?" Her eyes darted to the stairs and back to her mum. Stars help her if they had to continue up the devil stairs.

Her mum opened her eyes and held her hand up as Ada's lips parted like she had something to say. Her head tipped to the side as if she was listening for something, and then she glanced in each direction before settling on the left corridor. Her body stiffened, and something akin to horror contorted her face. "Dampen the light," she hissed, lunging from the wall.

Ada scrambled to obey as Dor's mum grabbed both of them by the arms and hauled them along the inky corridor that seemed to mock them as it swallowed them whole. The lantern light completely disappeared, and Dor kept close to her mum as she fought to swallow down the terror that was trying to spew itself from her mouth in noncoherent whimpers.

She stumbled along, stunned at how her mum moved through the darkness with complete ease, like she could see through the gloom. Dor reached her left hand out, touched dry stone, and skimmed her fingertips along the wall to try to orient herself in the debilitating gloom. As much as her body wanted to freeze in fear, her thoughts kept turning to what was coming for them. She fought the urge to look behind, knowing that it wouldn't reveal anything, but only serve to stumble her.

Her mum's hand tightened on her arm, signaling for Dor to stop. The hand on her arm tugged her to the right, and a door creaked. Her mum pulled them forward, and Dor could tell they had now moved into another section of the maze. She placed her left hand over her nose and pinched her nostrils shut as her mum closed the door softly. This room stank of dust and decay. When had the room last been used?

Her eyes watered from forcing back her sneeze. Her mum released her arm and moved farther into the room, her bare feet hardly making a sound on the stone floor. Dor inhaled through her mouth and grimaced when she could taste mildew and dust upon her tongue. *Disgusting.* The hair at the nape of her neck rose as tension seemed to detonate inside the room. Her mum sucked in a sharp breath.

"What can I do?" Ada asked softly from Dor's right.

"Prepare yourselves," her mum barely breathed, discomfort edging her tone. "I need a moment. The birth pains are coming more frequently. Dor, watch the entrance. We're being followed."

A cold sweat broke out between Dor's breasts as she spun and ran both hands along the craggy walls to the wooden door. She darted to the right when her hand touched metal hinges. If their adversaries came through the door, they'd receive a surprise. The silence in the room became deafening as her mum's birth pain passed. She pulled her dagger from her sheath and pressed her ear against the wood, listening. It was as if the room was holding its breath.

Tension bunched her shoulders as she strained to hear anything. Her heart stuttered when she caught a whisper of cloth against cloth from underneath the door. She squinted and waited for it again. A moment passed. Maybe she'd imagined it. Her eyes widened in the darkness though when steel against steel hissed as if a blade slowly slid from a sheath. That was a sound she'd never forget. She'd seen her father pull his daggers from his sheaths every time he'd visited, since Dor was a child. The sound was distinctive. Someone was definitely in the hallway. Just outside their hideout.

Dor held her breath and braced her shoulder against the wood, cursing the absence of locks on it that could barricade them inside and bar their enemy's entrance. Besides her weight, she had nothing but her teeth and nails. It wasn't like she even had time to search the room for any armor to help protect them. Determined to keep anyone from entering, she leaned further against the door. Perhaps, if they tried pressing on the door, they'd think it was locked.

But it wasn't meant to be.

Someone pushed on the door from the outside, and it edged open. Her pulse leapt, and she scrambled to find purchase on the floor with her bare feet without success and leaned into the door with all her weight, but it wasn't enough. The door slammed open, smashing her against the wall behind. Pain seared through her and white dots flashed across her vision. She groaned and pushed the door away from her and sunk to the floor, fighting to stay conscious.

A warrior covered in chainmail, sword in hand, pushed into the room, followed by a soft light that illuminated their haven. Dor swallowed the bile in the back of her throat as she stared at the corpses hanging from the walls. All these men had died long ago, but the corpses hanging from the walls by chains were a living nightmare she desperately wanted to escape.

Dor blinked as another man moved into the room. He carried a torch. She fought through the stars moving across her vision as Ada held her daggers tightly at each side, slipping into a defensive position in front of Dor's mum.

The warrior wearing the chainmail held up his hands. "There's no need for a fight. Clearly, you're with child. We'd never hurt the unborn."

Her mum's eyes narrowed as she took one step forward in challenge, putting herself in front of Ada. She casually removed a wicked blade from her hip and examined it as if she wasn't being threatened. "I will warn you once. You shall not take me or mine." A simple statement said softly, but it was as if she'd shouted a battle cry.

The warrior shook his head. "Swords don't have to come out and play. We can work this out. Isn't that right, Lazae?"

The warrior holding the torch nodded, but stayed mute.

"All you need to do is stand down," the warrior in the chainmail crooned.

But they all knew his words were false; the warlord never showed mercy. It was one reason he was so feared. If he let a threat go, that person became an enemy who might rise against him. Dor carefully tried to get her feet underneath her without drawing attention. The warriors had all but forgotten her.

She stilled as the second warrior moved farther into the room and angled himself toward her mum, exposing his back to Dor. That was his mistake. Her sire had always told her to never turn her back on the enemy. These weren't men trained by her sire, and that gave her an advantage.

She pulled in a deep breath and steeled her nerves. It was now or never. Dor leapt onto the back of the torch-holding warrior, cupping her right hand around his chin. She arched his head back and dragged her knife across his throat with her left hand. Disgust churned in her belly as he choked, staggered, and tumbled backward, crushing Dor against the floor under his body. Agony crashed into her, and she cried out as she was slammed against the stone. The torch tumbled to the floor and sputtered, casting ghoulish shapes across the room.

Darkness threatened to swamp her, but she forced herself to keep her eyes open. Dor squirmed, attempting to free herself. Ada's scream sent a shudder through her body, and she watched in horror as her mum launched herself at the warrior wearing chainmail, sword swinging to meet his with a mighty clash. Dor released a wheezed breath as another huge warrior moved into the room from the corridor. He stepped over his fallen comrade as if he was a bit of rubbish.

Dor's gaze darted back to her mum, just as the chainmail warrior pushed her mother's blade aside. Her mum twisted as he struck, leaning into her space. She surprised him and slashed across his belly with the blade in her opposite hand. He stumbled and clutched at his stomach for just a second before she swept the warrior's feet out from under him, dumping his body onto the mostly smothered flames.

The newest warrior released a war-cry that Dor swore she could feel in her bones and charged at her mum. Her ferocious mother sneered and stepped into his attack as Ada lunged forward and attacked in a series of parries that left Dor dizzy. As her mum and Ada both tried to take the warrior down, Dor cursed as she struggled to free herself from the corpse that weighed her down. Her breath stuck in her throat as her mother stumbled and clutched her stomach, sucking in a deep breath, her flowing movements halting. The warrior tossed Ada against the nearest wall, and didn't pause in his assault on Dor's mum as he went in for the kill.

Dor's pulse thundered in her ears, and she got her right hand free. Her sire had always told her to never throw her weapon, but his advice didn't matter now. She held her blade and clenched her teeth. Partly underneath the dead man's weight, she threw her blade. Her vision dipped as it struck true, right in the back of the shoulder of her mum's attacker. He bellowed and glanced over his shoulder, his eyes holding vengeance as he locked gazes with Dor.

The sounds in the room disappeared as she stared into the eyes of death. Her gaze moved to her mum's pain-filled face, and Dor smiled at her. It would be okay. By her estimations, the birth pains would subside and her mother would see justice done. She was the most formidable woman Dor had ever beheld. There was nothing that could conquer her.

Movements behind the warrior caused her to smile wider. His eyes narrowed as he took a step in the direction that would cost him his life. Ada launched at the warrior and slammed the butt of her dagger against his temple, her full weight crashing into him. The warrior's eyes blanked and rolled in his head. He fell forward and dropped onto his face.

Three bodies littered the floor, and only the sound of harsh panting could be heard. Ada groaned and sat up, rubbing her right shoulder, her nose wrinkled in distaste as she glared at the warrior she'd clouted, her face cast in shadow from the sputtering torches.

Dor glanced across the room and stared at her mum who looked no worse for wear, except for her torn skirt.

"Is everyone all right?" her mum asked.

"Fine," Ada muttered, wiping her dagger on her skirt.

"I'm okay," Dor said, finally wiggling out from beneath the warrior. Devil take it, the man was heavy. Wincing, she swayed on her feet, and the room spun as she pulled her dagger from the warrior's shoulder and stumbled over to her mum. "Are you sure you're okay?"

Her mum embraced her tightly and then pulled back, glaring. "Don't ever put yourself in danger like that again."

Dor touched the back of her head and winced as blood stained her fingers. "I could say the same thing to you."

"I'm your mother. It's my job to protect you." Her mum stepped to the side and hissed. She yanked her skirt up and revealed a blade wound high on her thigh that wept blood. "The bastard got me," she remarked, very put out.

Ada strode to her side and knelt, checking the wound on Dor's mum's thigh. "It's going to need stitches. You're losing too much blood. You should sit."

"I can't," her mum argued. "Another pain is coming. I need to be able to move through it."

"You'll faint long before the babe is born if you don't take care of that wound," a deep voice murmured from the darkness of the corridor.

Ada sprung to her feet, and both she and Dor stepped in front of her mum as she began to breathe through the waves of discomfort. Dor peered into the darkness, trying to see the newest threat.

A heavy sniff. "From the smell of this room, it'll need to be cleaned thoroughly or she'll breed infection."

Dor held her bloody dagger out in front of her defensively.

"Show yourself."

A muscled warrior materialized from the darkness, stepping forward into the dim light. His dark eyes swept the room, taking in the scene. Dor steeled her nerves as she assessed the warrior. This one looked hard. The way he moved reminded her of the jungle cats that were the monsters every child was taught lurked in the dark.

His gaze settled on her mum, and an emotion flittered across his angular face. "Thank the stars, I found you alive."

Her mum placed a hand on Dor's left shoulder and limped in front of her. She placed her hands on her hips and glared at the man. "It took you long enough. My children could have died. Where the devil were you?"

He arched a midnight eyebrow and hooked a finger over his shoulder. "Do you really think they'd only send three men for the commander's property and daughter accused of murder?" He shook his head. "Some from above are foaming at the mouth to see your demise and the commander's reaction."

He took another step forward, and Dor matched his step, keeping pace with her mother. Anyone who spoke of another person as property wasn't any friend of hers.

"Not one step further," she growled, surprising even herself with the menace in her tone.

"Dor," her mum called softly. She placed a hand on Dor's fist clenched around the dagger's handle. "It's okay, love. This is your father's man, the one I spoke of."

The warrior met her gaze, and Dor stared him down, not wanting to move one inch. "You really expect us to believe you're helping my sire? You're the one hunting us down!"

He rolled his shoulders and sighed as if aggrieved to have to explain anything to a stupid worker. She bit the inside of her cheek to keep her teeth from lashing out at him. She loathed the man already.

"If there was someone hunting you, who better than me? I needed to find you." He kicked one of the warriors on the floor. "These monsters made it faster and easier."

"How convenient for you."

"Dor," her mother chastised.

The warrior held up a hand. "It's all right. She has every right to doubt me after what you all experienced." He nodded toward her mum's bleeding leg. "But we don't have time for your doubts at the moment. Your mum is losing blood, and she's exhausted herself before the most critical part of the birth. She needs a healer's attention."

Dor's skin crawled at the mention of a healer, but she knew he was right. "I swear to all that is holy, if you make a wrong move, I will end you."

"Dark," he murmured, a strange twinkle entering his coffee-colored eyes. "I like it." Her mum cleared her throat and stared down the warrior, who pursed his lips like he'd tasted something sour. "Let's move before your mum births the babe in this hellhole," he said brusquely.

Dor nodded, slowly put away her blade, and took her mum's arm.

"That'll take too long," the warrior said, breaching the distance between them and gathering her mum in his arms as if she weighed nothing at all.

Her mum paled and sweat dotted her brow. "Hurry, girls. The babe will soon be here."

The warrior spun on his heel, stepped over the bodies of the fallen men, and strode out of the room. Ada kicked the chainmail warrior and followed. Dor blankly scanned the room, vaguely wondering whose family hung on the walls. She forced her legs to follow the others and glanced at the warriors she'd felled. The ugly red cut along the first one's neck looked like a demented smile. Her stomach rolled, and she stumbled against the door and puked on the stone floor.

She'd taken a man's life. *A life.* She heaved once more and wiped at her eyes and mouth. Not just one, but two. *She was a murderer.* There was no coming back from that.

Dor straightened and fled the room, but leaving the scene of the crime would not undo what had happened. She'd wear the stain of what she'd done on her soul for the rest of eternity.

Chapter Twenty-Three

Tehl

Mornings had become Tehl's favorite part of the day.

He stretched his back slightly and pulled Sage's warm, naked body more fully into the curve of his own. A smile tugged at his lips as she sighed and wiggled but didn't wake. Carefully, he propped himself up on one elbow and stared down at his beautiful wife. Every morning, it was a surreal experience to watch her slowly wake and sleepily smile at him, not even aware she was doing so.

His heart clenched as she snuggled closer, hugging his arm closer to her chest. In moments like this, he could almost forget the world around them. Tehl enjoyed the silence during the birth of a new day. In fact, silence had been his constant companion his entire life. Sharing it with someone else was an unexpected joy, especially seeing Sage without the constant weight she carried. In sleep, her hard edges fell away, leaving only the embodiment of warmth in its place.

"Are you going to keep staring?" Sage murmured, her lips barely moving, eyes still closed.

Tehl's mouth hitched up at the corner as he kissed her bare shoulder. Caught red-handed, and he wasn't the least bit sorry. "It's hard to look away."

His wife cracked one sleepy, green eye and arched a brow at him. "Compliments in the morning? Whatever could you be after, my prince?"

His smile widened. "Whatever indeed..." He pressed his face into the crook of her neck and bit down slightly before tightening his arm around her slim waist and rubbing his beard along her tender skin.

Sage squealed and writhed. "Noooooo," she laughed. "Make it stop."

Tehl rolled her toward him and onto her back. Her laughing, green eyes stared up at him, and he swept his gaze over her face and sent a silent *thank you* to whatever forces had sent this woman onto his path. Her mirth died away as she watched him.

"I've never had anyone look at me the way you do," she whispered into the chilly air.

He didn't know what to say to that, so he kissed her softly, hoping it conveyed his feelings. Actions meant more than words.

A cacophonous sound reached his ears, and he paused, staring down at his wife. Her brows slashed down, and a wrinkled formed between them.

"That's not good," Sage remarked.

Tehl kissed her once more, rolled off of her, and stood, the covers slipping from his body. His skin pebbled as the cold air rushed around him. He quickly slipped on his pants and groaned as Sage crawled from the bed, all bare skin and lush curves. Tehl eyed his wife and then the bed mournfully. What started out as a wonderful day was soon to turn sour, he was sure of it.

He yanked his shirt over his head, and grinned when Sage lifted her discarded corset from the floor and shook it at him.

"Look at what you did," she complained.

"You didn't mind so much last night," he countered.

She rolled her eyes, a small blush touching her cheeks, but smiled at him as she tugged her leather pants over her flared hips. "I won't argue that."

A touch of pride and possessiveness rolled through him at her statement. "You're going to be the end of me, woman."

She grinned impishly while pulling up her boots and then retrieved her leather breastplate. "I'm not sorry."

Tehl took the breastplate from her hands and slipped it over her head, careful to mind her long, loose hair. "Temptress," he said without heat as he tightened the armor to fit her figure.

"Beast," she replied.

He stepped back, and they stared at each other, acknowledging the playful moment before they settled into the roles they would both play when they left the comfort of their room.

Sage glanced toward the tent flap as the noise in the camp rose and seemed to move in their direction. "I fear what's coming."

So did he. Nothing was certain in war. "We'll do our best to get through it. Have no fear."

A small laugh fell from her lips. "There is much to fear."

Oh, how he knew. She'd shared some of her horrors from Scythia with him, but many others he'd experienced as she fought to escape them in her nightmares. Sometimes, he wished he could forget them, too. One too many times, he'd awoken with a racing heart, bitter fear coating his tongue, and his grip too tight around his wife.

He held his hand out. "We'll face this together."

Sage glanced down at his hand and slipped her small, calloused one into his and squeezed.

"To the end."

CHAPTER TWENTY-FOUR

Sage

Sage's heart thundered as loudly as Peg's hooves beneath her as they approached the remote keep near the Nagalian border.

Smoke singed her nose when she inhaled sharply as their riding group crested the hill and slowed. Her mouth dried, and her eyes stung as they approached the wreckage below them.

It was as if fire had rained down from heaven and scorched every part of the earth.

What remained of the blackened stone keep stood like jagged, rotten teeth amongst the ravaged remains of the village.

Could anyone have survived?

Tehl steered his black beast of a horse to her left side as Zachael pressed closer to her right. Their men formed a loose circle around them.

"My men have searched the area for enemies. It seems they came in like shadows and left just as quietly," Zachael said, his normally warm voice harsh and biting.

Sage watched her husband's cold profile as he scanned the area, his expression chillingly blank.

"Any survivors?" Tehl demanded.

"None so far, my lord," Zachael answered. "They pillaged and took what they wanted before burning everything else."

Her stomach soured, and her husband pressed his heels into the flanks of his horse and began the descent to the decimated village. She urged Peg forward and ignored how sweaty her hands felt inside the leather gloves she wore.

No survivors.

"Did they take captives?" she asked softly.

"We believe so, my lady," Zachael answered.

Her hands tightened on Peg's reins, causing her horse to snort. Death seemed preferable to captivity.

Ash and smoke swirled around them, falling like snowflakes. Sage's eyes stung, her nose wrinkling from the smell, and she blinked several times to keep from rubbing them as they entered the village, the noise of the horses' hooves against the dirt the only sound.

The hair at the back of her neck prickled as the gray cloud that surrounded the village kept thickening. She urged Peg forward and almost jumped from the saddle when a soldier coughed behind her, shattering the solemn silence.

Tehl eyed her but said nothing as she stared impassively back, hoping to convey that she was strong enough to do this. He already worried about her too much as it was. He nodded and continued deeper into the smoldering ruins.

Sage glanced to the left, and paused as a shadow darted past the remnants of what looked to be some sort of shop and home. Peg skittered to the side when Sage clicked twice, her attention on the alley. A familiar shape slunk by but didn't move any closer.

She blew out a relived breath.

Nali.

Her feline companion disappeared into the gloom, and Sage steered her mare to the left, trailing the rest of the group. Three soldiers still accompanied her, but she barely noticed them as they moved through the destruction.

The road opened up to a stone courtyard that led to the entrance of the keep. The men ahead had stopped, forming a line to block whatever was ahead.

"My lady, I don't think you should see this," the soldier to her right murmured.

Sage glanced at him, meeting his pained eyes that were just a little too close together to be handsome. She nodded. "Thank you for your concern, but I'll see for myself."

The men moved aside as she approached, and what was revealed caused flashes of hot and cold to run through her body. She gagged as the stench of burnt meat overwhelmed her senses.

One immense pole had been erected in the center of the courtyard and attached to it were bodies.

"Stars above," a young soldier breathed.

"Were they burned alive?" Sage forced herself to ask.

"We found no evidence of prior executions," Zachael said heavily.

Tears pooled in her eyes at the thought of the excruciating pain the men must have faced.

"Am I correct in assuming it was just men?" Tehl asked, his voice like ice.

"Yes. The bodies are too large to be women or children."

Sage inhaled through her mouth and tried not to breathe too deeply. It sickened her to think what she was breathing in – or whom. The young soldier to her right heaved next to her, and she met his ashamed gaze as he wiped his mouth.

"There's no shame in being sickened by something so heinous," Sage said softly, her own stomach rolling.

The young man nodded, his eyes glassy.

"Cut them down," Tehl commanded. "And bury them properly. They deserve that."

"It will be done," Zachael said.

The weapons master uttered commands, but Sage barely heard them as she counted the bodies. A hand touched her arm, pulling her from her morbid task. Deep, somber, blue eyes stared up at her from a face that could've been made from stone. Tehl placed his hand over hers but said nothing.

"I'm so sorry," she whispered, knowing the words would

neither help nor change anything. But they needed to be said, nonetheless.

Tehl's jaw clenched, and he swallowed once. "I'm going to help."

Sage nodded and moved to swing off her horse. It was a grisly task, but it had to be done. Tehl's hand on her thigh stopped her movement. She glanced askance at him.

"I would prefer it if you didn't help with this."

Her gloved hand touched his cheek. "I can do this."

"I know you can. I'm asking you not to."

She scanned his face and nodded. "Okay."

He pressed his cheek into her hand for an extra beat before straightening and striding into the fray of soldiers retrieving the bodies. The men made room for him and didn't comment as he began to work beside them. A surge of melancholy pride moved through her. He'd make a wonderful king someday.

The creak of a wagon alerted her to the soldiers moving in from behind. Sage nudged Peg to her left to move out of the lane so the soldiers could move the beaten-up wagon into the square. Sage longed to slap her hands over her ears as they began to cut down the corpses. Her nerves put Peg on edge, and, soon, she found herself near the keep.

She gazed up at the ominous soot-covered stones and almost wept. How long had this keep stood? How many lords and ladies, babies and grandchildren, weddings and funerals had it seen? So much was lost.

The ground groaned, and her brows pulled together. Sage

glanced down as Peg shifted, and sand slipped through a few cracks beneath her mare's hooves, revealing rotted wooden slats.

Wicked Hell.

"It's okay, sweet girl," she murmured to Peg as she inspected the ground around them. One wrong move, and they'd fall right through. She forced the tension from her limbs, and urged Peg to take one step backward.

Another crack.

Sweat beaded on her forehead. There was less distance to travel if Peg moved backward, but she was slower. If they moved forward...

The ground groaned and shifted.

"Yaw!" she commanded, her heels and knees digging into Peg.

Her mare shot forward as the wood began to crumble. Shouts exploded from behind her, but Sage focused on making it to the other side. Only a few more paces. Wood splintered, cracked, and gave way behind them. Sage leaned forward as Peg launched over a hole in the ground and narrowly made it onto the dirt waiting on the other side.

Air rushed out of her lungs as she let Peg run off her nervous energy, and then she spun her horse back the way they'd come. They approached the collapsed ground, and Sage shakily swung her right leg off of Peg and dropped to the dirt, clutching her mare's reins, her legs trembling. She stroked her hand along Peg's quivering shoulder.

"That's a good girl," she soothed. "You're such a good girl. So fast."

"Sage!" Tehl barked.

She glanced across the gaping hole in the ground and met Tehl's frightened gaze. His hands opened and closed as he stared at her.

"I'm all right," she called back, gesturing to herself. "Not a scratch." Her gaze dropped to the collapse, noting all the broken wooden pieces that could've impaled Peg or herself. *We were lucky.* She released Peg's reins and crept toward the gaping maw in the ground.

"Don't get too close," her husband cautioned.

"I won't," she said as soldiers arrived on her side.

She waved away the ash floating in front of her face and knelt next to the edge. Dirt and ash obscured what was far below. She squinted at the length and width of the space. It looked like...

"An escape tunnel," she murmured, hope blossoming in her chest. "Tehl, it's an escape tunnel!" She eyed part of the road that collapsed, creating an angled wall that disappeared into the dark. All she would have to do was slide down to investigate it.

"Don't you dare," the crown prince threatened.

Sage studied him. In that moment, Tehl was a commanding royal, not her husband. He was giving her an order as her sovereign, but if he was willing to bury the dead, she could surely make sure there weren't any people down there.

"Follow me," she called to the soldiers who had surrounded her. She tipped her chin to Tehl and slid down the makeshift slide into the darkness. Her boots slammed against the ground, causing dirt, dust, and ash to stir around her. She smothered a cough, and held her arm across her nose and mouth as she tried to make out the area around her.

"Coming down," a deep voice warned.

She stepped out of the way as Zachael descended into the tunnel and landed much more gracefully than she had done. He glared at her and reached for a chunk of wood.

"You're going to be the death of him," the weapons master muttered as he wrapped a piece of cloth around the top half of it, ready to create a makeshift torch as soon as a flame caught on. "And I think you took ten years off my life. You need to be more careful. I'm already old."

Sage snorted. He may have had children her age, but there was nothing old about him. He was as fit as any young man and could out-spar anyone. "I'm sure you'll survive."

Flint struck steel, and Zachael's torch caught fire. She squinted at the sudden light. The weapons master lifted the torch and swung it to his right, illuminating a huge stone door that sealed the entrance into the stone tunnel from the keep. There clearly wasn't anything in that direction. Sage turned to her left and eyed the wide, dark tunnel that stretched on. She was studying its ceiling, which had collapsed in several places, when something smooth and pale caught her attention.

Her gaze narrowed, and a warning screamed in the back of her mind. "Zachael, would you hold the light higher?"

The weapons master stepped closer to her back and lifted the torch over his head, casting more light around the tunnel. Icy disbelief trickled down her spine as the soft firelight highlighted a small pale arm. Dread filled her belly, and she wanted nothing more than to run away, and, yet, she found herself scrambling over the debris.

"Sage!" Zachael yelled.

She hissed as she tripped and grabbed a particularly ragged piece of wood, but she barely felt the pain as she ignored the weapons master's calls. She couldn't distinguish his words over the beating of her own frantic heart. A hand wrapped around her arm, halting her movement. Sage glared over her shoulder at Zachael.

"Let me go," she said with venom.

He gazed at her impassively, and then his eyes shifted over her shoulder, and horror and anguish rippled across his face. "You can't help them."

Them?

Slowly, she turned her attention back to the arm, and the world dropped from beneath her feet. Her knees crashed to the stone floor, and an inarticulate sound escaped her mouth.

They'd found the elderly, the women, and the children.

Tears dripped down her face, and she crawled to the little girl sprawled face-first on the floor. Her hands shook as she turned over the toddler. She placed her hand around the little one's cool wrist, praying for a pulse.

Nothing.

She hiccupped and placed her ear over the little one's chest.

Nothing.

"No," she moaned. Her eyes roved over the girl's round petite face and rested on her blue lips. There weren't any injuries on the child that she could see, but… the blue lips, and ten blue little toes.

Sage pulled the little one's hand into her own. "She suffocated." Her words echoed around them. At Zachael's silence, she glanced up to see the weapon master's own stricken expression. Carefully, she placed the little one's arm across her still chest and stood, her knees almost buckling once again at the sight that greeted her.

The other side of the tunnel was sealed as well, and from the bodies littering the tunnel, it was clear someone had locked them inside and then slowly suffocated them.

Her gut clenched and she turned to the side to vomit out all the contents of her stomach. She heaved and heaved, her heart breaking. Wiping her mouth, she stooped and picked up the toddler with care. Her body hardly weighed anything. Sage's hands shook as she held the child close to her chest and passed by Zachael, who'd not moved but stared at the crime with the horror it deserved.

Sage clambered over the rubble and found an easier way to climb up. When the soldiers saw what she carried, they reached down and helped her leave the tomb behind. She took a few steps and fell to her knees with a soul-rendering cry.

"How could anyone do such a thing?" she whispered, her bottom lip trembling as she looked at the wee one in her arms. She brushed a finger along the child's cool, downy cheek and once again turned to the side to dry-heave.

Hands touched her shoulders as she straightened, and then massive arms wrapped around her from behind.

Sobs wracked her body as Tehl sank to his own knees and began to rock her and the child.

"Why?" she cried. "Why?"

"There's no reason for such wickedness."

There wasn't. How could a human being treat another person in such a manner?

"She's just a baby," Sage wailed, the image of the silent tomb seared in her mind. "What was the purpose of this? I can't understand it."

Nali prowled closer and bumped Sage in the arm with her head, her golden eyes seeming concerned. She wished she could assure the leren that she was okay, but she couldn't get any words past her sobs.

Tehl said nothing but continued to hold her as she mourned. Eventually, her tears dried, and a sense of numbness and fatigue settled over her. She adjusted the child in her arms and forced herself to get to her feet, Nali shadowing her. She swayed and turned to face Tehl. Heartache and grief were etched into his face.

"Fix this." She knew that he couldn't.

"She's gone, love. You need to put her down."

Sage clutched the child closer to her chest and took one step back. "And leave her for the predators?" She shook her head. "No. She deserves better." Her gaze strayed to the soldiers pulling the too small bodies from the debris of the tunnel. "They all deserve better."

Oh god, she was going to be sick again.

"We'll make sure they're buried, and we'll get vengeance."

"Vengeance?" she asked dully. She glanced at the toddler once again. There was nothing—*nothing*—that could make this better. "It's not supposed to be like this. War. Books speak of honor, courage, and glory," she stated. "This is none of those things. This is the ugliest kind of evil."

Sage swallowed down another cry that threatened to break free as Tehl picked up a shovel and met her gaze.

"Where do you want to lay her to rest?" he asked softly.

She peered around the ruins and paused, spotting a lilac bush up on the hill behind the keep. "There."

Tehl said nothing else but strode toward the spot she pointed to. He hefted his shovel and began to dig a rectangular plot.

One that was all too small.

Sage followed him and stood by his side, Nali their silent sentinel. Time passed, but she couldn't be sure how much.

Her husband touched her shoulder and held out his arms. She released the child, her arms feeling oddly empty as he stepped into the small grave and laid the child down, each movement mindful. He placed a lilac bloom across her little overlapped hands and pulled himself from the plot. His chest and shoulders heaved as he sucked in deep, pained breaths.

Sage slipped her right hand into his and sunk her fingers into Nali's soft midnight fur. They stood there, both silently crying for the cruel, heartbreaking loss of so many innocents. She released Tehl's hand and picked up the shovel, then scooped up some dirt. For a second, she hesitated.

"I'm sorry, wee one," she whispered, tears thick in her voice. "I promise you that I'll kill the man who did this and that you'll never be forgotten."

It took all her strength, but she sprinkled the dirt over the child's body. With each scoop, her resolve solidified, and she buried a piece of her heart.

The warlord had crossed a line she never thought he would. He was a monster.

But by his actions, he'd created something worse: a consort as deadly as he was.

Chapter Twenty-Five

Dor

The floor lurched under her feet as she stepped into the hallway. Her breath hitched, and her throat dried at the sight of two warriors sprawled on the ground. Who had killed them? A chill ran down her arms as she hurriedly stepped over a motionless warrior, his sightless eyes blankly staring up at her. Her legs locked in place as she stared, stricken, at the warrior. He was dead. Death claimed him for following the orders of the warlord. It could have very well been herself lying in a pool of blood.

"Dorcus, come on," Ada pleaded.

As much as Dor wanted to follow her friend, she forced herself to stare at the warrior for a second longer. This was the price of rebellion. The consequences of fighting for one's life. The dark part of her knew that she'd exchanged the warrior's life for her mother's and Ada's, but even so, he was still a human being, and that deserved acknowledgement.

She knelt down and reached out with her right hand, ignoring how it shook when she gently closed his eyes. This man may have committed horrendous crimes for all she knew, but he could have hated the warlord as much as Dor. She didn't know his circumstances, and he deserved more than being left to rot in the godforsaken dark. She could do this much.

Dor straightened and glanced over her shoulder to find the warrior and Ada staring at her. A prickle of self-consciousness caused her cheeks to heat, which she ignored. She already knew she was particular, but she'd be damned if she let someone else's opinion of her determine her ideas on what was right and wrong.

She turned away from the fallen man, and scurried forward at the crumpled expression on her mum's face.

The warrior pulled her mum's face closer to his chest and lifted his chin at Dor. A clear command. "Follow me."

Dor's lips pressed together as she stared at his broad back as he stomped away, his steps quick and staccato-like. She didn't want to go after him. Every part of her screamed not to follow him or trust him. But he held her pregnant mother in his arms and was quickly disappearing down the hallway, so she didn't have much of a choice. Dor rushed to catch up, her skin tingling like a thousand spiders were running up and down her arms. When she'd awoken, it had been a normal day, but after this morning, she was sure she'd never have a normal day again.

"This way," he said gruffly, rounding the corner to the right.

The light from behind them slowly faded to a dull glow. She squinted into the dark and ran her hands along the wall, keeping her gaze on the warrior and Ada ahead of her.

"Grab the lantern," the warrior commanded, looking over his shoulder. His coffee-colored eyes flicked to Ada and then to the wall. Her friend scrambled to comply and quickly lit the lantern.

Their faces glowed eerily in the low light, and Dor blinked at how the light seemed to catch all the handsome angles of the warrior's face. Her lips curled as he faced forward and began moving without another word. *Rude.*

Her mum bit out a curse that had Dor speeding up and pressing closer to the warrior's right side. Her mother's face crumpled, and she hissed out a breath between her teeth, before panting and clutching at her belly. *Not a good sign.*

"Are you all right, Mum?" she asked, trying to keep panic from her voice. It wouldn't do to distress her mum even more.

Her mother nodded and gave a pained smile. "Women have been birthing babes since the beginning of time, love. I'll bear it as I have before."

Dor eyed her mum. They'd never had a babe come this early. It was happening a lot quicker than it should have been. But she kept her mouth firmly shut. It wasn't like *she'd* birthed babes before.

Her mum's expression cleared, and she opened her watery eyes and unclenched her hands. "I'll be fine, love. There's no need for so much concern. The babe will come, but I want to get to safety first."

Dor schooled her expression, smiled weakly, and jogged to keep up with the massive man carrying her mum, Ada keeping pace with her.

Safety. Was there even such a thing? In the world she was born into, there never had been.

Nothing was safe.

Ada squeezed in on her left side and looped her arm through Dor's. She clutched her friend's arm gently, and some of the panic loosened in her chest. None of them were in this situation alone. Ada scooted a little closer, as if seeking comfort, and lifted the lantern higher. A groan slipped from Dor's lips as they approached another staircase. Her legs were barely working as it was. It would be a bloody miracle if she got out of the maze of tunneled hallways alive.

The warrior cut her a look that spoke of irritation as he stomped up the stairs. Dor managed to keep from rolling her eyes, and swallowed back a sharp reply that would surely distress her mum and needle the warrior. Now wasn't the time. He was helping them and, even as tiny as her mum was, there was no way Ada or herself would have been able to carry her mum this far, let alone up the stairs. So, she swallowed back her complaints and trudged up the circling, black stone staircase. There were worse lots in life.

Thankfully, they only climbed a few more steps before they tapered off into a half-circle landing with tunnels leading in five directions. Ada set the lantern on the floor, pressed her hands to her knees, and panted while the rest of them caught their breaths.

Dor leaned against the wall and stared at the warrior. "So, since we're causing mischief and mayhem, are you going to share your name?"

"Names are a dangerous thing."

So, *no*. "I could easily identify your face," she argued.

He raised an imperious eyebrow. "Are you sure?"

He did look like most of the warriors, but there was something different about his eyes. She shrugged, neither confirming nor denying his words. If he wouldn't answer her, she wouldn't answer him. To some it may seem childish, but fair was fair.

"We need to move," he said, gently shifting her mum in his arms.

Ada snatched the lantern from the floor and rubbed at her back as she straightened. "Lead the way."

The nameless warrior dipped his chin and pressed into the far-right tunnel, disappearing into the darkness with her mother. Both girls locked arms once again and followed. The tunnel stretched on and on, curving left then right, up and down. It was disorienting, and goosebumps pebbled Dor's forearms as the temperature cooled. Her friend pulled the lantern closer as she practically plastered herself to Dor's right side.

"This tunnel creeps me out," Ada whispered, her words seeming to be absorbed by the inky darkness hovering just out of reach.

"I don't like it..." Dor trailed off as she caught sight of the end of the tunnel. It just *ended*. A flare of panic ignited in her gut. Had they made a wrong turn? Somehow, she doubted it.

Her heart began to pound in her chest as the man slowly lay her mother down on the floor and spun to face both Ada and her, his expression unreadable. Hell. She dropped Ada's left arm and palmed the blade at her hip. She knew they couldn't trust him.

Ada placed the lantern on the floor, stepped slightly in front of Dor, and effortlessly drew both daggers from her sheaths. No one spoke a word as tension filled the hallway.

"What do you want?" Ada asked, softly.

The warrior scrutinized both of them, letting no trace of his thoughts cross his face. Her mum moaned, momentarily pulling his attention from them, as she clutched her stomach and curled into herself, apparently oblivious to the situation around her.

Uneasiness coiled in Dor's belly. If they didn't get to a healer soon, the babe might not be born at all, or her mum could die.

The warrior's gaze narrowed and then moved to the wall behind his back. He heaved in a deep breath and then faced them once again, his expression cold as stone. "What is beyond this door will change your life."

"Hurry up," her mum grunted from the floor.

He glared at Dor's mother for a second and then focused back on Ada and Dor. "There will be no going back," he murmured quietly, his tone soft and low, carrying a deep warning. "This is permanent. Serious." A pause. "If you pass through this gateway, you must never speak of what you will see."

Dor's pulse accelerated even more. What could be so horrid

that she must never utter a single word about it?

"Decide now."

Decide now? "You've told me nothing." Dor wasn't about to agree to something when she didn't know the particulars. That was stupid. And stupid in her world led to death.

"I'm bound by the same laws you are. Decide or walk away."

"Walk away?" Dor wet her lips, her gaze bouncing between her mum and Ada. "You would let us go?"

The muscle in his jaw twitched. "I would allow you to walk away, but not to live."

Ada gasped, and dread twisted in Dor's belly. Her feet wanted to turn and flee, but she knew from experience she couldn't outrun a warrior, and there was no way she could leave her mum or Ada behind. They were family, and family stuck together.

"You would kill us over nothing?" Dor said flatly.

"This is not nothing."

A flare of anger ignited in her chest, making her a little bit reckless. She waved a hand at the invisible door. "I didn't ask for any of this. I don't even know who you are," Dor reminded him, her brain scrambling to find a way out of the situation. "*You* have a choice. You don't have to kill us. We'll disappear. You'll never see us again."

He shook his head. "I'm sorry, but that's not the way this works. You need to make a choice, but know if you do choose to walk the path ahead and you ever speak about what you see, your life will be forfeit."

"It's not really a choice. You're saying you'll kill us if we don't like what's on the other side," she pointed out. "Or if we ever try to speak about what's behind the door, we'll die. Death is on every path!"

"Lives are at stake," he said woodenly.

"Yes," she bit out. "*Our* lives."

"We cannot risk a breach."

We. Who was the *we* the warrior was referring to?

"Dorcus," her mum whispered.

Dor tore her gaze from the warrior and knelt beside her mum, careful to keep the warrior within full view.

"What, Mum?"

Her mum reached out and squeezed her hand, her hazel eyes filled with pain. "Go through the gateway. This is your future, love. You've never shied away from doing what's right. Take the path."

Dor swallowed, her tongue sticking against the roof of her mouth. She didn't want to admit it, but she was scared, not of death, but of whatever was on the other side of the door. Terrified of the change that would surely wreak havoc on her life.

She glanced at the dark, stone wall. Her fear drove her to back away, but she wouldn't give in. Fear had never ruled her in the past, and it wouldn't now. Even when she felt cornered, she still knew she had a choice. There was nothing to go back to. The only way she could go was forward into the unknown.

"You can do this, Dor," her mum whispered.

Dor nodded, pushed herself to her feet, and stood on shaking legs, meeting the warrior dead in the eyes. "I understand and agree to move forward." She inhaled then exhaled shakily. "But I want something in exchange. Care for my family-"

"Done."

"I wasn't finished speaking."

His lips twitched. "By all means, continue."

"I want your name."

The warrior blinked, looking a bit shocked. "My name?"

"It's only fair. I want to know whom I should hold accountable if things don't go well."

He cocked his head. "Darius." His coffee gaze moved to Ada. "Do you accept the terms as well?"

"Yes," her friend answered without hesitation.

Darius turned from them and pressed a series of spots and hollows on the door. Stone groaned and shuddered, then the door swung open silently.

"Enter."

CHAPTER TWENTY-SIX

Sam

Sam ghosted down the hallway to his chambers, his footsteps muffled on the lush carpets running the length of the arching corridors. A faint peel of laughter reached his ears as he arrived at the ornate, wooden door that led to his rooms. With care, he rested his forehead against the smooth wood and listened to the twins' squeals of happiness.

He loved listening to them laugh. They'd been through so much at such a tender age. Ethan was the more wary of the two, but he'd been warming up to Sam since he'd been bringing treats and little trinkets every time he visited.

Bribery at its best.

Jas, of course, had tried to keep the children away from him as much as possible. Sam's lips turned up in a devious smile. She may be stubborn, but her stubbornness was no obstacle for his plotting. Every time she turned her back, he made sure to spend time with the twins. It hadn't taken him long to win them over.

He reached for the handle and pushed the door open. As Sam stepped inside, his breath was knocked from him at the picturesque scene taking place in his chambers. A fire crackled in the hearth, and curled up on his bed were Jasmine, Jade, and Ethan. Both children had their cheeks pressed against Jasmine's swollen belly as she read from a storybook.

It was the picture of domesticity.

His heart swelled, and he longed to join them, to wrap his arms around his family and kiss his wife on the top of her head, but they weren't there yet. The children had accepted him, but their aunt had yet to do so.

Her gaze flicked up to his above her book, and he held a finger to his lips. The children apparently hadn't noticed his entrance yet. Jasmine pressed her lips together, but she didn't out him, so that was progress. She dismissed him and began reading the story once again, her voice changing pitch for each character.

Sam stealthily snuck up on the twins, who were enraptured with the story, and then launched onto the bed, snagging each child by their waist. Jade and Ethan screamed, and began to wiggle and laugh as Sam tickled them.

"What miscreants have invaded my lair?" Sam demanded in a

deep voice. "Do you seek to steal my treasures?"

Jade shook her head, her tawny hair flopping around her chubby face. "I would never steal, that's bad!"

Sam turned his attention to the little boy pummeling him with his fists. "And what about you?"

"Whatever does a dragon need treasure for?" Ethan retorted as he struggled not to laugh.

"Indeed," Sam whispered conspiratorially. "Dragons do like treasure, but do you know what they like better?"

"What?" the twins said in unison, their faces red from laughter and exertion.

"Dragons love maidens like your auntie. Maybe I shall keep her forever!"

Little war cries exploded out of the twins, and they began to attack him with fervor. Sam loosened his grasp on Jade and let her worm her way out of his hold. She hopped two steps and picked up a feather pillow, a wily gleam in her eye.

"No one takes my mama!"

Sam stilled as Jasmine's face paled and lost all expression at Jade's innocent words. It was like someone had punched Jas in the gut. He barely noticed as Ethan slipped from his fingers and launched the pillow-attack with his sister, the feathered blows skimming off of him.

"Are you all right?" he asked Jas.

Jasmine blinked and rolled from the bed, leaving the storybook forgotten on the brocade blanket covering the bed. She brushed the wrinkles from her dress and said softly, "It's time for bed, you two."

"Aw, come on," Ethan protested. "Sam just got here."

"I understand, but it's well past your bedtime as it is. I promised you could say goodnight and nothing more."

"But I want to—"

Sam placed a hand on Ethan's right arm, pulling the little boy's attention from Jasmine. "Don't argue with auntie. Do as she says."

His lip protruded as he stared imploringly at Sam. "I missed you."

Sam swallowed and pulled the little boy into his arms. "I promise to be here when you wake."

Jade sniffled, and he opened his other arm to the rambunctious little girl. She flung herself into him and wrapped her arms around his neck. Sam scooped the twins up and moved toward the door to their room. Jasmine bustled forward and opened the door for them.

Toys littered the room, along with books stacked haphazardly and drawings pinned to the walls. Leaning down, he placed Jade and Ethan onto each of their beds, and lit the lantern that stood on a small blue table between them. The soft glow warmed the dark room.

He leaned down and placed a kiss on the top of Jade's head as she snuggled into her covers. "Night, Sam," she said with a yawn.

"Goodnight, sweetheart," he replied, pushing the hair from her face.

Next, he moved to Ethan's side and sat on the edge of his bed as the little boy stared up at him, Ethan's expression grave. He latched on to Sam's hand with his little fingers.

"You promise to be here?"

"I promise," Sam said warmly.

"Not everyone comes back," Ethan whispered.

Sam swallowed hard and ignored Jasmine's sharp inhale at Ethan's remark. He squeezed the little one's hand. "You're right, not everyone comes back. That is a sad part of life. But there's nothing that would keep Jasmine or myself from you, if you needed us. That's what being a family means."

Ethan's eyes darted around the room before settling on Sam once again. "I see scary things in my dreams sometimes. It makes me scared."

"I'm sorry," Sam said gently. "That happens to me, too. Do you know what I do that helps?"

"What?"

"I say a prayer, and then I think about all the people who love me and will protect me."

"Do you love me?"

Sam's chest seemed to crack. "I do love you, Ethan. And I promise nothing can hurt you here. I'm a dragon, remember? Is there anything that can get through these stone walls and defeat a dragon?"

Ethan's brows furrowed as if he was in deep thought. "I suppose not."

"You'd be right. And not only do you have me, but you also have Tehl, Gav, Sage, Mira, Jasmine, and the king to look out for you."

"The king," Jade breathed from her bed. "Is he the king of

dragons?"

"He is," Jasmine said, rounding Jade's bed and sitting down next to the child to play with her hair. Jas glanced at Sam before looking back at the wee one. "He's the fiercest man I've ever met, and, yet, there's nothing that compares to the danger a dragoness poses when her kits are threatened. Myself, Auntie Sage, Mira, we're all dragonesses. We'll protect you."

Jade's eyes shone in the lantern light. "Will *I* be a dragoness?"

"One day, sweet girl." Jasmine bent down and kissed Jade's cheek. "Now, sleep."

Ethan squeezed Sam's fingers, and Sam turned his attention back to the boy. "Can we fight in the morning? I saw soldiers training, and I want to be like them when I grow up."

"I'll see what I can do."

Ethan squeezed Sam's hand one more time and then burrowed into his covers. Sam kissed his forehead and stood, staring between the two beds at the precious people who had been dropped into his life.

He'd never felt so lucky.

However, he did frown as he noticed how small the beds were. Where, in the devil, was Jasmine sleeping? He opened his mouth to ask, when she shot him a look, clearly telling him to leave. Sam crept from the room, but left the door open, hoping she got the hint that he'd like to speak with her.

They needed to discuss some things.

Chapter Twenty-Seven

Sam

Quiet footsteps padded into the room, and the door softly clicked shut. Sam didn't turn as Jasmine joined him, standing in front of the fire. She held her hands out to the flames but didn't face him. Regardless, he could still feel her appraising him.

"Do you want to talk about it?" he asked.

"Talk about what?"

"Whatever you're stewing about," Sam said, turning to face Jasmine.

The firelight played over her face, highlighting the spray of freckles across her sloping nose and sea-blue eyes. Eyes that were currently scrutinizing him.

"They're becoming too attached to you."

Not what he meant, but it was a start. "Should they not be? Am I not the man who will have a hand in raising them?"

Her rosebud lips pursed. "I don't expect *you* to parent them. They'll be fine without your meddling."

Meddling. He'd done a lot of meddling in his life, but this was *not* meddling. Every action he took regarding the twins and Jasmine served the greater purpose: building a family.

"You don't believe that they need two parents?"

She shook her head. "I've been doing fine on my own."

He nodded. "You've done an excellent job with the twins. They are remarkable."

A little color touched her cheeks. "Thank you."

"But—"

Jasmine groaned. "Must there always be a 'but?'"

"Yes."

She waved a hand at him. "Very well. I'm sure you'll tell me your opinion, even though I don't want to hear it."

Sam hid his smile. "I appreciate your never-ending suffering."

She snorted but said nothing else.

"I lost my mum well before I was raised," he said seriously. "Then, my father suffered greatly. It was like I lost both parents for years, and, even when my father was present, I longed for my mother. There's a reason the forces at will deem it best to have two parents. It helps the children thrive and gives each parent someone to lean on when things are difficult. Would you take that away from the twins?"

"So, you're saying I'm not enough?" she said flatly.

"No, I am saying that you're not alone. You don't have to be alone. You don't have to prove anything to the world. I am here." He stabbed a finger at the twins' door. "I love those wee ones already. I have not asked much from you, but I'm asking you now not to take them away and to let me in."

"Take them away?" She eyed him. "Who told you?"

"Told me what?"

"Don't play dumb. It's unbecoming, for you and I. How long have you known that we were planning on leaving?"

"For a little while," he admitted.

"And, yet, you've kept silent and not threatened me?"

Sam scoffed. "What did you expect me to do? Did you think I would chain you to my bed and keep you as my love-slave until you submitted to me?" Once the words passed his lips, the image flashed through his mind, and the darker part of him admitted he liked the idea of her as a love-slave, a willing one that desired him as much as he desired her.

Jasmine's eyes crinkled, and her lips twitched before her laughter spilled over. "Did you get that from a dark, romance novel or come up with that all on your own?"

He rolled his eyes but chuckled. "I made that up all by myself, thank you very much."

She wiped the corners of her eyes. "I'm sure your wicked mind has many such scenarios lurking in its depth."

Sam flashed her a devilish smile and inwardly purred as she

blushed. He tried hard to make her like him, but so much stood between them. Her unwillingness to trust, and his secrets, but this was simple, easy. He imagined this was what it would be like if each of them leaned on one another.

Jasmine sobered and cast a searching glance at the fireplace. "You've done much for the twins and myself. I admit, I hate how it happened." She glared at him and he winced. "Having a choice is very important to me. I understand why you did what you did, but it must never happen again."

"I promise." And he meant it.

"I miss the country," she blurted.

Sam blinked. "I suspect living in the castle has been somewhat jarring."

"It feels like a cage," she said softly. She peeked up at him from under her lashes. "I wish to return to the country." Sam held his breath. "But you've given me much to think on. I promise not to steal away in the night."

"Thank you," he said wryly.

She took in his expression and laughed. "If our positions were somewhat reversed, I'm sure you're not the one who'd be left. If I was to stake gold on it, I'd say you're the one to steal away in the night."

He forced himself not to grimace at her observation. He was aware of the rumors that circled the court around his behavior concerning the fairer sex. He'd encouraged it before, as it just obscured his true motives and actions, but having a wife… Well, it made the gap between them wider, filled with all of his lies, spoken and unspoken.

"She called me Mama."

Sam blinked at the change of subject. Obviously, she didn't want to discuss that, either. "How do you feel about that?"

"Confused," Jasmine said. "And hurt." She placed a hand over her heart. "My brother and sister-in-law were amazing parents. I remember them. I remember how they cared for the twins, how the twins were the light of their lives. But the twins barely remember them. Ethan has a vague idea of my brother, and Jade? She's lost all touch with them." Jasmine sucked in a breath. "The only person who truly remembers is me," she whispered, her voice cracking.

"Don't feel guilty for that."

Jasmine met his gaze. "How can I not? I survived, and they did not. I've taken their place."

Sam leveled a stern look at her. "I'm sure your family would be eternally thankful that you're living, so that you can care for the twins. Who better to raise them in their absence?" He reached out and touched her slim shoulder. "The twins may not remember your brother and his wife, but you do. You can teach Ethan and Jade about their wonderful parents who doted on them, and entrusted you to care for them."

Jas bit her bottom lip when it wobbled. "Even now, I fear I'm forgetting things about them."

An idea struck Sam, and he moved around the bed to dig through the top drawer of his dresser until he found what he was searching for. His fingers wrapped around a leather notebook, and he pulled it from the drawer and strode back to Jasmine. He held the notebook out to her. “Here. Use this to write down what you remember. Then they will never be forgotten.”

Jasmine reached out and took the notebook from him. Her hand shook as she brushed her fingers across the embossed cover. She glanced up at him, eyes glossy. “Thank you,” she choked out. “This is such a thoughtful gift.” But she held the notebook out to him. “But my writing and reading is poor.”

Tenderness flooded Sam. He pressed the notebook back into her hands. “I’ll help you. My handwriting is terrible, but we can work on this together.”

Jas placed her hand over his and squeezed. “Thank you.”

Warmth filled Sam at her sincerity.

She gasped and dropped the notebook, her face creasing in pain.

“What is it?” Sam barked.

She yanked him forward and placed his hand over her belly, her fingers splayed over his.

Sam’s jaw dropped as something kicked his hand. His gaze flew to Jasmine’s face, which was still creased in a grimace.

“She’s a strong one,” she breathed.

“She?” Sam echoed, his gaze dropping back to Jasmine’s moving belly.

“It has to be a girl,” Jas gritted. “Only a girl could be this vicious.”

Sam beamed as the little one continued to move and roll beneath his hands. “It’s a miracle,” he breathed.

Until this moment, the babe hadn’t felt real to him. He’d seen the changes to Jasmine's body, but feeling the child move? Well, it changed everything. Delight and joy filled him, along with a strong dose of protectiveness and possession.

That was *his* babe.

He peeked up at his wife who watched the little one move with wonder.

And she was *his* wife.

One day, she'd realize it, too.

All too soon, the babe settled down and Jasmine shifted on her feet, as if embarrassed. Sam reluctantly removed his hands and stepped away.

"It's amazing, isn't it?" she asked before yawning behind her right hand.

"There aren't words."

She smiled tiredly at him, which reminded him of something else he needed to speak with her about.

"Where have you been sleeping?"

"With the twins."

In the tiny beds. The beds designed for short, wee persons, not grown, pregnant women.

"I don't sleep much," he started.

Jasmine rolled her eyes. "I am aware."

He bit back his retort and gestured to the huge bed. "You're welcome to sleep in my bed."

"Your bed?"

"Yes, alone."

Her brows rose, and she eyed the bed.

"I guarantee you'll sleep better," he promised.

"And where will you sleep?"

"Somewhere else." Outside their door.

She glided to the side of the bed and ran her hand along the silky blanket before glancing over her shoulder at him. "The bed is enormous, and if I wasn't desperate to get away from the twins' kicks, I'd say no, but my back is killing me." She swung around to face him and crossed her arms. "I won't steal your bed. Our attractions both lie elsewhere, so we needn't worry about the other making advances. Do you agree?"

What devil had her attention? Sam fought to keep the scowl from his face. He'd had her followed since the night he found her by the docks. True to her word, she'd been careful. But it bothered him terribly to think she was seeking out another man.

"True enough," he admitted.

She didn't need to know how much her form appealed to him. The first time she'd scowled at him, all those months ago, it had been instant attraction for him, but her growing a child? He must have become some sort of deviant. He'd never found a pregnant woman attractive before, but, with Jasmine, he could scarcely keep his eyes off her.

"So, you're welcome to sleep in this bed with me as long as you stay on your side and don't kick me."

Sam nodded, keeping his glee at bay. "Agreed. But you need to promise not to steal my pillows. I tend to be territorial of them."

Sam was sure she didn't know it, but this was just the opening he needed. Close quarters usually bred intimacy, not always sex, but closeness, and that was what he wanted.

She rushed from the bed and flung her arms around him, hugging him tightly. Sam didn't hesitate in hugging her back and even dared to lie his cheek on the top of her head. Tonight had given him more gifts than he knew what to do with.

"Thank you," she whispered, her words heating his exposed skin at his collar. She inhaled and then pulled away, leaving Sam's arms feeling empty.

Her expression slowly cooled, and she bent to pick up the leather notebook, then trailed back to the bed and tugged back the covers, placing the notebook on the side table. "You might need a shower."

He barked out a laugh. This woman. She would drive him crazy with her mood changes. He strolled to the bathing room, deciding not to push his luck. "Your wish is my command."

It was a good thing she had no clue how true those words were.

Chapter Twenty-Eight

Jasmine

She watched him saunter into the bathing room and pause in the doorway. Sam glanced over his shoulder and wiggled his eyebrows.

"You could join me?" he trailed off.

Jasmine narrowed her eyes and placed her hands on her hips. "Not on your life."

He laughed. "You don't know what you're missing." Sam winked at her and closed the door behind him.

She stood stiffly until she could hear the water running in the bathing room. Her shoulders slumped, and she practically collapsed against the bed. Jas ran a hand over her face. What in the blazes had she been thinking when she'd invited him to sleep in the same bed?

The notebook. That was why.

She glanced at the book on the side table, picked it up, and couldn't help but bring it to her nose and inhale deeply. There was nothing she loved more than the smell of leather. The damned man had found her weakness.

Carefully, she placed the notebook back on the nightstand, and stared idly at the fire burning low in the hearth. Her gaze unconsciously wandered back to the bathroom door as her ears picked up the sounds of splashing. What the hell was he doing? And why was she bothered?

"Get it together, Jas," she chastised herself.

He might be her friend, possibly her partner, but he wasn't her lover, and most definitely wasn't her husband in the true sense of the word. She couldn't let herself get carried away with romantic notions. His familiar touches and flirtatious behavior meant nothing. She knew what he was when she married him.

A rake. Scoundrel. Sin reincarnated.

Jasmine forced herself to look away from the door and squeezed her eyes shut. When he'd hugged her, she'd detected another woman's scent on him. He made her no promises. She didn't expect him to be faithful, and, if she let herself get caught up in him, it would only end with her having a broken heart and a strain on their friendship—if that was what she could call it.

Forcing herself to stand, she rearranged the pillows to form a border down the middle of the bed and tiptoed to the closet.

Quickly, she stripped off her dress and tugged a nightgown over her head. The fabric fell to her toes. She scowled at the material.

Stars above, she hated sleeping in clothes, especially something so long. Every time she turned in her sleep, the garment would tangle around her legs. She sent a longing glance at one of Sam's lightweight linen shirts. What she wouldn't give to sleep in one of those.

Jasmine shook her head and hung up her day-dress. Her maid always got annoyed with her when she cleaned up after herself, but she couldn't help it. It bothered her to have someone clean up after her.

Jas poked her head out of the closet and tiptoed back to bed, sliding into the cool sheets. There was no better feeling than cool sheets. She snuggled into them, and peered drowsily at the fireplace. If she were smart, she'd stay awake until Sam came to bed, so she could keep an eye on him. A yawn snuck up on her, and she tugged the covers higher, her eyelids drooping.

Who was she kidding? She was pregnant with another man's child and getting fatter each day. She wasn't in any danger from the sultry prince. If anything, he should be worried about her mauling him in his sleep.

A smiled tugged up the corners of her mouth. He didn't have to worry about his pillows. Thank the stars he hadn't asked about snoring.

***

The feeling of being watched was what woke her. Jasmine blinked, disoriented. Where was she? She lifted her head to peek over the pillow and lay back down immediately.

Sam's bed.

A hand brushed her belly, and her eyes widened as she realized Sam's arm had pushed beneath the pillow-wall during the night, and she had curled herself around his arm.

One finger at a time, she released her death grip on his arm and slowly scooted backward, so he wasn't touching any part of her.

Two stifled giggles caught her attention.

Jasmine sat up and found the culprits crouching at the bottom of the bed like the early-rising monsters they were. She held a finger to her mouth, signaling the twins to be quiet, but the harder they tried, the louder they became, and pointing to the door to their room did nothing.

"Dear, I think we have an infestation of sniggering mice," Sam rumbled, startling her.

She glanced over at him and wished she had not.

His blond curls were mussed in a soft, sexy way, and he had a shadow of golden scruff growing along his jaw and cheeks. But that wasn't the worst of it. It was the way his blue eyes squinted as he beamed at her, like she was the reason he was so joyful to be on this earth.

Bastard. It wasn't right to look that perfect when one woke up.

She swiped at her face, hoping she didn't have dried drool around her mouth.

"Who could have snuck into our rooms?" Sam growled.

"We did!" Jade exclaimed as she clambered onto the tall bed, followed by Ethan.

The twins bounded across the blankets and pillows and settled themselves in between Sam and Jasmine.

"I'm hungry," Ethan proclaimed.

Jasmine blushed as her belly released a growl that could rival Nali's.

Sam grinned at Jade, and she snuggled closer to him, resting her head against his arm. "I'm hungry, too," she said.

"Well, that's settled. Let's get some breakfast!" Sam hoisted Jade onto his shoulders and plucked Ethan from the bed, setting him on the floor with care before taking the boy's hand.

Jasmine blinked as he started for the door. "They're in their nightclothes."

The impertinent man turned toward her with an impish grin. "And that is relevant, why?"

"It's not decent."

"There are many things in my life that are not decent, and this is the least of them. They're children. Now, get out of that bed before I decide to carry you, too."

Jasmine crossed her arms over her chest. "I need to change."

Sam rolled his eyes. "Please. I've seen what you wear to bed. It's more modest than most women's everyday gowns. Now, stop fighting me, and let's feed these children before they expire this very moment."

She tossed the covers away and slipped from the bed, her toes curling as they touched cold stone. He wasn't wrong, but she'd been given so many lessons on proper behavior since she'd become a prince's wife that she hardly dared doing anything she used to. She bustled into the closet, grabbing the first robe she spotted. She smiled as she pulled on the blue, silk dressing-gown with silver snowflakes embroidered along its hem and sleeves.

"We're positively wasting away," Sam moaned, and the twins giggled.

"I'm coming, you arse," she muttered as she secured the tie around her waist.

"I heard that."

Her lips twitched. She meant him to.

She exited the closet and moved toward the gaggle of starving individuals to open the door. "Let's be gone then. I can't have you starving to death."

The men stationed outside their room smiled and greeted them as the twins babbled and waved like they did each day.

"So, what would you like for breakfast?" Sam asked.

"Everything!" Jade exclaimed.

"Everything?"

"Yes. That's what Mama said yesterday. The baby was sooooooo hungry."

Jasmine shook her head at her niece. No one could keep a secret.

Sam cast a look her way, full of mirth. "Well, we'll see what we can do."

***

He was true to his word.

She didn't know how he managed it, but a feast arrived when they entered a cozy dining room Jasmine had never seen before. It was only after she'd gaped at the food, saliva pooling in her mouth, that she noticed there was one more occupant in the room. Her spine straightened as she realized he was looking at her over a sheaf of paper.

The king.

She pivoted and executed a curtsy. "My apologies, my lord."

He set his papers down and smiled, his arresting blue eyes, so similar to both of his sons, sparkling. "No need, my dear."

So that's where his son learned the endearment.

Her eyes widened as Ethan plopped himself in the chair next to the king and reached for the orange juice.

"Ethan, no—" she said, but it was too late.

The little one tipped the juice over, and it rushed over the king's papers and down onto his lap. Panic spurred her forward, and she snatched up napkins and began cleaning the table.

"I'm so sorry, my lord. Please forgive my son, he didn't mean any harm, he's only four..." She trailed off as a large hand settled over her trembling one.

She peered up at the king as he gently pulled the napkins from her fingers.

"There's nothing to forgive, my daughter. I raised wee ones myself. And, from experience, I know they make great messes that seem impossible for their size."

He lifted his papers from the table and shook them off before wiping himself down. He glanced at Ethan, who'd curled in his chair with wide eyes. The king held his hand out to Ethan. "Come here, little one."

Jasmine stepped back when Sam cupped her shoulder with his hand and squeezed gently.

Ethan slipped down from his chair and stood beside the hulking king.

"Are you still thirsty?" the king asked.

"Yes, I am."

"Do you know who I am?"

Ethan nodded. "My lord."

The king smiled, flashing straight white teeth. "To many, yes, but to you? I am just Grandad."

Tears flooded her eyes. *Stupid hormones.*

"Grandad," Ethan parroted.

The king held his arms out, and Ethan moved into them without hesitation. Jasmine could only stare as he poured what was left of the juice into a glass for the boy and plopped some food onto a plate for him, too. Once Ethan was settled, the king cocked his head and wiggled his eyebrows at Jade who watched him shyly.

"Would you like something, too, sweet girl?"

Jade nodded and scampered over to him. He made another plate, and once both children were eating, he turned his attention to Jasmine. Her breath seized at the massive smile stretched across his face and the emotion gleaming in his eyes.

"Thank you," he said roughly. "Ivy and I always dreamed of grandchildren. I didn't think I'd live to see the day, and what a wonderful unexpected blessing it is." He gestured to the chair to his left. "Please sit and enjoy a meal with me."

Sam's hand moved to her lower back and nudged her forward. She bit the inside of her cheek at the intimate gesture that didn't seem to faze the prince.

On trembling legs, she shuffled to the chair and sat just like her instructors had taught her. Carefully, she chose dainty portions of food and placed them on her plate. Stars above, she was hungry.

How she was going to make it through the meal without making herself look like a glutton, she didn't know.

A deep, male laugh rumbled from the king. She blinked at him.

He gestured to the food. "My Ivy was so sick for the first part of each of her pregnancies, she wouldn't touch a thing. But, near the end, she'd eat everything in sight. We don't stand on ceremony here, my daughter. Eat."

Jasmine smiled and tugged another hotcake onto her plate, as well as a few more slices of bacon. "Thank you, my lord."

"Marq," he said softly. "We are family now." His gaze narrowed on Sam who'd sat to her left. "Although, my son has kept you from me."

She shook her head. "The fault is mine. It's taken some adjustment, and I'm not overly fond of people I don't know. We've kept to ourselves, for the most part. I'm sorry if I've offended you, but it wasn't your son's doing." She snapped her mouth shut and shoveled a bite of buttery hotcake in her mouth so she wouldn't correct the bloody king again.

"And, now that you have met me, will you keep them from me?"

Swallowing slowly, she eyed the man who ruled their kingdom. "I would deny you nothing. You're the king."

"I'm giving you the choice, my dear. I won't force myself into your life."

Jasmine's attention drifted to the twins who were eating with gusto and getting syrup and God-knows-what-else all over the king, and he didn't even bat an eyelash. He seemed to be enjoying himself as much as the children.

"If you desire grandchildren, they are yours," she said softly.

"My own grandparents passed when I was young, and I always wished I had more time with them. The twins have lost much in their life, and I think they deserve all the family and friends who will love them as much as I do."

"I am glad for it," Marq replied.

She watched the king as he returned her regard. In that moment, she felt like she'd found a kindred spirit. He'd suffered pain, and, yet, he'd found joy in life. She hoped she could do the same. Jasmine turned back to her food and continued eating, savoring every delicious bite. Time passed, and the king chatted with the wee ones until they finished their food and the twins began to get antsy.

Jasmine eyed the food on her plate, sad to leave it, but if she didn't let the twins burn off some of their wiggles, it would become a warzone. Sam placed his hand over hers and her heart jumped as she began to push her chair back, and then he stood.

"I promised to take them to the training grounds. Finish your meal, and then follow us at your leisure." He looked at the twins. "Let's go!"

Ethan hugged the king, and Jade pressed a sticky kiss to his white-whiskered cheek, and then they both bounded from the room before Jasmine could even protest. She gaped at the door.

"He moves all too quickly," she muttered.

"He's been that way since he was a babe."

She startled and glanced at the king in surprise. How had she forgotten he was still there? "I don't doubt it. I aspire to have his stamina. I find myself worn out by the end of day."Her stomach soured, and she stared blurrily at the food before her. Of course, he knew. Everyone could see she was pregnant, but she didn't doubt that the king knew the real details of her shame, especially since she was so far along.

"Don't hang your head, daughter. Creating life is a wonderous miracle and a show of immense sacrifice."

She slowly looked up at the king. "You are aware of the circumstances of this child?"

He met her gaze and nodded. "I am."

Shame caused her belly to roll. "And what do you say?"

"I'm excited to meet my next grandchild, and I thank you for bringing such a gift into my life."

She couldn't contain it. Ugly sobs exploded from her chest, and she covered her mouth to muffle the terrible sounds escaping her. Jasmine pushed to her feet, determined to find the door, when giant arms encircled her, pressing her face into a wide, muscular chest.

"Let it out, my dear. It's okay," the king soothed. "Let it all out."

It should've felt odd to have a man she didn't know holding her—let alone her sovereign—but it didn't. She experienced a sense of acceptance and belonging she hadn't felt in ages. She sobbed and sobbed, but Marq never released her, just crooned softly, rocking her back and forth.

"How could they do this?" she cried. How could the men who'd protected her, do this?

"I don't understand it. It wasn't right, no matter their reason. And it wasn't your fault."

"I hate not remembering. Mira says it's a blessing, but the blankness terrifies me. What else did they do when they drugged me? I'm sure my imagination is worse than anything they could've done."

The king didn't answer but held her as she lost the shame, tears, and pain that had gathered in her heart for months.

Her tears slowed, her face hot and swollen. She pulled back and winced at the mess that was the king's shirt. It was stained with orange juice, syrup, and now, her tears. "I'm sorry about your shirt." She hiccupped. "I'll replace it."

"The shirt means nothing." The king tipped her chin up and scanned her face. "Did you get it out?"

Jasmine heaved out a breath and nodded. "For now, at least." Embarrassment started to creep up on her, but she batted it away. She and the king were kindred spirits. "If *you* ever need a shoulder to cry on..."

He hugged her and then moved back to his chair and leftover breakfast. "You will be the first person I seek out." He smiled at her. "Just be prepared, my crying is ugly—nothing like yours."

She snorted. "That is a damn lie, my lord."

"Marq, if you please."

Jasmine resumed her seat. "Marq."

His smile grew. "Now, tell me about my grandchildren, please."

Chapter Twenty-Nine

Jasmine

It was too easy, slipping into her new life with Sam. Only ten days had passed, and the children were completely enamored with him.

The man was all too charming, and she couldn't help but love his father. The king was nothing like she'd expected and was everything she'd been missing from her life. Plus, the twins absolutely adored him. And for the past week, he'd visited the children every day, and Jasmine couldn't help but love someone who loved her twins.

She wound around the small tavern just outside the castle gate and entered into the palace courtyard, strolling toward the training yard, her homespun dress rustling with each step and her cane whistling as she twirled it through her fingers. Soldiers circled the fenced-in training area, shouting at the men who were fighting in the middle. She watched in interest as the smaller man twisted and rolled, out-maneuvering the large one with sinuous movements. Familiar sounds teased the air: the clashing of swords and canes, curses, and the ever-present commands of battle instructors advising their men to disengage, straighten the arms, and engage in cleaner footwork.

Jasmine's fingers curled around the top of the fence, and she rested her chin against the smooth wood to observe. Stars above, she missed bouts with her father. He'd never turned down a chance to spar and play with her. Her hand rubbed the exposed skin above her heart like she could get rid of the grief that struck her at the oddest moments.

The dark-haired soldier to her right straightened as he noticed her and cleared his throat. She ignored him—and hid a smile as the small man slipped beneath the larger man's guard and swept his opponent's feet out from underneath him. The smaller soldier pounced on the prone form of the other and wrenched his opponent's arm behind his back, holding him pinned to the ground.

Jasmine smiled, set her cane down, and began a slow clap. The small man's head snapped up, and he grinned back at her, his crooked, white teeth bright against his amber skin.

Kylir.

She'd been wandering around the palace nearly a month prior, completely lost, when she'd spotted him. Normally, she would've kept moving on, but the way he moved while training had caused her to halt in her tracks. It was like watching water flow over stones. The fighting style was so foreign and unique, and, yet, so familiar. She used to sit on the floor of her bedroom and, through the crack of her door late at night, with only a small candle for light, she'd watch her father practice. Every move was so precise, so smooth. It seemed magical.

That day, she'd found herself entering the small training room and settling into a place next to Kylir. If he'd noticed her, he hadn't shown it. She'd stretched and then begun to follow his steps. Her body had burned and stretched, and sweat had drenched her immediately. Her breath had been billowing from her lungs when he finished. Kylir had turned to her and smiled, his chocolate eyes so very warm. He'd said two words that day, and they'd changed everything: "Hello, sister."

From then on, she'd snuck away every day to stretch and train in companionable silence with Kylir. After they finished, sometimes they'd talk. She'd learned that he was Zachael's ward, and that he had a Nagalian ancestor somewhere in his bloodline. He was kind, quiet, and seemed to have more wisdom than most who were triple his age. She was so grateful she'd met him. It was luck that he was still training at the palace. Soon he'd be summoned to the war front. Her heart sank at the thought, but she shoved it down and focused back on the bout.

Jasmine whooped when the man beneath Kylir slapped his

hand against the ground. Her spry friend sprung from the soldier's back and held his hand out. The larger man grinned and slapped his massive paw against Kylir's.

"I almost had you," the soldier said, his tone teasing and breathless.

Kylir nodded. "If you continue with those exercises, I have no doubt that you will next time." He patted the soldier on the shoulder and called, "Next."

Jasmine blinked but kept silent as another tall man entered the ring, his blond curls shining in the light like spun gold.

Sam.

Jasmine pressed a little closer to the fence as he pulled his sweaty, linen shirt over his head and tossed it over the fence, into the dirt. He took off his boots and stripped off his socks, so he was wearing nothing but his tan leather pants. Despite her husband's reputation of wickedness, she'd never seen any part of him bare. For a moment, she averted her eyes and blankly stared at a round pebble near her left toe.

No wonder women flocked to him.

His face wasn't the only thing that was attractive.

She couldn't unsee what he'd flashed to the world. Jasmine swallowed hard and shook her head at herself.

"Get it together," she whispered, startling the soldier to her right. She'd seen half-dressed men before. Sam was nothing new.

Lies. There wasn't *anyone* like her husband.

Steeling herself, she lifted her chin and pasted a bored expression on her face. Sam's back still faced her as he accepted a cane from a nearby soldier on his left. Kylir held his staff out, and both men tapped their canes against each other's.

Her eyes widened as Kylir attacked immediately in a sustained sequence of combination blows. She winced as their canes met in a series of harsh cracks. Her hands flexed on the fence as she imagined what the impact must have felt like. She could almost feel the vibrations moving through her arms.

Sam retreated, the muscles in his back straining as he met another of Kylir's blows. His legs flexed as he leaned into the smaller man and pressed forward, his feet digging into the soil of the training ring. He disengaged and spun, darting under Kylir's staff as it swung just above his head. Kylir adjusted his attack and struck again in flawless, easy movements.

To her surprise, Sam was just as precise as his opponent. However, his style of fighting was unlike anything she'd ever seen. He never allowed the match to settle into a familiar rhythm. He attacked unexpectedly and retreated before Kylir could strike. There was something catlike about his movements, a vicious grace that raised every hair on Jasmine's body.

Fascinated, she lifted a foot onto the bottom rung of the fence and stood to get a better look at the match.

The night Sam had found her near the docks came to her mind. She hadn't seen him attack those men. Hell, she hadn't even heard him attack. But, in a matter of seconds, those men had been taken out. The prince hid much from the world.

Or, is it, you don't really want to know him?

She ignored that thought and tried to memorize one of his more complex movements.

"My dear, it makes me very uncomfortable to have you leaning into the training ring," Sam grunted as he blocked another one of Kylir's strikes.

Jasmine narrowed her eyes on his back, and, for some reason, her heartbeats seemed to collide as his deep voice curled around her in a delicious way. What in the world was wrong with her? She lifted a hand to her forehead. She wasn't sick. Her lips pursed as she glared at his back. And how did he know she was leaning into the ring?

"It would soothe my frayed nerves if you would step back."

She didn't move.

"I've warned you. If you don't heed my warnings, you may need to call for the smelling salts."

The soldiers around her chuckled, and Jasmine smirked. "Certainly, not for me?"

"Of course not," Sam huffed. "I have a delicate constitution."

She snorted as the men guffawed, supremely amused with his antics.

Sam dropped low and attacked beneath Kylir's staff, tapping her friend on the ribs.

"Stop," Kylir said, his voice soft and melodic as usual, his accent lilting.

The two men disengaged.

Chocolate eyes moved from Sam and met her own. "Would you like to try next?"

Jasmine grinned and nodded, but she froze in place as Sam

whirled and glared at her. It felt like he was trying to set her on fire.

"Train?" he asked, his voice deceptively soft.

Forcing herself to move, she loosened the ties at the front of her dress and tugged the garment over her head, exposing the pants and loose linen shirt she wore beneath. Some of the men clapped and whistled, but one glare caused the whoops to turn into coughs.

She rolled her eyes. *Men.*

Jas popped her neck and smiled brightly at Sam. "Good evening, my lord," she said cordially. "I train every day with Kylir. Now, if you'd be so kind as to exit the sparring ring…" she trailed off as she noticed where Sam's attention was pinned—on her shirt.

Well, technically it was his shirt, but she'd stolen it and claimed it as hers. It hid her bump well, and it kept her cool.

She cleared her throat, pulling his attention to her face. "If you'd please move."

Sam eyed her and leaned on his staff, the picture of laziness. "I had reservations about Kylir training you, so I figured I would test out his skills to judge his abilities."

"Are you serious?" The words popped out of her mouth, and indignation burned inside her chest for her friend. "Kylir is one of the best weapon-trainers I've ever had the pleasure of sparring with. And how did you know I was training with him?"

"You've never asked *me* to spar with you," Sam said with a chuckle, not answering her question.

She ignored his comment and gave Kylir a lopsided smile. "I'm sorry."

Her friend smiled back at her, and a playful gleam entered his gaze as he looked between Sam and herself. "Thank you for your kind words, but I have to tell you, your husband is a rake, and I cannot condone your association with him. He'll ruin every method you have ever learned."

"I hope so," Sam snorted. "Some ruffian from the street won't hold back for her, as she's well aware." He stared her down as if challenging her to remember the night by the docks that could have ended very differently than it had.

Jasmine pressed her lips together, and leaned against the post behind her, raising her brows. "Are you going to leave so I can have my turn? Or will I have to throw you out?"

Sam arched a haughtier brow at her and faced Kylir. "We weren't finished."

Kylir settled into place just as Sam uttered, "Go."

Her husband attacked, and another duel commenced so lightning fast the two men blazed and burned. A large hand helped her through the fence, and she glanced up, meeting identical eyes to her husband's.

She jabbed a finger at Sam and rolled her eyes, conveying to the king how much his son annoyed her. Marq smiled, his white mustache hitching up at one corner.

"Boys," he muttered.

It was just one word, but Jasmine felt like it summed up everything. She turned her attention back to the ring as Sam twisted out of Kylir's hold and deliberately shoved a shoulder against the other man to knock him off balance. After making a strike, Sam dropped to the ground in a roll, then sprang to his feet, and jabbed her friend a second time.

Her hands curled into fists. He'd cheated. "This isn't a tavern brawl!"

Jasmine yanked her incensed gaze from her poor sport of a husband and paused as Kylir beamed, his smile so big it seemed to take up his entire face. What the devil? What was he so bloody happy about?

Turning to face her, Sam lowered his staff. "Isn't trying to win the objective of a bout?" Sam said calmly.

"The goal is to train. There are some rules," she said.

"And who taught you that?"

"It's a well-known fact."

"Answer me this: have you ever seen a spontaneous fencing match break out in the slum, or a tavern, or on the battlefield?" Sam asked with blistering sarcasm. "The rules are just a courtesy for those we train with." He pointed his finger toward the castle wall. "You won't be fighting gentlemen outside this training yard. They won't wait for you to catch your breath, and they won't play by the rules. They're ruthless, and the best defense anyone has is to fight with everything they have."

Embarrassment colored her cheeks at his public chastising. Then anger rose swiftly behind it.

Sam cleared away the blond locks of hair that hung in front of his eyes with a quick shake of his head, the blond layers seeming to come alive before settling into place. He skewered her with a hard stare.

"You have no idea what to do when it comes to the scum that would harm you. You may have pretty little cane twirls, but they mean nothing when your life is on the line. Your ladies' parlor exercises are picturesque, but they won't help you fight for your life. One day, you might be doing just that, armed only with the skills and values you hold dear. If you cannot let go of your preconceived notions, you'll end up on the street with your throat slit."

Jasmine shivered at his gruesome words. The man didn't pull any punches.

Sam shot Kylir a dirty, angry look. "And you! You've been training her? In her condition?"

A deep-seated rage flamed in her belly. She was pregnant, not stupid, and no one—*no one*—attacked her friends.

Marq placed a hand on her arm, and she glanced up at him, not realizing she'd started to climb the fence.

"How dare he!" she whispered harshly to the king. "I am not an invalid."

The king smiled softly. "My son is worried about you. And he's not handling it well."

Jasmine patted his hand and pulled away. "I'm not going to let him carry on. I'm going to prove him wrong."

Worry lines creased Marq's forehead. "Be careful."

"I will."

She clambered over the fence and dropped into a crouch on the other side, dust puffing up into the air. Slowly, she straightened and stormed toward her husband who was threatening Kylir with passive-aggressive comments.

"Why have you been training her?" Sam barked.

Kylir blinked slowly but didn't react to the prince's hostile tone. "My lord, she has been trained well. I didn't realize that I needed your approval to train a willing soldier, or I would have come to you."

"She's not a soldier," Sam said, his tone cutting.

"Could have fooled me," Kylir said mildly. "She has advanced training that has nothing to do with my skill. She's been sparring lightly, which is good for a woman in her condition, from what I'm told. I visited Jacob."

Jasmine winced and scanned the ring, noting all the soldiers leaning closer to watch the maudlin scene unfolding. Stars above, this would be all over the court by morning. So much for keeping her pregnancy a secret. Her stomach rolled. The rumors were going to be worse than the actual truth.

The two men stared each other down, apparently having a silent conversation.

"I don't appreciate both of you speaking like I don't exist," Jasmine hissed.

Sam pivoted to watch her with blue eyes practically spitting flames.

"Did you forget our prior conversation?"

His lips thinned but he didn't answer.

"I informed you that my father was a retired soldier. He taught me how to wield the staff, cane, and bow. I'm not the most skilled, but my skills are not something to be tossed aside."

Sam's blue eyes narrowed. "I don't like it." His gaze dropped to her belly and then back to her face. "You need to be careful."

She huffed. "Believe me when I say I am. If you'd spoken to the healers, you would know they encourage physical exercise and stretching—which is what I have been doing." A nasty smile touched her mouth. "But I'm more than ready and able to show you what I've been doing with Kylir for the last month."

Enjoy that innuendo.

Her husband stilled. He slid his attention to Kylir and then back to Jasmine.

"Just what has he been teaching you?" he asked, his voice soft and savage.

One look at him told her he wouldn't hear anything she had to say. One could not reason with an unreasonable person, and until he calmed down, she wouldn't be speaking with him. Disappointment tugged at her, and she slowly roved her eyes up and down his form, making sure he saw that she found him lacking.

She spun on her heel and climbed over the fence, collecting her discarded dress and her cane. Jasmine pressed a kiss on Marq's cheek and walked away. She kept her chin up and shoulders back, trying to project a regal demeanor. She hated walking away from a fight, but, sometimes, walking away was the best thing. And, right now, she wanted to rip Sam's head from his shoulders and she was pretty sure that was against the law.

Insufferable lout.

"Jasmine!" Sam called, his tone sharp with a touch of darkness.

A shiver skated down her spine, but she ignored him and didn't look back.

Never had she been so mortified in her whole life! If he wanted to speak with her, he damn well better be on his knees, apologizing and bringing a honey cake with him.

Her stomach growled.

Honey cake first, then she'd deal with her irritating husband.

CHAPTER THIRTY

Dor

Every instinct Dor had honed over the course of her entire life begged her to turn around and leave the dark, haunting place that seemed like it would gobble her up. What disturbed her the most wasn't the complete darkness lurking just past the dimly lit hallway. It was the way the wide, heavy stone door swung silently open as if it was holding its breath for what horrors were to come.

Ada lifted the lantern higher, the light stretching just a bit farther into what looked like a small room and highlighting the paleness of her friend's face. Dor wasn't the only one who was terrified. Her eyes moved to the warrior who once again watched her like she was his prey. There was something in his gaze she didn't like, no matter what her mum said. She needed to be careful of him. Dor knew when she'd discovered a predator.

She pulled her gaze from Darius and stared at the white stone floor. Then, she started abruptly, her attention on the floor by the entrance. Her eyes narrowed. She'd never seen a creation that was so smooth, so flawless, *perfect.* This time, she couldn't hide the shiver that raced down her spine. This wasn't the Pit any longer. They were entering the domain of the most sinister enemy she'd ever come across. The warlord. Only he'd have something so atrocious and unnatural gracing the rooms of his abode.

"Are you quite done gawking?" Darius said, sarcasm coloring his tone.

Dor pursed her lips to keep a nasty comment from bursting free and turned her attention to her mum, who shivered on the floor. "By all means, let's go."

The warrior glared at her and then addressed Ada by jerking his chin toward the wall. "Leave the lantern on the hook."

Ada glanced at Dor and reluctantly followed his command.

Darius bent at the knees, gently pulled Dor's mother into his arms, and walked past the threshold. Dor didn't move as she watched him step onto the alien, white-stone floor, his boots making not one mark on the ground. Frowning, she peeked at her dirty blood-spattered feet. They'd leave a mark for sure.

Dor, stop thinking about things that don't matter.

"Enter at your leisure," Darius snapped at her.

She clenched her jaw and bared her teeth at his back, hating how scared she was to follow him. Digging deep, she swallowed down her fear and followed the man into the darkened room. Her toes curled as they met the cold stone floor beneath her feet. It was so smooth, it almost felt wet. *Focus, Dor.*

Ada stepped closer and slipped her hand into Dor's. "We have each other."

Dor squeezed her friend's fingers, grateful to have her company. They'd known each other since they were young and had always had each other's backs, no matter what. It was fitting they were entering this together. Dor squinted as they moved farther into the dark.

Ada gasped, and Dor followed her line of sight, her own gasp falling from her lips as the stone behind them slammed shut. She lunged for the wall, releasing Ada's hand and scrabbling in the dark. The sound seemed to echo around her as she blinked repeatedly.

"Ada?"

"I'm here," her friend's soft voice trembled from Dor's left.

Swinging her arms toward the sound, she moved in Ada's direction. "Don't move," she barked. "I'm coming to you." Her left hand smacked into flesh, and she jerked back, fear thundering through her veins. That wasn't Ada.

She blindly scrambled away from the flesh she'd touched, her feet slipping on the floor, so disoriented. She yelped when a small hand grabbed her dress.

"Dor?"

Just Ada.

She spun toward Ada's voice and hugged her friend close, as her heart did its best to beat out of her chest. Her friend's slight frame trembled against her own as they clung to each other. Despite the utter darkness, Dor kept her head up, eyes open, and tried to see through the darkness. There were others with them, but how many? Were they in another torture chamber? Did the flesh she'd touched belong to someone alive or dead? And where in the hell was the warrior?

"Darius, so help me, you better light the lantern right this instant or I will reign Hell upon you." She just managed to keep the tremble from her voice in the silence. "Answer me."

Silence.

"Did he leave us?" Ada whispered, her voice seeming hollow in the room.

"He couldn't have," Dor reassured her. He couldn't have left without them. Or could he? What did he do with her mum?

The complete darkness surrounding them seemed to surge forward and slither around them. Her breaths became shallow, and her panic rose. They were trapped. Who knew how large the space was? Her breaths turned to pants as the suppressive panic began to scream at her. She was trapped. The nothingness around them was suffocating.

"Are you all right?"

Dor shook her head, then stopped, knowing the gesture was wasted in the dark. Her fingers dug into Ada's arms as she pulled away slightly and bowed her head. She couldn't let her panic get the best of her. She needed to use the breathing techniques her mum had taught her. She pulled in a slow deep breath and held it while counting to five, then repeated it again and again until she was breathing normally, and her pulse had slowed from a thundering of a hundred horses to a short, fast staccato. Not great, but better than passing out.

The deafening silence around them crept in once again, and she began to focus on what was most important. They needed to figure out where they were and where her mum was.

"Mum?" she called, hoping she would answer her.

Nothing, not even a whisper of sound. Surely if Darius was still in the room, she'd hear her mum breathing? If it hadn't been for Ada holding her, Dor would've thought she was the only one in the entire room.

Either the warrior was gone, or he was playing with them. Neither was a great option, but the latter made anger burn in her veins like fire.

"Mum, please answer me."

Nothing.

Dor inhaled deeply before speaking. "Darius, speak up now or face my wrath when I find you," she said a little bit louder, trying to hide her fear. *Still* nothing. "We need to move."

"Move? We can't see," Ada said, her voice trembling slightly.

"We can't stand here forever. Close your eyes and hold your hand out in front of you. It might not be so off-putting."

Dor couldn't tell if her friend would follow her advice, but Ada squeezed her hand once and Dor straightened and lifted her chin. From the echoing of their voices, the room was large. She wouldn't be hitting her head on the ceiling any time soon. She held her left hand out and shuffled forward, through the dark. Each step was terrifying, but at least they were moving. She blew out a breath when her hand touched stone. Her fingers explored its texture, and she determined it was a wall.

"Ada, let's move to our—" She paused, cutting off her words as a foot scuffed against stone. The hairs on her arms rose.

They weren't alone.

That was even worse to imagine. What sort of creature could stay that still for so long?

Dor slowly pivoted to face in the direction of a foot against stone and closed her left hand around her dagger at her waist. She didn't want to scare Ada, but she needed to know what was going on. "Ada?"

"I heard it," Ada said softly. "We're not alone, are we?"

"No."

Dor's softly exhaled word seemed to stir the tension in the room, and beads of sweat broke out along the back of her neck, despite the cold. Her feet slid apart as she braced herself for whatever nightmare stalked them. Carefully, she pulled her dagger from its sheath, with a soft hiss of leather against metal, and held it ready at her side. She strained to hear any new sounds, and her eyes frantically searched the dark, but she spotted nothing. In the back of her mind, she knew what it was.

A man-eater. A leren.

And, in all likelihood, she and Ada would end up dead.

"We don't taste that good," Dor crooned. "I promise, we'll make for a very nasty meal."

"Devil, take it," Ada cursed. "You think we crossed into a leren's territory?"

Dor listened harder for any clue as to where the large jungle cat lurked. "I don't think we crossed into anything. I think we were led here to die." Her tone was still lilting.

"An execution?"

Dor nodded and then spoke, knowing Ada couldn't see her. "Yes." She turned so the stone wall was to her back, tugging Ada along. This was so the leren couldn't sneak up on them. "I'm not one for games," she cooed. "I'd rather you just attack than lie in wait for us."

Ada snorted, and a nervous giggle escaped her. "Leave it up to you to bait the leren into killing us in a sing-song voice."

"If death comes for me, I'd rather face it head-on than have it catch me unaware and stab me in the back."

"Words spoken like a true warrior," a female voice said, her tone velvety soft and yet somehow as strong as steel.

Dor jerked. Not a leren. Something much more devious. With the jungle cat, she knew what it wanted. But a Scythian had motives she couldn't pretend to understand or guess.

"Show yourself," she barked, her voice echoing in the space around them.

Stone striking stone pierced the silence, and a small spot of light erupted directly across from them, illuminating the woman's face. Firelight played over the woman's formidable features that were much like her voice: feminine but sharp. Caramel-colored eyes seemed to glow like twin flames as she stared impassively at Dor. A small smile touched her full mouth and drew attention to her high cheekbones and straight nose. Feathers and beads adorned her coal-black hair and plinked together in a soft symphony as the woman tilted her head back, obviously studying Dor as well.

With care, the woman took the small flame in her hand and lit a lantern hanging from the wall behind her. Dor swallowed as she was able to see the woman fully. Her thick, black braid hung over her shoulder, and silky furs draped over her back in a becoming manner. Tight leather pants ran down long legs and into sturdy boots. But what alarmed her the most was the vast array of weapons the woman had strapped to her lithe body. Everything screamed danger with this woman. The woman smirked, and her gaze bored into Dor's like she could see the deepest parts of her soul. One thing was certain, the woman was not to be trifled with.

Most assumedly, this woman was every Scythian's dream of perfection, of purity. And while the woman was beautiful and terrifying to behold, there was something repugnant about her because of what she stood for. A deep-seated fear made Dor want to cower away from the woman and the warriors that melted from the shadows like wraiths and stood in a circle around the room. Perfection like the woman's came at a cost. Only those closest to the warlord could afford such perfection. Even the tilt of the woman's chin spoke of a regal bearing.

This woman wasn't just Scythian – she was something *more.* Dor wanted to cower against the wall, to seek a way of escape, but fear and stubbornness kept her feet rooted to the smooth floor beneath her toes. In that moment, Dor made a choice. She wouldn't be a coward. Chances were she'd end up dead by the end of the encounter, but she'd go out with integrity and honor.

Swallowing, she forced her tongue to work. "Where is my mother?" she asked in a careful tone.

The woman tilted her head to the side and scrutinized Dor. The woman's eyes scanned Dor from head to toe, and she pursed her lips in a way that betokened disapproval or deep thought.

Dor lifted her chin and threw back her shoulders, determined to hold the woman's gaze. She had nothing to be ashamed of. If anyone should be ashamed, it should be the creatures standing proudly before her. The perfection-seeking monsters from above the Pit were the ones that had caused the pain and the suffering she'd experienced her entire life. They were the blight on the world, not her or the laborers in the Pit.

She dared to smile at the woman and almost dropped into a mock bow. She wouldn't let a perfect intimidate her, not in this moment. Dor may be covered in dirt and grime, her hair matted, and her clothes old and worn, but she still had value, despite what she looked like. She would not feel shame for her poverty. In fact, the woman should feel shame just looking upon *her*. To see the wreckage their people had caused.

The woman spoke, breaking through her thoughts. "Your mother's fine."

A snort escaped her. She didn't believe her one bit. "I want to see her."

The woman smiled slightly and nodded.

Searing light exploded around the room, causing Ada to cry out and drop Dor's hand, and Dor squeezed her eyes shut and covered her face with her hands as colors flashed across her vision. Tears leaked from the corners of her eyes as she squinted and tried to get her bearings. Now was not the time to be blind.

"Not nice," she said, blinking repeatedly in an attempt to see the room. She vaguely detected that the woman had moved closer, and Dor lifted her blade higher despite her seared eyes. She held the blade defensively as she tried to get her damned eyes to stop watering.

"There's no need for that."

Dor laughed. "So says the woman who debilitated her prisoners."

"You're not prisoners."

She chose to stay quiet as she was able to finally get a good glimpse of the room. Terror was too small of a word to describe what sank down to her very bones. Immense warriors circled the oval-shaped room, silent sentinels whose attention was completely focused on them.

The woman had moved to the left and up a set of stairs that led to a dais. Dor's pulse kicked up as she noticed her mum's prone form laying near the woman's feet. Her red hair was strewn across her face and draped down the white stairs like dripping blood. Her face was completely blank of all expression, eyes closed as if she was asleep.

Dor rushed forward and sprinted up the stairs to her mum,

dropping to her knees. She was highly aware of the warriors moving closer to her, but she ignored them as she checked her mum's pulse. It thrummed beneath her fingers as she clasped her hand around her mother's wrist.

Carefully, she laid her mum's arm across her swollen belly, and glared up at the woman only five paces away, barely managing to keep her tone civil. "What have you done to my mother?"

The woman stepped closer and Dor lifted her blade, her lip curling as Ada moved to her side. "Not one step closer, or you die," she threatened. She'd never been more serious about anything in her whole life. The woman shifted, cocking a hip, and Dor held her blade a little higher. *Try me, wench.*

The woman studied her for what seemed like hours. Dor's arm trembled as she fought to keep her blade held aloft. If they kept the staring contest going, Dor was going to lose in a spectacular fashion.

"Your mother is close to birthing the babe. I gave her a moment's reprieve from the pain, to rest before she begins her battle."

Everyone lied. Surely, this woman wasn't an exception.

"And you expect me to believe that?"

"You will have to trust me."

"I don't trust anyone." Trust meant betrayal. Betrayal meant death.

A throaty laugh spilled from the woman's red lips, the corners of her caramel eyes crinkling in mirth. "I see your sire didn't hesitate to train you well."

Dor stiffened at the mention of her father and stayed silent.

The woman held her hands up and slowly dropped to her haunches. Her liquid gaze held Dor's until she glanced at her mum's swollen belly. "Your mum trusted me and my men, and you would not be here unless she wished it. She's guarded you zealously all your life. So, it seems you have no choice in the matter."

Bitterness and fear left a bad taste at the back of Dor's mouth. The woman wasn't wrong, but hearing the words out loud made it that much more frightening. She was trapped, but all wasn't lost. The woman obviously held power. The question was what she wanted with Dor.

A clammy hand touched her arm, causing her to jerk and glance down. Her mum wetted her lips and gazed up at her, strain pulling the skin covering her cheekbones taut. "Love," she said, her tone soothing. "Listen to Maeve."

Maeve. So that was the woman's name. Dor squinted as she tried to remember why that name was so familiar. Where had she heard it before? It was uncommon. Her brow screwed up as she strained to place it. Nothing.

Dor met Maeve's direct stare and bluntly asked, "Who are you?" She swore every pair of eyes in the room seemed to focus on her at the moment.

The woman stood fluidly to her full height and smiled. "Now, that is an interesting question. Do you want an interesting answer?"

"I want the truth."

A feline smile graced Maeve's face, making her seem infinitely devious and cunning. "I am the warlord's right hand."

The air from the room was sucked away, leaving Dor gasping for breath in the silence. The warlord's sister. Death would surely come for all of them. What was her mum thinking, dealing with such a deadly predator?

"Leren got your tongue?" Maeve asked, her eyes sparkling. The woman was enjoying her discomfort. Dor forced herself to focus and glared at Maeve.

"What do you want?" Dor's tone was far from respectful, but she couldn't find it in herself to care. The monster before her was a mass murderer. The warlord's handmaiden.

"Everything."

"Sorry, not on the menu."

Maeve cocked her head and arched a brow. "We'll settle on one thing then."

She had a distinct feeling it would destroy her. "What is that?"

"You are the future."

"I don't follow," Dor said slowly.

"You, my dear one, are going to start a rebellion."

Dor's blood turned cold.

Maeve's lips hitched up in a sharp smile. "You will be the end of everything."

Dor didn't know about that. But one thing she knew for sure:

The warlord's handmaiden would be the end of her.

Chapter Thirty-One

Sam

He was an idiot.

And his spies were turning against him.

Sam trudged up the hidden spiral staircase that led to the docks. Water dripped from his clothes as he wove his way through the long-forgotten passages deep in the bowels of the castle. Next time he visited Mer, he needed to leave a stash of clothing in the cave. He was sick and tired of moving around in cold, wet clothes.

He frowned as he thought of his meeting with Mer. She'd looked more haggard than usual. It seemed that war was being waged on all fronts. Tensions were at an all-time high below the surface of the sea. Mer had revealed that one of her generals had broken rank and challenged the king publicly, which had led to the Sirenidae's very humiliating execution.

Thank the stars Mer hadn't been exposed, but Sam worried it was only a matter of time until all was revealed. Mer's men had moved into place, shadowing the Aermian fleet as they created a blockade around Sanee's port. The Scythians had launched their armada and, all too soon, come to their capitol's door.

Sam turned to his left and sprinted up the next three flights of stairs. His heart pounded, and his breath came in short pants as he crested the stairs leading to his office and training room. He spied several of his girls, including Gem, peering into the training room. He crept closer and looked over Jacie's broad shoulder.

His lips thinned as he got an eyeful of what had captured their attention.

His wife.

Jasmine stood alone in the middle of the room, practicing hand-to-hand combat. Her eyes were closed, and her expression was one of complete peace as she flowed from one exercise to another.

"What are you all doing?" he asked softly.

Gem shrugged a shoulder but didn't glance in his direction. "Watching the show."

"It's like she's made from water. I wish I could move like that," Jacie whispered.

"You can," Sam said. "If only you practiced more."

The younger girl tipped her head back and smiled impishly, her crooked teeth somehow endearing and not appalling. "Perhaps."

He rolled his eyes at her sass.

Ruth, the redhead to his left, grinned at him. "You sure do take dangerous ones to bed." She flicked a finger toward Jasmine. "Your wifey could kill you in your sleep."

"As could any of you." He shook his head dramatically. "What have I done?"

A small smile flickered across Gem's mouth, and mirth entered her eyes. "Apparently, everything."

Sam scowled, his eyes narrowing on Gem. She definitely knew something. Jasmine had practically fled from him every time she was in his company for the last two days. The only time he'd actually spent time in her presence was when they put the twins to bed and when Jasmine shared his bed to sleep.

Thank the stars for small miracles.

She hadn't left his bed, and, every morning, he'd find her in his arms, her belly pressing against his stomach, or she'd wrap herself around him with her belly poking his back. It delighted him to have the wee one kick him until she woke. Still, each time, he'd pretend to be asleep when she woke, because, as soon as she realized what had happened, she'd wiggle to the other side of the pillow wall she built every night and pretend it never happened.

"Don't you girls have something better to do?" Sam whispered with fake exasperation.

"Better than spying? I think not," Jacie piped in. "We're just doing what you taught us to do."

"I didn't mean spying on my wife." He shooed them away from the door. "Unless you have something you need to discuss with me, get out of here, you wenches."

His girls rolled their eyes at him and reluctantly followed his orders. He watched them disperse between the tunnel that went to different parts of town until he was sure they were gone. Sam swiveled back to the doorway and crept a little closer to admire the way his wife moved.

He held his breath as she bent to pick up the staff lying at the edge of the mat, the image of her climbing into the training pit flashing through his mind. He knew now what possessed him to act like a total ass, but, at the time, he was too angry to understand what had spurred him into action: he'd been surprised when he'd noticed her lurking next to the soldier. His urge to impress her had been strong, so he'd fought harder than was necessary. What he didn't expect was for her to be absolutely furious with him and accuse him of being unsportsmanlike. It had rankled him, but not as much as her defending Kylir had.

His jaw clenched.

That damn traitor. Kylir had been training with her for a month and had never said one word about it.

Then she'd tossed her dress aside, showing off her curved thighs and small waist despite the babe. Everything about her looked tousled. She looked like a well-loved woman, and he knew all the other soldiers were imagining it, too. Then there was the matter of the babe. He couldn't believe she was being so careless with *his* child. He may not have been the one to put the babe in her belly, but, once he'd felt the wee one dancing beneath his palm, the babe had *become* his.

And that was what had turned him into an idiot.

He'd let jealousy and overprotectiveness override his common sense and vast knowledge of how to handle a woman. As the aggressive and chastising words had flown from his mouth, he'd wanted nothing more than to snatch them from the air, shove them back into his mouth, and swallow them down.

He knew better.

Then she'd walked away.

Panic had flared in his chest.

He'd planned to go after her, but his father had pulled him aside and given him a stern talking to. Feeling like a little boy, he'd stayed silent until his father had finished. A little raw from his father's words, Sam had exploded. His father had listened to his side of things, acknowledged his concerns, and given him wise advice. But as much as Sam had tried to put it into practice, the words stuck in his throat each night Jasmine had crawled into bed and turned her back on him. It was like she'd cut him off.

And he *hated* it.

He'd always understood the female sex. Hell, he even got along with them better than he did with men—but Jasmine? She confused him. She was unlike any woman he'd ever met before.

But enough was enough. His father said not to go to bed angry, and Sam had let it happen for two days. Two days for things to fester and stew.

He stepped through the doorway, and Jasmine faltered, her rhythm slowing as she noticed him. Immediately, she appeared to dismiss him and focused on a stone on the wall across from her.

Oh no, you don't. They were going to fix this now.

She spun her staff in an elaborate twirl.

"Those are a waste of motion," he murmured. "But very pleasing to the eye."

His wife slammed the tip of the staff against the floor and glanced at him. "I'm not sure if you're insulting me or trying to pay me a compliment. But, if it was the latter, you're doing a poor job."

He edged closer.

Prickly. That was how he'd describe her.

It was if she had invisible spines surrounding her, keeping anyone from getting too close.

Time for a different tactic.

"When did your father start training you?"

She squinted, and her jaw set. For a second, he thought she wouldn't answer him.

"I was young. Maybe three years? I remember going to the square, and two older boys picked on me. They knocked me down into a puddle, and I skinned my palms. My father found me crying in the dirt. He didn't say anything as he'd picked me up, but he told me to dry my tears. After that, he began training me. It was games at first, but then they got consistently harder." She glanced away from him.

"Sounds like a good father."

Jasmine barked out a laugh. "He wasn't much of a father. He was my commander. The man was cold and distant and hardly showed any amount of affection." Her expression softened. "But I loved him anyway. He gave me the tools to protect myself. I've never been at the mercy of a man because of that."

Her fingers turned white as they tightened around the wooden staff, her lips thinning. He didn't think she'd noticed as her left hand moved to her belly.

"At least not the ones that I knew to be monsters."

"I'm sorry for what you suffered," he offered, knowing the words weren't enough.

Her brows furrowed, and her gaze blanked as if she'd gone to some distant place.

"Suffering," she whispered, her voice hollow. "I didn't suffer, not like Sage. I wasn't beaten, tortured, starved, forced to kill, or accept another's touch." Her eerily placid gaze disappeared as she blinked, her stormy eyes clashing with his. "My suffering is nothing compared to some."

Sam balked. "It's not fair to compare what you've been through to that of others. It's okay to mourn what you've lost. It's not something to be brushed aside."

"And how do I even know what I've suffered?" she challenged. "Let's be honest. I don't know what happened." Her eyes became glassy, filled with unshed tears. "I've seen how others act when they've been into their cups too much. Drunks are freer with their actions, and, sometimes, they don't remember their actions in the morning. How do I even know that I didn't ask for it?"

"No!" Sam said vehemently, slicing his hand through the air. "You aren't accountable for a man's perverted choices. You must never blame yourself. I know you. You wouldn't have done that."

"Don't you remember how you found me? Maybe that's who I am."

"No, that's not you," he said gently as he approached her and grasped her upper arms with care. "During the time we've spent together, I've been able to discern one of your driving factors. Do you know what it is?"

Jasmine shook her head.

"You are one of the most caring and compassionate people I've ever had the pleasure of knowing. You put others' needs above your own, and you go out of your way to help those in need. That is not someone who seeks pleasure above all at the expense of someone else."

"You can say it." A tear dripped down her cheek. "I was raped."

The ugly word rattled around in his head. He lifted his left hand and brushed a sweaty strand of hair from her face, while figuring out how to phrase his next words. "Yes," he murmured. "And that was not your fault. No one—no man, woman, or child—deserves to be abused in such a demonic way. The fault lies with the disgusting men who took advantage of you when you deserved their protection."

Her bottom lip quivered, and she leaned closer, placing her forehead against his chest. "It's so confusing," she confessed. "I keep going over everything I remember, and they were good to me. My warriors," she paused. "The warriors cared for me and protected me. How could they do this? I just can't understand. I don't understand. I thought they were my friends." Her voice dropped to a whisper. "I loved them a little bit."

Jasmine pulled away from him and dropped her staff, spearing her fingers through her tangled hair.

Sam kept his expression placid, even though he hated the thought of her caring at all for her abductors. He understood what captivity could do to a mind, but watching the aftermath of such a trauma? Well, it was heartbreaking.

"How can I still feel this way?" She dropped her hands and rubbed at her arms. "I want to scrub the shame from my skin. I want the ugly, disgusted feeling to go away."

Sam held his empty hands out. "What can I do to help?"

Her bleak gaze met his. "There's nothing you can do to remove this stain from me." She bent to pick up her staff. "But you can help me train. It quiets my mind, and I feel more in control."

"Okay." Now, he felt even more like an idiot. He'd been so angry two days ago that she'd put herself and the babe at risk, and all she was doing was trying to find a way to feel safe. "If you'd like, I'll show you a way to protect yourself in close quarters." He pointed at the staff. "You won't need that."

Jasmine wordlessly set the staff along the wall and turned toward him.

He smiled. "This will be easy for you. Hell, you might enjoy it after the last few days. In a few minutes, I'll let you throw me to the floor."

Her formerly haunted gaze narrowed, and a spark of interest lit in her eyes. "You're twice my size. How could I do that?"

"I'll show you. But, first, we'll start with something simple. Did your father ever teach you about the most common ways women are attacked?"

Her lips pursed. "They're choked from the front."

"Yes. Usually against a wall." Slowly, he stepped closer to Jasmine and placed his hands carefully on her shoulders. He waited for her to tense or step back, but she just looked up at him, waiting for the next instruction. Sam guided her backward until her spine was pressed against the stone wall. When her breathing didn't accelerate, he slid his calloused hands to her neck.

Jasmine stiffened.

Instantly, he let go, his brows drawing together in concern.

"No," Jasmine assured him. "I'm okay. I've just never had anyone wrap their hands around my throat before."

"You have nothing to fear from me. Ever."

Her expression softened. "I know."

Sam could tell she meant it. He edged closer and placed his fingers around her delicate neck. He focused on the front of her neck where his thumbs rested. "In this situation, you only have a few seconds to react after he takes hold."

"Breathing is important," Jasmine huffed, amusement lifting her lips into a dark smile.

Sam barked out a laugh. This woman. Her hands snaked up to grip his elbows.

"If I yanked down on his arms, like this, could I get out?"

He shook his head. "Not if he was my size. You wouldn't be able to budge him. So, tuck your chin down to protect your neck and then put your palms together like you're praying. Then push your hands through the circle of my arms."

She followed his instructions.

"Good," he murmured. "Now, push higher, until it forces my elbows to bend. Can you feel how it loosens my hold?"

She grinned, clearly pleased with herself. "Yes."

"Now, grab my head."

She cocked her head. "Do what?"

"Go on. You heard me."

Tentatively, she placed her hands on his head.

"Take hold of my face, so you can push your thumbs into my eyes."

"That's brilliant," she hummed, adjusting her grip so the pads of her thumbs rested at the outer corners of his eyes. "Show the bastard no mercy."

Sam grinned at his bloodthirsty little wife, but he quickly sobered as the image of three men attacking her near the docks rose in his mind. "That's right. As he will show you none," he continued. "As you apply pressure to the eyes, you'll be able to push the head back easily. Then jerk it down until the nose meets your forehead, thus breaking the nose." He cupped a hand over his nose. "But please show me mercy."

Jasmine rolled her eyes. "I'd hate to mar such beauty."

"You think I'm beautiful?" He winked at her.

"Oh hush, you vain creature. You and everyone else knows you're devilishly handsome."

She pulled his head down so his mouth and nose rested on her forehead. The contact only lasted an instant, but something powerful rocked through him. Her feminine scent teased him, and all he wanted to do was hunt for the source of it like a bloodhound. But he tugged on his self-control and drew back slowly.

"You could follow that with a knee to the groin if your skirts aren't too heavy." His gaze dropped to her leather pants. "But, as it seems, your choices in attire are as conducive to fighting as they are inappropriate."

His wife snorted. "As if you've ever acted appropriately or made apologies for it."

Here was his chance.

"Speaking of apologies. I owe you one."

Jasmine's mirth melted away, and she cocked her head,

studying him. "For what?"

"I acted like an utter arse at the sparring ring." He sighed. "When I saw you climb over that fence intending to fight, I lost my mind. I was worried for the babe and for you. I didn't handle it well, and I embarrassed you. I'm sorry for it."

Sam held his breath when her expression revealed none of her feelings.

"I ought to let you suffer," she muttered. "I was so mad at you."

"I know. My reaction was out of line, but can you understand how it looked to me? Then there was Kylir." His brows lowered as he remembered the silent conversation that seemed to flow between Jasmine and one of his best spies. He wanted to gouge the man's eyes out for just staring at his wife. "And I allowed my jealousy to get the best of me," Sam admitted.

Jasmine surprised him by laughing. "*You* were jealous?"

"Out of all of that, that's what you focus on?" he demanded.

"I just find it ironic that you were jealous of me. You literally have hordes of women who follow you around and pant at your heels, and yet I have just one male friend, and you lost your temper?"

He shifted uncomfortably. Wicked hell, he hated feeling guilty. It was a feeling he rarely dealt with. "I sound very ridiculous when you say—"

"Utterly ridiculous," his wife cut in. "I'm a peasant woman carrying the bastard child of monsters. Believe me when I say your fantastical ideas have no basis in reality. I don't chastise you for your liaisons."

He winced. If only he could tell her the truth. There weren't any romps or rendezvous, but how his meetings appeared to others served his purposes in protecting his spy ring. He bit the inside of his cheek. It hadn't bothered him terribly before, but now it affected not just himself, but his entire family.

"But I can let that go. Men are volatile creatures with too many feelings that they're not willing to deal with. And, as for the training, well, I'm not going to stop. I feel better than I have in a long time."

"I don't expect you to stop," he spoke up. "I visited Mira."

Her brows rose almost to her hairline. "You did?"

"I did, and if you want to keep training with Kylir, I won't stop you. All I ask is that you be mindful of your limits. I don't want to see you in pain." He held his left hand out toward her belly. "May I?"

She nodded slowly.

Sam placed his calloused hand on the top of her belly and marveled at the life growing there. "I don't want anything to happen to this wee one."

Jasmine dropped her hands from his face and proceeded to stare so hard at him, he was surprised she didn't bore holes through his head.

"Is there something on my face?" he asked.

"Your nose."

He cracked a smile and pulled back. "You and that mouth."

She winked at him and brushed her hands over her shirt. "My father always said it would get me into trouble, and you know what?"

"What?"

"He was right."

Sam sniggered.

She smiled and then shifted her stance, her gaze flickering to his crotch and then back to his eyes. "So, back to our lesson, you want me to use my leg to..."

"Well, not to me, per se, but if you feel threatened by any man, you do it. It's the most impactful target on a man. The pain shoots through all of our innards."

"Hmmm... My brother was apprenticing as a healer before he died. We had many interesting conversations, including what he referred to as nerves that run from the groin and into the belly."

Sam blinked at her. She wasn't shy, that was for sure.

Jasmine smirked at him. "Have I made you uncomfortable?"

Rising to her challenge, he stepped closer, laughter glinting in his eyes. "Never. There isn't much in the world that can make me blush. I've just never met anyone like you, my lady-wife."

She threw her head back and laughed. "I'm no lady. The twins will be the first ones to tell you that."

Chapter Thirty-Two

Jasmine

Jasmine flitted around the room she shared with Sam, cleaning up items he'd abandoned. For a man who was relatively organized, his clothing seemed to find homes wherever he tossed them. She sighed as she picked up his boots from beside the bed and placed them inside their closet. Why he couldn't just walk the few extra paces to put away his boots, she would never understand.

Her silver, silk robe flared around her bare feet as she spun to survey the tidy room. There were a few things still lying on his side table, but she wasn't about to touch a man's weapons. Her father had been very particular about that when she was growing up. She rubbed at her eyes, weariness blanketing her. Blearily, she glanced at the doorway that led to the twins' room. Sam had disappeared to say goodnight to them, but he hadn't reappeared.

She crept toward the cracked door and listened. Nothing. Well, he wasn't telling them a story. Jasmine pressed against the wooden door and peeked into the darkened room. Moonlight streamed in from the window above the twins' beds, illuminating the room just enough for her to make out everything. Her breath caught as she tiptoed farther into the bedroom.

Sam sat in the chair between the twins' beds, each of his arms reaching out to hold Jade's and Ethan's hands. His head lolled to the side, and he released a deep snore. Jasmine's heart clenched at the precious picture they made. Her eyes watered. Somehow, they'd created a family. She wiped her cheeks and snuck around Jade's bed to place the soft blanket over her shoulder. Her niece snuggled deeper into the covers and sighed.

Jasmine glided around the bed and paused in front of Sam, admiring him. The moonlight transformed his golden locks into silver waves. His dark lashes swept downward and rested on his cheekbones. The man was stunning. She reached out and brushed a wayward curl from his forehead, tracing his dark-blond brow in the process.

Sam's eyes popped open, and awareness filled them immediately. Jasmine leaned over him, her fingers still on his skin. They watched each other in the silence, neither of them moving. She continued her exploration and skated her fingers down his face to cup his cheek.

In that moment, she made a decision. Jasmine bent down and

pressed a kiss against his opposite cheek. Sam might have his flaws, ones she didn't care for, but, all in all, he was a good man.

One she loved.

She wasn't sure if she was *in love* with him, but she couldn't help but have love and affection for the man who was so good to the children.

Jas pulled back, her lips tingling as she met his deep, blue, fathomless eyes, almost silver in the moonlight. "Come to bed, love," she whispered and straightened.

She turned her head and looked over her shoulder to see if he was following her as she moved into their room. Nerves caused her belly to quiver as she edged around their bed. Sam closed the twins' door and quietly moved to his side of the mattress. He flicked back the covers and began constructing a pillow wall down the middle.

It took a great amount of effort for Jasmine to pull back her side of the covers. She watched Sam crawl into bed and yawn.

Be brave, Jas.

She fumbled as she untied the sash fastened below her breasts and shrugged off the robe, letting it slither to the ground. She hiked her nightgown up and clambered into the bed as awkwardly as a newborn foal.

Sam squinted and rolled to face her fully. "Something wrong?"

Jasmine blinked, realizing she was staring. Instead of answering, with trembling hands she grabbed the pillows that ran down the middle of the bed and tossed them onto the floor. Her breathing increased as Sam seemed to quit breathing entirely. Tension filled the space around them, and her doubts crept in.

What if he wanted the wall there? What if he didn't want her near him? What if—

Sam lifted the covers and extended his arm toward her, from beneath his pillow.

An invitation.

Relief swamped her, and she carefully scooted closer to snuggle into him. Her nose pressed against his chest, and her pulse pounded as his arms draped over her loosely. Yet, he still said nothing. Slowly, her tension melted away as his breathing deepened and the stiffness in his body disappeared. She wasn't sure how much time had drifted by, but she tipped her head back to peek at his sleeping face.

Her mouth parted as his blue eyes opened and looked over her head toward the fireplace heating her back. Then, his eyes dropped and locked on to hers.

"Thank you," she blurted.

"For what?" he asked, his tone like velvet.

She swallowed hard. "For taking care of the children and me. It means the world to us."

"I'm happy to do it." His jaw tightened, and his gaze bored into hers. "You know you don't owe me anything, right?" Sam's arm cinched on her waist. "This. You don't owe me this."

Jasmine snorted. "I know."

"So, you're not doing this out of a sense of obligation?" he asked cautiously.

Dumb man. She rolled her eyes but smiled at him. "I would never cuddle you because I felt obligated. I just wanted to cuddle because I like you." Her cheeks heated at her admission.

Her husband's face lost its edge, and something tender moved across his expression that made her palms sweat. His hand smoothed up her back and then down her braid. "I like you, too, Jasmine."

"Jas," she said.

"Jas," he rumbled and smiled.

Stars above. It was downright cruel that he possessed such a smile. Surely, the angels looked on with envy.

She bit her bottom lip as he leaned forward to kiss her forehead. Her eyes closed, and, in that moment, she'd never felt safer.

"Sleep, dearest," he breathed across her skin.

He turned onto his back and pulled Jasmine against him, tucking her into his side. Her head pillowed on his bicep, and he drew her left hand onto his chest to rest over his heart, where he tangled their fingers together. He squeezed her hand once and settled in the nest of blankets.

Each of her muscles slowly relaxed, and a contentedness she hadn't felt in forever seeped into her bones.

Home.

She finally felt like she was home.

***

Awareness crept in, in increments, along with a familiar feeling of being watched.

"Jade," Jas grumbled, not opening her eyes. "Must you stare?"

"I'm hungry."

"Me, too!" Ethan piped in.

A deep chuckle rumbled against her right cheek. "You beasts are always hungry."

Jasmine's eyes popped open, but she didn't move. It shouldn't have shocked her that she woke up snuggled with Sam. She'd woken up that way since they'd decided to share the bed. The only difference was that she had made the *conscious* choice to do so this time. She felt her cheeks scorch at how she'd thrown her leg over him.

She moved to pull her leg back but gasped when Sam's hand wrapped around the back of her knee and held her in place. He pushed up onto one elbow and peered down at her.

"Don't," he said in a hushed tone. "The babe has been saying good morning."

"What?"

He beamed down at her as the little one in her belly stretched and pressed into his side. "See?"

"How long have you been awake?"

Sam shrugged and lay back down. "A while."

She tilted her head back to admire his profile. He wasn't normally an early morning person. "Did the babe wake you?"

"Something like that," he said wryly.

"I'm sorry."

"Don't be. I liked it."

Her chest warmed.

"Mama?" Jade trilled.

Jasmine stiffened and lifted her head to look at the twins peeking over the bottom of the bed at them. "Yes, baby?" It still bothered her that Jade called her that. Even Ethan had called her

"Mama" two days prior.

"I'm hungry."

She grinned. "Go and get dressed in proper clothes, and we'll go find something to eat."

"With Grandad?" Ethan said with excitement.

"He wouldn't miss it for the world," Sam said. "I'm sure he's waiting for you already."

The twins screeched and scrambled to their room, bickering with each other to move faster.

Jasmine reluctantly rolled away from Sam and sat up, swinging her legs over the side of the bed, the linen nightgown tickling her calves.

"It's okay, you know," Sam murmured.

"What?" she replied absentmindedly, rubbing at her temples.

"They're very young. You're the only mum they might remember."

Guilt and sadness warred with each other in the pit of her stomach. "It catches me off-guard every time it happens."

"That's understandable." Sam shifted in the bed behind her and rested his chin on her right shoulder. "But, it's okay if they do. You're the one raising them; it's only natural that they think of you as their mum."

His hand curled around Jasmine's right bicep, his thumb running back and forth over her skin. Absentmindedly, she placed her left hand over the top of his and squeezed, thankful for the comfort.

She turned her neck to thank him, but the words died on her tongue when her lips brushed his chin. When had he gotten that close? She pulled back, her eyes connecting with Sam's deep pools.

"What is it?" he asked, his deep voice sending a shiver of pleasure down her spine.

Jasmine had always liked kisses, and, in that moment, all she wanted to do was touch her lips to his. She wanted more from him, but those were thoughts for another day. She couldn't deal with that now, but a kiss she could handle.

Instead of answering, she twisted to fully face him and leaned forward, brushing her lips softly against his. Her belly quivered when he didn't move away and his hands lifted to cup her cheeks, seemingly content with her taking the lead.

A spark of excitement and something much deeper flamed in her chest. There wasn't guilt, self-loathing, or numbness, just a complete and utter sense of rightness. Her pulse picked up its pace, and she gathered her nightgown in her hands and slipped onto his lap, straddling his thighs, *needing* to be closer to him.

Sam's arms wrapped around her and pressed their bodies together. Jasmine paused to run a finger along the prince's face, admiring his high cheekbones, sharp jaw, and beautiful blue eyes that promised things Jas wasn't sure she was ready for.

Once more, she returned to his lips and sank into the kiss. There were many unknowns in her life, but Sam had been one of her constants. He never asked for anything from her, but she could give him this, give *them* this.

Jasmine ran her hands along the hard planes of his body that seemed to fit her just right and sighed against his lips. Sam froze and then groaned, the sound vibrating against her own chest.

She gasped as his hands wrapped around the backs of her bare thighs and he jerked her impossibly closer with a growl, her round belly pressing insistently into the firm muscles of his stomach. Her hands sank into his gilded waves as his lips trailed down her neck and stopped to lavish the spot above her collarbone.

Stars above. This man was going to wreck her.

Her skin prickled as he pushed her nightgown off her shoulder and brushed more kisses against her skin.

"So beautiful," he murmured, his hands clenching on the backs of her thighs, like he was holding himself back.

A wildness filled Jasmine, along with a sense of reckless urgency. She'd never done anything more before that she remembered. Jas pushed the thought away and focused on the man all but worshiping her.

But she wanted to. With this man. Only this man.

Jasmine yanked his head up and crushed her lips to his, her hands running along the bands of muscles hidden beneath his clothing. What would it be like to have his skin pressed to hers? Brazenly, she reached beneath his linen shirt and scoured her nails up his back.

Sam's breaths came faster, and he exploded into action.

His hands were everywhere, like he was trying to touch every part of her that he could. Gooseflesh rippled down her arms as he bit her bottom lip before soothing it with his tongue. He glanced up into her eyes, and what Jasmine saw caused her heart to accelerate.

Pure heat.

Raw want and rapture.

"I've wanted to be this close to you for so long, love," he whispered.

Love. That's what they had—love and companionship—everything.

Jasmine closed her eyes and pulled her hands from his tempting body to lift the edge of her nightgown. The choice had been taken from her the first time, but this time, she got to choose.

And her choice was Sam.

"No," Sam whispered, slightly breathless.

Jasmine stilled, her eyes snapping open. "W-what?" she stuttered.

Sam's hand slipped over her clenched fist, and he lowered her nightgown. A crushing sense of disappointment and embarrassment rushed over her at his gentle refusal.

Tears flooded her eyes, and she dropped her head, trying to hide them. What was she thinking? He may have enjoyed her company, but that didn't mean he *wanted* her. Stupid, she was so stupid. She tried to backpedal, but Sam's left arm banded around her waist, holding her in place.

"I need to check on the twins," she said thickly. "Please let me go."

"No. Look at me, Jas."

She shook her head. If she looked at him, surely, she would sob all over the man. How embarrassing. "Let me go."

"No."

Her head snapped up, and she glared at him through her tears. "Let me go!"

"Not until you listen to me," Sam said, infuriatingly calm.

Jasmine threw her hands in the air. "I'm sorry I accosted you. Now, let me go."

"No."

He reached out and sank a hand into her hair before yanking her close, his mouth slamming against hers, his other arm crushing her against him. It was desperate, hot, and messy, like he was trying to imprint himself on her skin.

Sam pulled back, releasing a shuddering breath as Jasmine trembled from head to toe. She touched her swollen lips and stared at him in shock. The wicked man had the audacity to grin at her.

"What in the wicked hell was that for?" she demanded.

"To get you out of your head. I could see rejection and hurt dripping from you like you'd just taken a dip in the sea."

"I'm sorry if my feelings bothered you so," she sniped, wishing she could leave the room.

Sam rolled his hips, and her eyes widened in shock. He laughed. "You bothered me alright. You plague me every damn day."

"What a romantic way to be described. A bloody plague."

He narrowed his eyes at her. "You're not listening." He removed his arms from around her waist and clasped her face between his calloused palms. "I want you, dearest, I do," he ground out, "but we don't need to rush this. We have time. And that's what I want with you—time—not just a quick romp between the sheets." He tilted his head toward the twins' doorway. "It's lucky they haven't burst through the door already."

Her cheeks burned even hotter. "I'm an idiot."

"No, you're human." A slow smile spread across his face before it melted into something completely sinful. He leaned forward and pressed his lips against her ear. "Be thankful our children are in the other room. I don't think you're ready for what's in store for us."

A thrill went up her spine at his words. She jerked when he bit her ear and then pulled back, looking way too pleased with himself.

Bastard.

Two could play that game.

She arched her back and stretched, hiding her smile when he hissed and then cursed. His hands grabbed her hips as she crawled off of him, making sure to give an extra wiggle. He smirked at her.

"Wench."

"Rake," she retorted.

He winked at her and brushed a surprisingly sweet kiss along her brow before stiffly climbing from their bed. He strolled to the bathing room and glanced over his shoulder. "Just remember, love, I always give as good as I get."

A good kind of shiver trickled over Jasmine's skin.

She didn't doubt it for one second.

Chapter Thirty-Three

Jasmine

Sweat beaded on Jasmine's forehead and slid down her hairline. "Don't go so fast!" she called to the twins. Ethan paused while Jade continued to scamper ahead. He held his hand out to Jasmine, and she took his little hand in hers as they clambered down the last of the porous sea rocks to get to the tide pools.

"Jade, you best turn around right now, young lady!"

Her niece paused in her explorations, then skipped back to them, her feet kicking up white sand as she crashed into Jasmine's legs and almost bowled her over.

"Good gracious, baby. You almost knocked me down." Jasmine

laughed as she patted Jade's head.

"Don't go so far," Ethan chastised. "Jas is slow today."

Jasmine narrowed her eyes at her nephew. "I'm not that slow."

He smiled at her and nodded. "It took you *forever* to climb down the rocks."

"Well, I had to make sure I was careful. If I fell, it could hurt the babe."

His eyes rounded and dropped to her midriff. Her heart fluttered as he pressed his little hand against her belly.

"The baby is okay?" he asked, worried.

"The babe is happy," she said reassuringly. She released his fingers and dropped her slippers from her other hand into the sand. "I don't think I'm the only slow one." Jas lifted her skirts just a touch and glanced conspiratorially between the twins. "I think we need to have a race!"

The twins flashed her excited smiles. And Jade took off running.

That child.

"You have to wait for everyone else," Ethan shouted at his sister. "You're cheating!"

Jasmine waved Jade back. Again. "Okay, first, we need to make a starting line."

Ethan nodded, his brows furrowed. He bent down on his hands and knees and methodically began to draw a straight line to the left. Jade watched him for a moment and then dug her foot into the sand, dragging it behind her to create a line the other way. It never ceased to amaze Jas how different the twins were.

Once both children were satisfied with their lines, they

tromped through the sand to get back to her. Jas hid her smile when Ethan caught sight of his sister's very crooked line and scowled. She ran her hand over the back of his head and smiled at him.

"It's okay. Your line looks very nice."

He stood a little taller at her praise.

"Are you ready?" Jas asked.

Both twins nodded and lined up.

Jasmine hitched her skirts up and looked from one twin to the next. "Get set." Both children tensed. "Go!" she shouted, and she burst forward. The twins screeched in joy and ran alongside her.

She laughed breathlessly and ran with the children until the docks disappeared and the castle loomed above them on the cliff. Jas hissed when a stitch formed in her side. She slowed and threw her hands up in the air.

"You both won," she huffed, collapsing into the sand. Ethan and Jade plopped down next to her.

Jade lay on her back and began to move her arms and legs like she was swimming. Jas groaned as sand collected in her niece's hair. *That will be a nightmare to get out.* But they'd worry about it later.

Jasmine ran her hand over the warm sand and wiggled her toes in deeper, sighing when the cooler earth touched her overheated skin. She always used to be cold, but something had changed once the babe had begun to grow. Now, Jas was perpetually hot.

A cool ocean breeze ruffled her hair, chilling the sweat on her face and arms.

Ethan stood and held a hand out to her. "Can I take you to see the tide pools now?"

What a little gentleman he was turning out to be. She grinned at him and placed her hand in his. "Why, thank you, kind sir."

Ethan kicked his foot in the sand, his cheeks pinking slightly as she pushed herself up and then offered her other hand to the sand mermaid who was attempting to bury herself alive.

"You ready?" Jas asked.

Jade scrambled out of the sand and placed her gritty fingers into Jasmine's. The three of them slowly weaved around the huge, white rocks that jutted out of the sand like giant broken teeth. She kept an eye on the surf as they attempted to find the perfect pool—it was still receding, so they had time.

Ethan jumped up and down as they rounded a particularly huge rock, and they discovered a beautiful cove. Rocks rose up on each side, protecting it from the wind. The water lapped gently on the shore, and little tide pools were scattered around the edges.

"We've found our own secret world," Jasmine said excitedly. "Let's see what treasures we can discover!"

Time passed as they moved from pool to pool. Ethan exclaimed over all the variations of crabs he found, and Jade had to touch every sea anemone she could get to. Jasmine smiled as she ran a hand over a rough pink starfish, marveling at the texture. She'd abandoned all attempts to keep the twins out of the water. They were happy, and that's all that mattered. One could always wash them later. A bit of sea water and sand never hurt anybody.

"Look at this shell!" Ethan exclaimed, holding up a huge fan shell.

"It's beautiful. Are you going to keep it for your collection?"

He nodded and placed it on her lap, along with other treasures the twins had collected.

"We needed that for our gate," Jade objected and gestured to the sand castle they were building.

"I've found something better." Ethan handed her a piece of curved driftwood.

Her niece eyed it and then nodded. "It'll do."

Jas stretched her back and slowly stood, making sure to keep the sea trinkets safe in the top layer of her skirt. "The sun is going down, loves. Only a few more minutes until we have to leave."

A chorus of groans reached her ears.

She took a step forward, and her eyes widened as her bladder protested the movement. Devil take it. She had to use the bathroom. *Right now.*

"Stay where you are," Jas called as she hustled to the edge of the cove. "I need to relieve myself."

Ethan's nose wrinkled. "Gross."

Jas ignored him and rounded the edge of the rock so that she could see the twins but they couldn't see her while she did her business. Jasmine finished up and sighed in relief. Every day, she learned something new about pregnancy. Women glamourized it, but from her experience, her body was falling apart.

She snorted and adjusted her dress. *If they actually told us what it was like, no one would have children.*

She'd taken one step toward the twins when hushed voices

reached her ears from behind her. Jasmine frowned and backtracked, very aware of the dagger strapped to her thigh beneath her dress. She never went anywhere without it.

Carefully, she peeked around the huge boulder she'd relieved herself behind and frowned as the setting sun temporarily blinded her for a second. Jas held her hand up to shield her eyes and froze, her mind not able to comprehend what she was seeing.

She whipped back around the rock and squeezed her eyes shut. It couldn't have been...

Look again.

Jasmine glanced around the rock and swallowed hard as she got an eyeful of the lurid scene. A stone settled in the pit of her stomach as she watched Sam pick up a beautiful pale woman with scarcely a stitch of clothing on. Her mouth dried when he dropped to his knees, the goddess straddling him. The woman took his head in her hands and murmured something to him. Bile flooded Jasmine's mouth as his hands ran up the woman's back and tangled in her silver-white hair.

She couldn't watch anymore.

Jas stumbled back into their cove, her heart feeling like it was breaking into a thousand pieces. She closed her eyes to keep the tears from falling, the image of her prince and the flawless woman seared into her mind.

Jasmine gasped as pain washed over her and wrapped around her heart like thorns. How could she be so stupid? Her sight blurred as more tears filled her eyes. No wonder he didn't pursue what she'd offered two days before. A bitter laugh escaped her numb lips. Why in the blazes would he want a pregnant woman when he could have a goddess like that?

She knew better. He'd made her no promises, and yet she'd gone and let herself get attached to him. Hastily, she wiped her eyes and strode to the twins. She forced a wobbly smile onto her lips. They'd had a wonderful day, and she wasn't about to ruin it for them.

"Time to go, sweet ones," she rasped.

Jade moaned, but Ethan studied her in his quiet, contemplative way. He stood and walked to her and took his shells from her skirt and put them in his own pockets. She stared down at him, not even realizing she was still holding her skirt up.

"Let's go, Jade," Ethan said.

Her niece eyed Ethan and then acquiesced. "Could we see Vienna today?" She reached for Jasmine's other hand.

"That sounds like something we can do," Jasmine said and squeezed both of the children's hands as they walked back the way the, came.

The walk back was a quiet one. The sun continued to sink low in the sky, and Jasmine kept looking over her shoulder expecting to see Sam running after them. But the beach was empty of all life.

She bit her trembling lip and tried to get herself together as they neared their abandoned shoes they'd hid behind a rock, which was shaped like a heart.

"Hurry," she said, eyeing the sinking sun. She squinted as she noticed familiar shapes on the horizon. More scouting warships. The navy had spread out their ships in and around the port to protect Sanee from a sea attack. But there'd been no news about a sea attack, so she wasn't too worried. Maybe she should ask Sam. She sucked in a sharp breath like someone had thrown icy water over her.

Sam.

How in the world was she going to face him?

Mortification washed over her as she and the twins hiked back up to the marketplace that was on the edge of the docks. She'd made a fool out of herself. Why had she made the first move?

Because you're all alone and lonely.

Jas shook her head at her maudlin thoughts and pulled the twins closer to each of her sides, their tiny hands wrapped in hers.

No, she wasn't alone.

As much as she wanted to disappear and never face him again, she'd made him a promise. He may not love her, but he loved the twins, and they loved him. She couldn't do that to either of them.

Her throat tightened as they turned left and moved down another cobbled street toward the apothecary, sand chafing her toes in her tight slippers.

Sacrifice. That's what love demanded.

Even if it hurt her going back to him after what she'd seen, she'd do it for the children and, damn him, for Sam.

One lone tear escaped.

Because as much as she didn't want to, she loved him.

CHAPTER THIRTY-FOUR

Sage

"He won't stop until we meet."

Sage rubbed at her burning eyes and coughed. She had scrubbed herself twice and yet the stench of smoke seemed to still cling to her.

"We've discussed this before," Zachael said. "It's too dangerous."

"You're right. It is too dangerous, but the longer we wait, the more people die!" Her voice rose. "More men, women, and children," she croaked. "We can't keep going on like this. People are suffering because of us."

Little blue toes flashed through her mind.

"Not because of us," Gav corrected gently. "Because of a mad man."

She nodded. Logically, Sage knew he was right, but all the deaths weighed heavily upon her, regardless. "Not because of us, but we can do something about it. We need to meet him."

On her left, Tehl hung his head and shifted from foot to foot. "I don't like it. I don't want to give in to his demands. It gives him power."

"No, we are taking the power back from him," Sage said. She had to make him see. "He wants to see me, and he will, but we won't give him the reaction he expects."

"And what does he expect?" William asked, running his fingers over his white beard, his expression shrewd.

"He thinks I will go crawling back to him with a bleeding heart. And while I am broken inside for what he's done –" she swallowed, "I will never cower before him or go back. He crossed a line I didn't know a human being could." Her smile was bitter. "He also changed me in ways I'm not sure he understands. He's the one who should be afraid."

Rafe pushed through the tent entrance with a missive in his hand, his hair rumpled from his flight with his fiilee. "I've just received word. Mother and the Methi army are a day's travel away. More soldiers will be arriving tomorrow."

A sigh of relief seemed to move through the entire group. They needed the soldiers badly.

Tehl eyed Sage and then the map spread out before them. "Sam says that the Scythian fleet approached Sanee. Soon we'll have war along the southern region of Aermia. If the Methian soldiers are arriving tomorrow, then I want the third battalion moved back to Sanee now. Gav, I want you to go with them."

"I will leave now and arrive before the army to inform Sam." Gav moved around the table to clasp forearms with Tehl, and then he scooped Sage into his arms. "Be strong and brave, sis."

She nodded as a lump lodged in her throat. What if this was the last time she saw him? "Take care. I'll see you soon."

"That you will."

Gav waved at the group and left the command tent.

Sage stared after him and said a little prayer. *Please keep safe.* She focused back on the conversation as Tehl gave William instructions.

The older commander nodded. "It'll be done, my lord." He bowed and left the tent, a gust of cool wind following his departure.

One by one, their people were disappearing, and it sent unease down her spine.

Her husband focused back on the map. "We will send a message to the warlord."

"He won't refuse us," Sage added, swallowing down her morbid thoughts. "This is what he's been waiting for."

"Zachael, we'll need protection."

The weapons master pushed his black hair streaked with white from his face. "I will arrange it."

Tehl turned to Raziel. "It would help if we had a view from the air."

The crown prince of Methi dipped his chin. "Our warriors, including myself, will protect you."

"Thank you," her husband whispered. "Is there anything else anyone can think of?"

"We all need sleep," Lilja muttered from the chair in the far corner. "Tomorrow will change everything." She stood with a stretch and wove around the table to pull Sage into her arms. "If you need me, all you have to do is send for me."

Sage nodded and hugged her aunt fiercely. She didn't know what it was, but it seemed like the air held a charge, like it was trying to tell her something. So, she held on to Lilja a little longer, and made sure to hug all of their friends and advisors as they left.

Rafe was the last to leave. He pulled her into a bear hug.

"We will win, little one. My people will protect you from the sky, and I will stand at your side. He will never touch you."

Sage squeezed him back as hard as she could. Sometimes, it felt like he could read her mind. It was one thing to imagine seeing the warlord, and another completely to be in his presence.

"Thank you," she whispered against his heavy fur jacket.

He dropped a kiss on top of her head and pulled Tehl into a hug before he left.

She gazed at her husband, feeling like she was about to fall apart.

Tehl said nothing, but approached her and swung her into his arms. He pushed through the rear flap that led to their sleeping quarters. Gently, he set her on the bed and pulled her boots from her feet. Next, he unbuckled her breastplate and set it next to the bed. Tehl dug around in the bag next to her side of the pallet and unearthed a brush.

"Turn around, love," he murmured.

Sage stared at him as love and affection for the amazing man before her threatened to drown her. She'd never been one for decorum, so she abandoned all pretense and launched herself at him, upsetting his balance. Tehl caught her and braced a hand on the bed as they toppled forward onto the blankets.

"I love you," she murmured.

"I love you more."

She arched against him and kissed him with everything she had. Sage twisted her fingers in his black hair and pulled him closer, needing his skin against hers, the assurance that he was with her.

"We're not going to die tomorrow," Tehl murmured against her lips. He didn't let go of her as he hauled her up the bed, and then with some finagling, he yanked the covers from beneath them with one hand and pulled the quilts over the top of them.

Sage tipped her head back and smiled at Tehl. He grinned at her, and her heart flipped.

"You and I 'til the end?" he murmured.

"'Til the end," she promised, snuggling into the cocoon of warmth he'd created.

She'd cling to life with everything she had.

The warlord would take nothing more from them.

CHAPTER THIRTY-FIVE

Sam

"Sam, you need to breathe through it."

He dropped to his knees and gazed up at Mer in awe. How could one woman be so heartbreakingly beautiful? He ran his hands up the sides of her bare thighs and onto her back, her skin as soft as silk.

"Stars, you're stunning," he whispered in awe. His eyes dropped to her pink lips, and he leaned closer, determined to find out what they tasted like.

Mer's hands cradled each side of his face and held him captive, her magenta eyes wide and her expression pinched. "It's the Lure,

Sam. You don't want this."

Oh, he very much did. He wrapped his hand in her hair and pulled her closer to his chest, the saltwater from her skin seeping into his clothes. "I know exactly what I want."

"Do you?" she whispered, her voice somewhat painful. "Because I know you don't want me. You want your wife. Jasmine is who you want."

Sam blinked slowly, and a small voice in the back of his mind that he'd been ignoring grew a little louder.

You don't want Mer. What about Jasmine? What about the twins?

He shuddered and pressed his forehead to Mer's chest, his body trembling as rational thoughts began to filter back in. He'd just accosted his friend, a friend he wanted nothing to do with romantically—nor she him, she'd made that clear before.

"I'm sorry," he panted and released her hair, his arms still staying wrapped around her. He tried not to inhale her scent, but it curled around him like a lover, intoxicating him with each breath.

"It's okay," she whispered. "It's not your fault. You've done nothing wrong, but if you don't get yourself under control, I think we're going to have company."

"Company?" he said groggily like he'd just awoken from a deep sleep.

"I heard children laughing, and I'm pretty sure a woman saw us."

"Damn," he growled and forced himself to release Mer. When he'd received her urgent message, Sam had dropped everything and come running. Whatever she was here for, it wasn't good.

The Sirenidae scrambled back and clutched at her stomach, red liquid seeping through her fingers.

He cursed. "By the stars, what in the bloody hell happened?" he demanded. Disgust and horror rolled through him as he still felt a carnal pull toward Mer. He'd been so absorbed in his attraction to her, he hadn't even noticed her injury.

Damn Lure.

Mer threw a sealskin pouch at him. "I need you to help me and listen. There isn't much time."

He nodded and put all his attention into opening the pouch instead of staring at the woman he desperately wanted to kiss. Sam pinched the bridge of his nose. That wasn't right. He didn't *want* to kiss her. She was his friend. He was only reacting to her Lure, to the pheromones her body created when it came in contact with air and seawater.

His hands shook as he pulled out a vial that held pink flowers. "What do you want me to do with this?"

Mer coughed and pointed to the nearest tide pool. "Gather some algae and crush the flower into it. Please."

Sam forced himself away from her and followed her directions. He approached her and breathed through his mouth as he gently applied the paste to her pale skin. Paler than usual.

"What happened?"

Mer blanched as he pressed some of the paste deeper into the wound. "Depths below, that hurts!" she snarled. She dropped her head back into the sand. "They're almost here."

He nodded, not surprised in the least. "How long do we have?"

"Hours," she whispered. "I came to warn you."

"Thank you," he said, brushing her silvery hair from her face. "I'll alert my captains immediately." He eyed her wound. "How did that happen?"

"A spear."

He winced. "What else can I do to help?"

Mer sat up and wrapped a hand over her wound, her face creased in pain. "You've done everything you can." She grabbed her sealskin pouch off of the sand and stood, swaying.

Launching to his feet, he steadied her. "Are you sure?"

"I need to get back to my people, and you need to prepare yours. War is upon us." Her mouth twisted into an angry, ugly line. "And they're just as barbaric and monstrous as we expected." Mer pressed a kiss to his cheek. "I'll see you on the battlefield."

She turned on her heel and strode straight into the water, disappearing from Sam's sight, just as the last vestige of the sun sank below the horizon.

Sam allowed himself one minute to calm his racing heart before he transformed into his role as spymaster and general. He spun toward the palace and then sprinted for the secret entrance.

The time for preparations was over.

War was here.

CHAPTER THIRTY-SIX

Jasmine

Jasmine rocked back and forth in Vienna's rocking chair, blankly staring at the fire in the hearth. For the hundredth time, she wondered how she was going to act when she saw Sam again. She rubbed at her chest as the expression of devotion and pure hunger on the prince's face floated to the forefront of her mind. Her heart seemed to shrivel. He'd never looked at *her* that way.

She hung her head and covered her face with her hands. For the last four hours, Jas had been berating herself for getting attached, for letting him in, for trying to help Sage in the first place, for being a sad excuse of a mother. Basically, for breathing.

Vienna's rosemary scent teased her nose right before her old friend placed a hand on the back of Jasmine's neck and kneaded.

"It seems you have much on your mind tonight. You've not spoken more than ten words. What's on your mind?"

Jas dropped her hands and studied her palms while trying to come up with an answer that wouldn't make her look like she was a sniveling, lovesick pup. "I have decisions to make," she said slowly. "But I am not sure which course of action I should take."

"Well, you're not alone. Have you spoken to Sam about what's bothering you? He's known to be fair and levelheaded, which is rare in a husband," she said wryly.

Jasmine squeezed her eyes shut, and her hands curled into fists.

"So that's how it is," Vienna said with sympathy. "The prince is the problem."

"Vienna, I made vows," Jas choked out, her eyes unconsciously seeking out the twins who played quietly in the corners of the living room. "He loves the twins and is a good person, but there are other sides to him that I don't know I can live with. I thought I could, but things have changed. And it… it hurts *so* much."

"That's love, my girl. At times, you feel like you could float above the ground, and, at other times, all you want to do is bury yourself in a hole to escape the horror of it. You have to be willing to take the good with the bad. Real love is not all flowers and romance. It's gritty, and it's hard. Those that are brave enough to really see the flaws of another person, and then accept them for it, will suffer pain like they've never felt before—but they will also experience love, friendship, and laughter like nothing the world has seen. And I've never known you to be a coward, Jasmine."

Jas lifted her head and craned her neck to look up at the older woman. "I don't feel very brave right now. I feel broken."

Vienna dropped her hand from Jasmine's neck and pulled up another rocking chair next to hers. The healer groaned as she lowered herself into the wooden seat and took Jasmine's left hand in hers.

"You are one of the bravest women I've ever had the pleasure of meeting."

Jasmine scoffed.

"You've shared with me bits and pieces of your life, but don't forget, the whole kingdom has heard what you did for our princess."

"I'm sure what you've heard is greatly exaggerated," Jas said softly.

Vienna narrowed her sky-blue eyes at Jasmine. "I'm an old woman, Jasmine Ramses, and a healer at that. I know what you did for Sage, and I know what it cost you," she said gently.

What it cost her.

Everything.

"I wouldn't change it," Jasmine admitted. "I hate, *hate,* how everything's happened, but—" Her gaze slid to the twins. "They're happy and thriving. Before, in the village, each day was just about surviving. But they're happy here, and I would give my own life for that."

"You're a good mother and friend."

"I don't feel like it," she muttered.

Vienna patted her hand. "And that is the curse of being a woman. We feel guilty about everything and rarely believe we are good enough for any task we complete, but that is just our skewed perception of ourselves. It's not the truth."

"What is the real truth?" Ethan said, abandoning his toy and crawling up into Vienna's lap.

The healer cuddled Jasmine's nephew close and kissed the top of his dark head.

"Listening in, again?" Vienna said with exasperation, but her smile betrayed her true feelings.

Ethan shrugged and squinted into the hearth. "I like your talks. They're interesting." He tipped his face back to stare up at Vienna. "So, what is the real truth?"

"The real truth is that—"

A screech followed by a bone-jarring boom rocked the room. Dirt from the thatched ceiling drifted down in puffs.

"What in the wicked hell?" Vienna blurted.

Another screech followed by an explosion set Jasmine's teeth on edge. She jumped out of the rocking chair and strode to the window. "Stars above," she whispered as a macabre scene played out before her eyes.

Flashes of light from cannon fire illuminated warring ships in their harbor. Her stomach bottomed out as a trebuchet released a huge, flaming rock toward Sanee. The ground seemed to roll beneath her feet as the stone crashed through a tavern five streets from Vienna's apothecary.

Good god, they needed to get farther into Sanee and away from the floating war machines.

She scanned the chaos in the streets. People had abandoned their homes and were screaming and stumbling away from the ensuing battle. Jasmine covered her mouth as a woman tripped and fell to the ground. The woman cried out as a man trampled over her.

Jasmine spun away from the window, panic starting to rise up. Vienna placed Ethan in her rocking chair and stormed toward the back room.

"Barricade the entrance, Jasmine!"

Jas hurried to the front door, slipped the heavy wooden slat into place, and stared at it as an ear-splitting scream pierced the air. Her pulse picked up, and she eyed the heavy trunk next to the door. She grabbed the handle and heaved, moving the blasted piece of furniture a few inches.

"What are you bloody doing?" Vienna barked, storming into the room.

"Helping," Jas gritted out, and she pulled again.

Vienna reached for the other side and helped move the enormous trunk. Once they'd managed to move it in front of the door, the older woman wiped the sweat from her brow and gestured at the windows. "We need to board them up."

Jasmine pulled herself to her knees and hugged each of the twins, who were watching with wide, fearful eyes.

"It'll be okay, loves," she whispered. "Vienna and I will keep you safe. Cover your ears, okay?"

The twins nodded, and Jas hurried to help Vienna lock the

shutters over the large front window, then yanked the curtains closed. Jasmine moved to the children and stumbled as another explosion rocked the earth. She dropped to her knees and wrapped her arms around Ethan and Jade, their little bodies trembling against hers.

"We can't stay here, Vienna. It's not safe."

"We can't go out there, either," the older woman replied, peeking through her keyhole. "It's utter madness." She sucked in a sharp breath. "No."

The hair rose on Jasmine's arms, and a tingling sensation began at the base of her neck, a sixth sense of foreboding, and she knew what the healer was going to say.

"They're here." Vienna glanced at Jasmine with fear in her eyes. "We need to leave *now*."

A hysterical laugh threatened to escape Jasmine's mouth. "We've no place to go." The palace was the safest place to be, but... She peered down at the whimpering children in her arms. They couldn't drag the children through the nightmare outside the door. They'd never make it.

Vienna stood from her crouched position and gestured for Jasmine and the children to follow her.

"Come on, children," Jas urged.

The twins followed her, completely silent.

They entered the back room of the apothecary. The rows of tinctures, tonics, and salves rattled against each other due to the raging conflict outside.

"Help me move this table," Vienna barked.

Jasmine hurried to assist her, and her brow wrinkled in confusion as the older woman dropped to her knees, her fingers pressing along the grooves of the wooden floor.

"Come on," the healer breathed.

Vienna pressed harder, and a faint click sounded beneath the floor. She dug her fingernails in between the floorboards and pulled. A trapdoor lifted, revealing a pitch-black hole.

"An escape route?" Jasmine asked.

"My grandfather's father was a paranoid man." Vienna gestured to the children. "This will get us into the sewers and close to the palace. Once there, we can—" She snapped her mouth shut as gruff words spoken in a foreign accent echoed down the alleyway.

Scythians.

Jasmine began to tremble as the voices neared the back door to the apothecary. She held her finger to her lips. Ethan nodded and hugged Jade closer to his own body. The room seemed to hold its breath as the warriors paused, and then their footsteps faded away. They waited a minute before Vienna moved into action.

She snatched a small lantern off the shelf and gestured to the trapdoor.

"Down you go, my girl."

Jasmine eyed the escape route. If Jas went first, there was no possible way for Vienna to hide the trapdoor after her, but if Jasmine went last, she could probably shove the table over the trapdoor and squeeze into the escape route.

"You go first. I can move the table and hide our escape the best

I can," she said in a hushed tone, too spooked to speak above a whisper. Scythians had uncanny hearing. Who knew what monsters might be listening in.

Vienna eyed her and then the table. "You're right. I wouldn't be able to move the table myself."

The older woman handed Jasmine the lantern. Jas held the light up, illuminating a short ladder that led to a tunnelway covered in cobwebs. Vienna didn't hesitate in lowering herself into the rickety-looking ladder. She reached the bottom and held her hands up. Jasmine lowered the lantern into the healer's waiting hands and turned to the twins.

"Come on, loves. It's time to go." Her heart picked up its pace as another explosion sliced through the air.

They scurried forward, but Jade clung to Jas's dress.

"There might be spiders down there," her niece cried.

Ethan hugged Jasmine but climbed down to Vienna.

Jas grabbed each side of Jade's precious face and stared into her eyes, so like her own. "I need you to be brave right now, baby." She swallowed down a sob. "Can you be brave for me?"

"Y-yes, Mama," Jade stuttered, before crawling into the tunnel.

Jasmine closed the trapdoor and pushed up from her knees, then yanked on the table with all her might. She gritted her teeth as the wooden legs scraped against the floor. Jas panted as she sprinted for the broom in the corner and swept away the evidence of her having moved the table.

She placed the broom against the wall and hustled back to the trapdoor. Carefully, she felt for the edge and lifted. Jas shifted to her side and slipped her legs down into the space. Her nerves were so shot that she almost screamed when a hand clasped her ankle and directed it to the ladder.

Her teeth chattered as she eased herself lightly onto her belly and wiggled backward, her flesh scraping against wood, Her muscles trembled and her jaw clenched as she managed to get her belly into the opening, her chest still pressed to the apothecary floor like she was prostrating herself before an altar.

Jas sucked in a deep breath and froze, her brows furrowing. Ripples of unease rolled through her. It was quiet—too quiet.

The back door to the apothecary exploded inward. Shards of wood flew across the room. A piece struck her in the forehead and cheek, but she barely felt the pain. Terror froze her screams of horror as a Scythian stepped into Vienna's home.

Recognition washed over her as she got a good look at the warrior's face.

Phoenix. One of *her* warriors.

She must have made a sound, because his chocolatey eyes dropped to hers, and a triumphant smile spread across his face.

It was the smile that had her scrambling back.

"Go!" she screamed, ripping her dress as she managed to get farther into the tunnel. Her foot slipped on the rung below her.

A roar of fury, followed by a crash and shattering glass, had her moving down faster, the trapdoor slamming above her.

"Run, Vienna, run!"

The trapdoor was flung open above her head, flooding the tunnel with light. She didn't look up but jumped. It may hurt to fall, but she didn't have time to climb all the way down.

Jas cried out as Scythian hands caught her hair and dress.

God, no.

She reached up and raked her hands along the arms pulling her upward, away from her family. But it was no use. They didn't release her.

With tears streaming down her face, she met Vienna's eyes. "Go," she mouthed. Her eyes moved to the twins. "I love you."

The arms jostled her and yanked her out of the tunnel. She gaped at the trapdoor that had been torn completely off its hinges. Jas squeezed her eyes shut and focused on slowing her breathing.

She couldn't escape monsters, but maybe she could divert their attention from her family. A strange calm settled over her as a large hand brushed the hair from her face and settled her on the floor of the back room.

Jas opened her eyes and shrank back from the men who surrounded her.

Phoenix's immense form stood in the entryway, eyeing the alleyway. Orion crouched next to her side, his raven-colored braids hanging around his face as he slipped a finger under her chin and lifted it, examining her face.

"She's bleeding," Orion growled.

Another Scythian pushed past Phoenix and stood before her, his expression one of relief and disgust.

Mekhl.

Her most volatile warrior.

Jasmine blinked and looked away toward the door. Not her

warrior. Her *captor*.

"We need to move," Phoenix rumbled from the doorway. "Time is short." He glanced over his shoulder and pinned her to the spot with his gaze. "Hello, consort."

She bared her teeth at him. "I'm *not* your consort."

His gaze dropped to her pregnant belly, which was on display, because her dress was pulled taut against the bump.

A smile full of male satisfaction, and a touch of something else, transformed his serious face into something hauntingly beautiful.

"The babe says otherwise."

Bile flooded her mouth.

The babe.

Orion smiled and reached out to touch her belly. She slapped his hand away and curled her arms around her belly.

"Don't touch me."

Orion tucked a braid behind his ear and glared at the floor. "We're trying to help you," he whispered in his quiet way that was so familiar.

She touched her bleeding cheek where the wood had struck her. "This is not helping," she hissed.

"She's going to be a problem," Mekhl snarled. His brown eyes narrowed on her. "Orion?"

Jasmine scooted backward as Orion pulled a cloth from his leather trousers.

"Don't fight it," he said softly.

Jas scrambled backward and attempted to get away.

An arm wrapped around her, just below her breasts and above

her belly.

"No!" she screamed. "Please, no."

"I'm sorry," Orion said, and he shoved the cloth over her face.

A sickeningly sweet scent invaded her nose and mouth. She kicked and screamed, but as her eyes drooped, she knew it was all for nothing.

Jasmine had always had a feeling they'd come for her.

Her last thought was of the twins as everything faded to darkness.

Sam would take care of the twins.

They'd be all right.

Chapter Thirty-Seven

The Warlord

Coming, coming, coming, the voices sang, completely satisfied.

Zane stood tall, his left hand resting on Nege's motionless black head. The feline's muscles were tense as he watched the party approach on horseback, their army standing guard in a solid wall of blue and white.

She comes.

Pride blossomed in his chest as his consort galloped toward him, her brunette hair shining like polished wood. Warpaint cut bold black lines down her eyes and high cheekbones. Her emerald eyes seemed to glow in her heart-shaped face and held him rooted to the spot. He tucked away the triumphant smile that threatened to break across his face as he studied the fine figure she cut in her armor and her silver breastplate that gleamed in the morning sun. The Aermian banner whipped in the air behind her, a great sapphire dragon.

She looked like a warrior angel, one he was happy to play the part of the devil with.

The warlord arched a brow at her as their party halted just over twenty paces away. Sage gazed at him as the rest of her warriors dismounted and circled her, her expression giving nothing away.

"Magnificent," he breathed, his praise lost in the bitter wind.

Something flashed across her face, and she blinked, breaking the spell that had been woven between the two of them.

His gaze dropped to the hands that circled *his* consort's waist, helping her from the spirited mare.

Ours, the voices snarled.

And he couldn't help but agree.

Nege growled lowly, and Zane ran a soothing hand over the maneater's head in an absent manner, letting none of his feelings leak out from the raging chaos that swirled inside his mind. He lazily observed the Aermian party as they arranged themselves into a barrier around *his* consort and the boy who thought himself a king.

This time, he did smile at the group of children playing at war. They were children in comparison to him, at least. His gaze snagged on a pair of cool magenta eyes that appraised him with indifference. Zane's smile deepened as he moved on, ignoring the reflective amber eyes that held hate.

So, they brought the Sirenidae and the Methian beasts. That was significant. They feared him.

As they should, the voices hissed.

Blair shifted closer to his right side.

"They reek of aggression," his commander spoke lowly, so only Zane could hear his words. "This will end in war."

"So be it," he whispered.

His heart picked up its speed as his consort stepped to the front of the group with the royal pup at her side. Zane appraised the Aermian prince and admitted that he was a handsome man, but too pretty and innocent for *his* Sage. He had an eye for those who knew true suffering, who were broken, but the man almost shone with wholesomeness.

Disgusting.

He dismissed the man who practically towered over his consort and let his gaze truly feast upon her figure. She was exactly as he remembered her. Although... his eyes narrowed slightly at the paleness of her complexion. His consort looked tired.

Pleasure unfurled in her chest when Nali sunk into place next to her mistress, her feline gaze alert. They were two parts of a whole, he and his consort, almost mirrors of each other. Nege huffed at his side but he ignored the beast, his eyes only for Sage.

A fissure of delight ran up his spine when she held his gaze, not cowering in his presence. For a long moment, they stared at each other, and the only sound was the wind whistling through the meadow and trees.

He took one casual step forward and grinned at how the warriors guarding his consort tensed. Zane wanted to scoff.

As if he'd hurt *his* woman.

"Consort," he murmured, practically purring.

Sage's eyes flashed, and an emotion broke free from her face for just one second before she tucked it away. But it was too late. He'd seen it.

Worry. Worry for *him*.

Try as she might, deny it all she could, but in the end, she was still his.

"Warlord," the prince muttered, his tone somewhat bored. "We've come as you've requested. You spoke of peace --" he cocked his head and looked past Zane, "--and yet you have an army that has encroached upon my land."

"My apologies, but it's been difficult to get your attention, my lord," Zane said.

The prince had held out longer than the warlord had expected. The young pup had a bit of backbone, which was as surprising as it was thrilling. There was nothing he loved more than a fierce opponent. Zane hadn't enjoyed burning the villages, but he gained a grain of respect for the man who wouldn't bend to him.

And yet, *she* was here.

"Another simple note would have sufficed," the Sirenidae said, her husky, sensual voice washing over him. He closed his eyes and savored it. There was something he loved about their rich musical voices. The Sirenidae voice was a thing of beauty.

It was too bad their kind were the children of beasts, whores, and cowards.

"The first wasn't taken too kindly." He opened his eyes and pursed his lips. "Decisions had to be made."

Pleasure swelled in his belly when his consort took one step forward and Nali appeared at her side. Sage braced her feet apart, one hand on the maneater's head, the other hanging loosely by her side.

A mirror of Zane's posture.

It was almost poetic.

Her green eyes glittered with rage and sorrow. She swept over him with her gaze, lips thinned like she found him distasteful. But he knew the truth. Sage was an excellent actress. Like called to like. With time, she might become as skilled as he. But that wasn't something he wanted for her. He wanted her just as she was.

"We're here. Will you consent to peace and retreat to your lands?" she asked, her voice sharp like a steel blade.

"I will consent to leave your lands under one condition." He held his hand toward her, palm up. "Come home and all shall be forgiven."

The warlord stilled, and the hairs on his arms rose as the prince pressed against Sage's back.

OURS! How dare he touch what is ours?

"You are a liar." Her voice rose and thundered in the space between them. "There will never be peace between us as long as you plague this earth."

"What an interesting term, plague," he replied. "Plagues have an essential use. They weed out the old and weak. They help control the population, so that people won't starve. Plagues have a purpose, and so do I. The world will be a better place, wild one. *We* can make it better."

"And what of the children?" she flung at him. "What did they ever do to deserve your wrath?"

Sorrow twisted his guts. War was ugly and violent, and sacrifices had to be made for the greater good. It didn't mean it was easy. "It pained me as much as it pains you."

A shudder worked through her body at his words. A guttural scream exploded from her chest, and the rest seemed to happen in slow motion.

One lone tear dripped onto her cheek.

His consort tore two daggers from the sheaths at her arms.

Her gaze latched onto his.

"Death comes for you," she shouted. "For Aermia!"

And then she attacked.

Like water bursting free from a dam, his warriors sprinted past him to meet the Aermian army that burst forward at their mistress's command, voices raised in battle cries.

One simple silver blade lodged in Zane's shoulder; the other he caught by the blade. His palm began to burn and dripped blood. He beamed at his consort as her warriors dragged her back from the bloody fray that had begun.

She had struck first blood. He was a lucky man to possess such a woman, such a champion.

Zane slipped her dagger into his belt and pulled the dagger

from his shoulder with his cut hand, warm liquid leaking from the wound. He dipped his chin to her in respect.

The warlord of Scythia would only ever bleed for his consort.

And she for him.

Both broken but made whole together.

A deep chuckle passed his lips at the mayhem of clashing swords, grunts, horse screams, cries of terror, bellows of triumph, and the thunder of thousands of footsteps.

Beautiful.

An Aermian soldier broke through his guard. He knocked the sword from the man's hand, swept his feet out from underneath him, and clenched his head beneath his palms. One swift jerk and the man fell to his knees like a marionette with its strings cut.

Zane lifted his head and met his consort's tumultuous gaze. "I'll see you soon, wild one," he whispered.

Her eyes widened before a Methian beast yanked her back from the front line. Sage disappeared from view, but he didn't worry.

No one would hurt his consort.

She'd be back.

And he'd be waiting.

He lifted his hands to the heavens.

"Bring forth the fire! Let us scourge the earth of those who are not worthy!" the Warlord bellowed.

Chapter Thirty-Eight

Sage

Absolute chaos reigned around them.

Her breaths seemed abnormally loud in her ears as men crashed together, screaming for blood. Bile burned her throat as a Scythian warrior cut down a young Aermian soldier with hardly a flick of his sword. He charged toward her, his war cry rattling her very soul.

She stared into his dark, bloodthirsty eyes as he closed the distance between them and pulled her sword from her scabbard. Her fingers wrapped around the metal hilt of her blade, her palm slipping from sweat.

The warrior bared his teeth at her, and she braced for the strike that never came. Rafe slammed into the warrior from the side, both men crashing to the ground in a heap of limbs, armor, and deadly weapons.

Her skin prickled, and sweat dripped down her spine as she watched them grapple. An inner bell went off inside her mind, telling Sage that she should be more aware of her surroundings, but she couldn't look away from the warrior who was howling for her death.

The Scythian spun and managed to slash his blade across Rafe's arm. He roared in pain and his attacks grew tighter, more focused. As if her body belonged to someone else, she pulled a dagger from her hip and crept forward, the anarchy around her fading into nothing. She focused on the vulnerable spot just below the warrior's ear.

He didn't notice her coming as he was so hellbent on killing Rafe.

Rafe met the enemy's downward strike and locked swords with him, a slow smile creeping up his face. Her friend never even looked at her, but he knew she was there. Sage jumped onto the warrior's back and struck true.

It was over in an instant.

She released the warrior and landed in a crouch as the Scythian crashed to the ground between her and Rafe. Sage lifted her dagger and stared at the scarlet tip.

She'd taken a life.

Someone she didn't even know.

Her gaze moved back to the felled warrior.

He was Scythian, by all accounts a soulless monster, and yet he bled the same color she did. A shiver worked through her and the dagger slipped from her shaking hands.

Murderer. A cold-blooded killer. Just like the Warlord.

Sage jerked as fingers lifted her chin and she met Rafe's burning amber eyes.

"This won't be the last life you take," he said gruffly. "This is war. If you don't get it together, you and I will both die on this field. Remember your training. Now is not the time to feel."

He stood abruptly and spun to meet another enemy, one who was clearly less experienced. She watched dispassionately as he dispatched the man, and once again knelt beside her, ignoring the bedlam around them.

Rafe leaned into her, his face mere inches from her own. "Snap out of it! I will drag you back to the war camp by your hair if I have to," he growled. He plucked her dagger from the ground and wrapped her bloodied fingers around the handle. "Can I trust you to protect yourself?"

She blinked slowly and nodded once, some of the fog around her mind dissipating. Her hand tightened around the blade while the other dug into the earth, grounding her. She bowed her head and inhaled deeply. This is what the Warlord had wanted. He'd forced her hand.

Sage stood and lifted her head, the cool numbness seeping through her veins, but not keeping her prisoner in her own body any longer. She scanned the immediate area, looking for potential dangers, but none approached her. Rafe, Zachael, and a few guards had formed a loose ring around her as the battle surged like waves around them.

A screech cut through the air, followed by a bone-jarring boom. The ground rolled beneath her feet, and Sage stumbled. Her eyes watered as smoke filled the air. Slowly, Sage spun in a circle and scrutinized the mayhem. An unbidden chuckle burst from her lips at the indescribable horror unleashed upon their people.

Blood soaked into the ground, creating a garish, unholy painting. War machines lined the edge of the Mort wall, catapulting burning orbs that shot across the sky like hellish shooting stars, leaving destruction in their wake. Her breath seized as a rain of whistling fire descended from the sooty sky.

"Shields!" Zachael bellowed.

Sage yanked a discarded shield off the ground and held it above her head. Men cried out around her as fiery arrows pierced flesh, earth, and shield. She bit the inside of her cheek and fought not to cover her ears. A haunting melody of thwarted arrows clinked against metal like a chilling version of ice clinking against glass.

She hefted the shield back up until she formed a triangle of protection with Zachael and Rafe. "This is madness," she said woodenly, hardly able to comprehend the destruction around her. How had so much carnage happened in such little time? It was unthinkable.

Too much violence.

Too much death.

And it had only just begun.

"We need to fall back," Zachael muttered.

Sage's heart thumped painfully in her chest as she spotted Tehl and Lilja more than twenty paces away. "Not without them."

Rafe and Zachael exchanged a look but nodded.

"On my command," the weapons master said.

Another explosion rocked the earth.

"Now!"

Chapter Thirty-Nine

Tehl

He gritted his teeth as he slammed his sword against the wicked blade of the lanky Scythian warrior who seemed to appear out of thin air. His muscles trembled with strain as the warrior growled and pressed forward. Tehl's heels dug into the dirt beneath the soles of his boot as he leaned into his strike, trying to unbalance his opponent.

He gasped when the enemy spun away quickly and darted forward in a serpent-strike that had him on his toes. Lilja cried out from his left, but he didn't dare take his eyes off his opponent for one second. The Sirenidae could handle herself far better than he could.

"You're going to die today," the warrior snarled. His gaze slid over Tehl's shoulder. "And then, everything you hold dear will be ours."

"Over my dead body," Tehl gritted out, meeting each bone-jarring strike.

"Your wish is my command," the warrior whispered with glee.

Tehl gasped as the Scythian caught his thigh with the tip of his blade. He ignored the burning pain and lunged forward, pushing the Scythian backward. From the corner of his eye, Lilja emerged from the fray and attacked his opponent from the left side.

The warrior growled and disengaged, then spat on the ground as he got an eyeful of the Sirenidae.

"Disgusting," he hissed. "Unnatural."

Lilja arched a haughty white brow. "If anyone is unnatural here, it's you. You're a mongrel." She sidled farther from Tehl, keeping the Scythian's attention on her. "Who do you think your warlord experimented on to get your precious elixir, hmmm? He coveted us, our abilities. You're nothing but a poor replica."

The hair on the nape of Tehl's neck rose as the warrior began to tremble. His whole body seemed to vibrate, and his muscles bulged. Tehl moved cautiously to his right, searching for a way to attack the dangerous man who looked like he was one moment away from jumping out of his skin.

Lilja laughed, the sound condescending and sharp. "So, you're one of those? Are you going to let your berserker out? Come on, let him out to play with me," she taunted.

Tehl paused when the Scythian's head whipped in his direction, his braided hair slapping against his burnished skin. The warrior's wrathful gaze pinned him to the spot before moving back to Lilja. Tehl released his breath and shoved his terror down. There hadn't been anything human left in the warrior's face, only rage and hunger.

The Sirenidae shifted her stance and batted her lashes at the unraveling warrior. "It must gall you that you're so weak. What would your Warlord say? I bet he hasn't even gifted you with a woman yet." She let her sentence hang and then smirked. "I'm sure he never will. If I can see that you're lacking, I bet your leader can, too."

That was the final straw.

The Scythian bellowed and lunged. Lilja met him blow for blow. Her magenta eyes caught Tehl's for one moment, and he knew what he had to do. He attacked from behind. The warrior swung around and slammed his fist into Tehl's stomach. He wheezed and hunched over, knowing he'd suffered a few cracked ribs.

Quickly, he yanked his dagger from his bicep and swiped at the man's hamstrings. He rolled out of the way and hopped up onto his feet as the warrior spun with a cry. He took one limping step toward Tehl when Lilja swept under the Scythian guard and slammed her dagger into his neck. The warrior gurgled, clutched at his throat, and dropped to his knees. He gave them one more hate-filled glare before his eyes rolled into his head.

"Are you hurt?" Tehl panted as he scanned the pandemonium.

His guards had formed a barrier between him and his advisors. He exhaled and wiped the sweat from his forehead. The ground shuddered beneath his feet with an explosion. Smoke singed his nose.

"No."

A screech of pain caused him to glance upward. His stomach bottomed out as a fiilee and his rider plummeted from the sky in a ball of flame. "Hell." He prayed that it wasn't Raziel plunging from above.

"Remember this feeling," Lilja said in a hollow voice. "It will keep you from ever seeking war again."

Tehl nodded. He'd never forget the horrors of this day.

"How is your leg?" she asked, wiping her blades on her pants.

He glanced at the seeping wound. "It's nothing." Tehl lifted his head and scanned the fray, looking for his wife. Sage stood back-to-back with Rafe, fighting their way back from the front line. Somehow, they'd gotten separated. "We need to move." They needed to regroup and plan.

"I agree." Lilja straightened and lifted her chin toward Sage and the sea of warriors between them. "If you can, goad the warriors."

Tehl fought a shiver. "Into the rage?"

"Yes. They're less coordinated."

He nodded. That was something he'd noticed. "You lead, and I'll follow."

The Sirenidae flashed him a bitter smile from a dirt-smeared face. "Age before beauty?"

"More like experience before ignorance."

Lilja sobered. "I'll protect you with my life."

"As will I." He rolled his shoulders and hefted his sword higher as another warrior broke through the makeshift ring. "Let's be done with this."

CHAPTER FORTY

Lilja

She stepped over the warrior she'd dispatched and locked eyes on the Warlord.

His sword flashed as it reflected the liquid fire that the war machine catapulted through the sky. He looked exactly the same as when she'd met him years prior, before she knew the extent of his depravity, cruelty, and corruption.

Devastatingly handsome, even covered in blood and grime.

As if he heard her thoughts, his face turned toward her, and a handsome smile tipped up his lips. Everything began and ended with him. He curled a finger toward her in a "come closer" motion.

His words floated to the front of her mind like he'd just whispered them in her ear.

Animals deserve to be chained.

She smiled at him and began to carve a path in his direction. The only animal that needed to be put down was the Warlord. His brand of unhinged delusion could not be allowed to live any longer. He'd played god for long enough.

Her stride lengthened as she drew closer to the Warlord.

A warrior charged her but halted when the monstrous ruler of Scythia held his hand up. The warrior backtracked and entered gleefully into the battle.

She stared at him, an ax in one hand and a sword in the other.

He brushed his raven hair from his face and grinned impishly. "I was wondering when we'd speak again. It's been far too long."

"Indeed, it has," she murmured, eyeing her greatest enemy. "I was quite hoping you'd be dead by now."

The Warlord barked out a laugh. "I forgot how frank you are. I remember a time when you were quite innocent."

"Those days are long gone," she said honestly. The warlord and his men had made sure of that.

"I have to say, I like you this way better." His black gaze wandered down her figure. "Jaded vengeance looks good on you, Captain Femi."

She batted her lashes and moved to the right with slow, cautious steps. "You've heard of my antics?"

The Warlord mirrored her actions and shrugged a shoulder. "You've been plaguing my ships for years now. It's hard not to notice an irritation that won't dissipate. But I wonder... was it worth all of the lives you lost in the process? Do they weigh heavily upon you?"

"They lived their lives the way they desired. I miss them, but they ultimately chose their way of life," she replied evenly.

"What a refreshing answer. I can't tell you how tired I am of sniveling guilt mongers."

"I'm not sure you know what guilt is," she whispered, slinking closer to his right side. "You'd have to have a conscience."

She swung her ax, and he danced away, delight burning in his soulless eyes. Revulsion and rage filled her as she eyed the ancient creature masquerading as a man. Lilja had lived a very long time, but she was a pup compared to him.

Keep focused. Don't let your emotions get the best of you.

Her lips twitched with the smile that she smothered. He'd been stealing her people for as long as she could remember. To experiment on, to breed, to retrieve precious herbs from the sea. Even seemed appropriate that retribution come from the Sirenidae.

She eyed the vulnerable side he'd left open, but she didn't take the bait. He was an expert weapons master, and even if she was young compared to numerous years, she hadn't been born yesterday. She knew a trap when she saw one.

Lilja didn't delude herself into thinking it would be easy to vanquish her ancient enemy, but she'd be satisfied if she shed just a bit of his blood.

"I can see your mind working behind those ethereal eyes of

yours. Will you not share your thoughts?"

"How I am going to rejoice over your dead carcass," she purred, her boots sinking in the mud beneath them.

He tsked and shook his head, the feathers in his hair quivering in the wind. "So violent and naughty. Come closer and put those hands to good use." He sank into a defensive crouch. "It's been so long since I killed a woman."

She bared her teeth. "I'll not die this day."

Then, she sprung.

CHAPTER FORTY-ONE

Sage

Stray hairs that had escaped her braid were plastered against her face and neck.

Sage scrambled out of a warrior's path and attacked with everything she had.

Rafe had been the first one to notice the pattern.

The warriors never attacked to kill her. They were trying to capture her. And as terrifying as that idea was, it gave her an edge. There was no way she was going back to the Warlord.

She'd die first.

A roar pulled her attention to the right. Another Scythian cut his way toward her, atop an Aermian mount. Ice trickled down her spine at the expression on his face.

Pure loathing and hatred.

This man she wouldn't trust to capture her. He was out for blood.

And he had the high ground.

Her heart picked up its pace when she saw that she was alone. Rafe and Zachael were both locked in battles. She was on her own.

She braced her legs and readied herself.

Stars above, this would hurt.

He thundered closer, trampling all in his path, and her mind screamed at her to run, to find escape. But there was none.

Sage cursed when he dropped his sword right before he was upon her and grabbed at her breastplate. She sliced down with her own sword, only managing to scrape the bracer on his forearm. Her breath whooshed out of her as he yanked her off her feet and continued to ride. She dropped her sword and pried two of his fingers from her breastplate until they cracked.

The warrior yelled, but he didn't release her. Roughly, he tossed her over the saddle.

The horn of the saddle pressed relentlessly into her belly. Nausea rolled through her, but she managed to rip the necklace from her throat which hid a petite blade Lilja had gifted to her. Sage pressed a hand against the horse's sweat-streaked side and slammed the dagger into the warrior's calf.

The Scythian brute grabbed her by the hair and yanked her head up. She gritted her teeth and barely managed to keep ahold of her blade.

"Aermian whore!"

He lifted his hand as if to strike her, but she didn't care. Her eyes were focused on the soldier riding toward them like the devil was chasing him.

Garreth.

And he wasn't slowing as he approached.

Sage slid her hand back and sliced at the warrior's hand before pushing from the horse. Pain burned from her scalp as the Scythian tore hair from her head. She wrapped her arms around her head and crashed to the ground. Agony slammed into her as she tumbled, praying that she wouldn't be trampled by the beast.

She lifted her head, and the world blurred and tilted around her. Breathing seemed almost impossible. Through watering eyes, she forced herself to focus. It wasn't safe to lie about on the ground.

Garreth, wielding a long sword, had cut his way through the fight. Sage watched as the huge warrior closed in on her friend, hacking at him from horseback. She crawled to her knees and snatched a sword from a dead soldier.

Frantic to get to her friend, she used the sword as a cane and stood on wavering legs. The men crossed swords, and their mounts kicked at each other. Garreth slashed at the Scythian's saddle, and time held still for a second.

The warrior's saddle slipped, and for a moment, all she could see was Garreth's intense expression before the brute tore her friend from the saddle with him. The warrior was on his back, his hand reaching for a dagger. Garreth lodged his blade through an opening in the warrior's armor and cut deep as the brute plunged his blade into her friend's chest.

Sage shrieked and clawed her way toward the two men who stared at each other, both in shock. Garreth glanced to her and gave her a small smile, a look of peace crossing his face.

"Everything is going to be okay," she chattered as she slid her way through the muck and mud to get to him. "We'll get you to Jacob, and you'll be healthy before you know it." Her voice wavered as she tried to keep her sobs at bay.

"I'm so sorry, Sage." He tipped his head back and roared in a voice that could be heard over the clash of weapons and shrieks of warriors. "For our future!" he bellowed.

Garreth wavered, his gaze blank, and his body tumbled onto his already slain enemy.

"No," she whispered. Sage didn't realize tears streamed down her cheeks as she stood on shaking legs. She swiped at her face and brandished her sword.

Zachael pressed past her and placed his fingers over Garreth's pulse. His grief-stricken face told her what she already knew.

Her friend was dead. Gone.

And he'd saved her life.

A broken sob tried to pass her lips, but she swallowed it back. If she started now, she wouldn't stop.

"We must move," she said dully, wrapping an arm around her bruised stomach. A brush of black fur tickled her cheek. She blinked into fierce feline eyes. "Where have you been?" she whispered.

Nali's ears twitched and she bumped Sage's chest with her head as if she was trying to offer comfort.

The weapons master closed Garreth's eyes and stood, tears

tracking lines through his soot and dirt-covered face. They gazed at each other, not ashamed of their sadness, and then tucked it away.

Distractions would get them killed.

She studied the raging battle for allies. Fiilee and their riders soared through the sky, loosing arrows on the enemies below. Sage dropped her gaze and paused when wind whipped around her, clearing the smoke for one precious moment.

Her heart ceased to beat as she was given the perfect view of the Warlord and Lilja. Panic and terror washed away her pain and sadness, spurring her to pick up a shield and sprint farther into the battle. Zachael cursed and ran beside Sage, her constant protector and shield on her left, and Nali right side, snarling at any enemies that dared approach from the direction.

Lilja slammed sword to sword with the Warlord, her arms straining as he used his larger frame to upset her balance. Her braided white hair whipped around her in a silvery flash, much like lightning. Sage panted and pushed herself harder when he broke away and kicked her aunt in the knee. Lilja grunted but stayed upright, her face creasing in pain.

Sage stumbled but caught herself on shaking legs.

Only a little farther. You can make it.

The Warlord laughed and struck again. Her aunt held her own, but even Sage could see that her strength was waning. Sage slammed her shield against a warrior, and swung under his sword arm as she kept moving through the bedlam warring around her.

Lilja danced closer and slashed her sword toward the Warlord. He danced out of the way. The Warlord paused and touched a hand to his cheek. His smile turned dark as he held up his blood-covered hand.

Sage's stomach dropped. She'd seen that smile once before. When he slaughtered Rhys before her very eyes.

"No!" Sage screamed. *He wouldn't.*

The Warlord met her panicked gaze with devastation in his own. He was done playing with Lilja. The demon was about to make his appearance. He lifted his weapon and blurred into action. In the span of a heartbeat, he stepped behind her aunt.

"Please, Zane," Sage begged. "Don't!"

She tried to move faster, but it was like her feet were stuck in quicksand, each step too slow, too late.

Lilja thrashed, dropped her ax, and pulled a blade on the Warlord, but he was so much faster. Her aunt swung toward Sage, and her magenta eyes widened. Lilja gasped as a blossom of red bloomed across her chest. She coughed and shuddered. With care, the Warlord pulled Lilja into his chest and wrapped an arm around her, his lips resting near her ear as he observed Sage. For all intents and purposes, they looked to be two lovers.

"Please, no!" Sage screamed, plowing through the nightmare around her. A Scythian screamed as Nali pounced on the warrior creeping up on her, but Sage couldn't look away from Lilja.

Tears slid from her aunt's eyes, and she smiled softly at Sage. "It's alright," she mouthed. But Sage knew down to her very marrow that nothing would be okay.

Lilja's eyelids slid closed, and her body collapsed against the Warlord's form. Sage tore her eyes away from her aunt and regarded the devil himself. Her eyes filled with liquid heat, and the world turned to a haunting watercolor hue.

Lilja was gone.

Gone. Gone. Gone.

Sound faded like someone had shoved cotton into her ears. Her heart pounded in time with the war drums as she watched the monster who continued to destroy her, one broken piece at a time.

Time blurred as they studied each other, his gaze filled with remorse and triumph, hers with devastation and disbelief. She trembled as he lay Lilja gently on the ground and stood.

He lifted his arm and held his hand out to her.

Even though a battlefield still separated them, it felt like he stood just in front of her.

"Come to me," she read upon his lips. "End this."

End this.

A tremor worked through her body, and she took one choppy step forward. He would never stop. He'd burn the world around them to get to her. The longer she fought, the more deaths and blood would be on her hands.

A bellow broke through the fuzziness in her ears. She slowly turned to the left and gasped. Hayjen plowed through soldiers, Blair at his side, cutting a swath through the warriors. Her uncle's gaze was pinned to the Warlord.

The heartbreak on his face was enough for Sage's knees to weaken.

A hand curled around her arm. "That's far enough. It's time to retreat, Sage," Zachael said tightly.

She shook off his hand and turned back to the Warlord, then blinked at the distance she'd traveled toward him. It was if he had some sort of power that drew her to him. Sage straightened her spine and locked her knees.

He took one step closer and raised his hand higher. "Come to me," he commanded.

Nali hissed at her side and growled, the sound sinister enough to rise the hairs along Sage's arms.

Her fingers clenched around the sword in her right hand, and she stared blankly at his handsome face. There wasn't anything she could do to keep him from his ambitions. Even if she went to him, the bloodshed would continue. He was too broken, too warped.

Sacrificing herself would fix nothing.

It would only give him what he wanted.

She forced herself to remember the little one she'd buried. He would never stop. Sage lifted her chin and leveled her gaze at the demon destroying her kingdom and shoved the broken, abused little boy he used to be in a box deep inside her soul. Trauma didn't turn you into a monster, a person's choices did. He'd had ample opportunities to change, but he chose the dark path each time.

"Never," she said.

His eyes glittered in excitement. "Never is sooner than you think."

Chapter Forty-Two

Sage

She crashed into the tent, her broken heart threatening to fall from her chest. She gasped, tears pouring down her filthy face.

Lilja.

Cut down in just a moment. There one second and gone the next.

Sage stumbled farther into the room, her blood-slicked boots catching on the rough-sewn rug. Pain bit into her hip as she bumped into the table holding the spirits. In a fit of rage, she swept her hands across the surface, scattering goblets and spirits across the dirt floor.

How could he take Lilja away from her?

Her fingers clutched at the heavy wooden table like the solid piece of furniture would keep her grounded. Salty tears burned down her wind-chapped face and lips, tasting like bitter loss and hopelessness.

"How could you?" she whispered brokenly.

Even after all this time, a small piece of her believed there was some part of him that wouldn't harm her so intentionally. But he proved her wrong once again.

Lilja's cry echoed in her mind, causing her to spin around and lean against the table for support. She slammed her eyes shut to keep the memory from replaying in her mind, but it stopped nothing.

A white braid.

A dark smile.

Blood.

Pained magenta eyes.

An ugly sob burst from her chest as the tent flap rustled. She opened her watery eyes and absorbed Tehl's shattered expression. He unlatched his dented chest plate and let it fall to the floor with a clatter. He brushed his sweaty hair from his face and opened his arms, striding toward her.

Sage pushed from the table and launched into his arms with a cry. He wrapped her in a crushing hug and sank to the ground, cradling her against his chest.

"I'm so sorry," he choked out.

Sage sobbed louder, her fingers clutching at his stained linen shirt.

"I'm so sorry, love," Tehl whispered, his voice hoarse. He swallowed hard. "I don't have any words."

Neither did she. There weren't words for the agony coursing through her veins. It felt like part of herself had been ripped apart.

"I hate him," she cried. "I hate him so much that I can't breathe."

"I know," Tehl crooned, running a hand down her tangled hair, and hugged her even closer, like he could keep all the cracking pieces of herself together by the ferocity of how he held her.

"He won't stop. He'll never stop," she wailed.

She pressed her face against his chest and held onto him with everything she possessed, her body trembling. How could she bear so much anguish?

Her husband pressed a kiss on the top of her head and rubbed his nose along her temple. "We'll find a way." His tone was so sure.

Sage shook her head, glanced up at his dear face, and released the shame she'd harbored.

"He beckoned me, and I almost went to him."

They were the softest words, but they felt like they rocked the room. Tehl's chest stilled under her hands as he held his breath, seeming momentarily stunned. His deep blue eyes scanned her tear-soaked face. He brushed the sweaty strands away from her wet cheeks.

"You didn't go to him."

"No," she stuttered. Had she made the right decision? Everything was so muddled.

Tenderness softened the sharp angles of his face as he leaned his dirt-smeared forehead against hers.

"You know I'm terrible with words." Frustration creased his brows, and his jaw clenched. "How I wish I wasn't. But know this, it's okay to break down. Just hold on to me, I'll be the light to guide you from the darkness, your sanctuary when it seems like you'll drown." He placed both of his hands on her cheeks. "Hold on to me, and I'll never let go."

Tears of gratefulness rushed from the corners of her eyes. How did she get so lucky? "I love you."

"I love you," Tehl said softly. "Always and forever."

For a man of few words, the ones he did express we're more than enough.

"Always and forever." She hiccupped. That was what Lilja and Hayden had. "How can she be gone? It's not right."

"Death is not something we can ever make sense of. Believe me, I've tried," he said solemnly.

She swiped at her face, hating her tears, but didn't try to stop them from flowing. Lilja deserved that. "I'm going to kill him." It was an oath.

Her husband said nothing but kissed each damp cheek.

She soaked in his support and wrapped his love around herself like a warm blanket on a winter day. She wasn't the only one suffering.

"How's Hayjen?" she questioned.

"I had him sedated."

Sage jolted and stared up at the prince in shock.

Tehl shrugged a shoulder, his eyes suspiciously shiny, before he glanced away. "He was going to get himself *killed.*" His voice broke on the last word. "I couldn't lose two friends today."

Stars above, she was selfish and completely blind. She wiggled until she straddled his legs and wrapped her arms around his neck.

"I'm so sorry, Tehl."

He dropped his head and rested his face in the crook of her neck. Warm liquid dripped onto her throat and slid down her collarbone and into her shirt. Her husband's fingers knotted in her shirt and pulled her tighter against his body as he shook with silent tears.

They'd both lost someone they'd loved dearly today.

It was on the tip of her tongue to tell him what befell Garreth, but she couldn't. He protected her from so much, it was the least she could do. Tomorrow would come soon enough.

Sage sank her fingers into his hair, pressed her cheek against the side of his head, and cried with him.

At some point, they ended up cocooned in furs on their pallet. Tehl wrapped himself around her body, his lips resting against the back of her head.

She stared blankly at the side of the canvas tent as exhaustion threatened to swamp her.

"He's going to die."

"He is," Tehl answered simply.

She'd let herself mourn tonight, and tomorrow, she'd scheme to end the monster's life.

No one hurt her family and lived to tell the tale.

AUDIOBOOKS

Are you an audiobook addict? I'm happy to announce that all books in the Aermian Feuds are available now in audio! Listen now!

REBEL'S BLADE

CROWN'S SHIELD

ENEMY'S QUEEN

KING'S WARRIOR

ALSO BY FROST KAY

THE AERMIAN FEUDS

Rebel's Blade

Crown's Shield

Siren's Lure

Enemy's Queen

King's Warrior

Warlord's Shadow

Spy's Mask

DOMINION OF ASH

The Stain

The Tainted

MIXOLOGISTS & PIRATES

Amber Vial

Emerald Bane

Scarlet Venom

Cyan Toxin

Onyx Elixir

Indigo Alloy

Thank you for reading SPY'S MASK. I hope you enjoyed it!

If you'd like to know more about me, my books, or to connect with me online, you can visit my webpage https:// www.frostkay.net/ or join my facebook group FROST FIENDS!

From bookworm to bookworm: reviews are important. Reviews can help readers find books, and I am grateful for all honest reviews. Thank you for taking the time to let others know what you've read, and what you thought. Just remember, they don't have to be long or epic, just honest. ♡

FREE BOOK

How do you feel about free books? Personally, I love em. I collect books like dragons hoard gold. Feel free to grab the first book in the series, Amber Vial, for FREE at your favorite retailer < 3

Happy reading,

Frost

Fact #257-Allie Sai should have been named "Unlucky."

Fact #372-Sometimes moonshine is not the answer.

Fact #401-Pirates aren't princes. They're extortionists.

NEW FANTASY SERIES

Have you read the Tainted?

It's an ENEMIES TO LOVERS post-apocalyptic fantasy perfect for Sarah J. Maas and Holly Black fans.

Check out what readers are saying: "With a refreshingly unpredictable plot, real and relatable characters, and a deliciously magnetic romance, I devoured THE TAINTED in one sitting." USA TODAY Bestselling Author Raye Wagner

www.ingramcontent.com/pod-product-compliance
Lightning Source LLC
Chambersburg PA
CBHW030549310726
48979CB00010B/2086/J

* 9 7 8 1 6 4 6 6 9 4 3 9 6 *